THE SAME RIVER

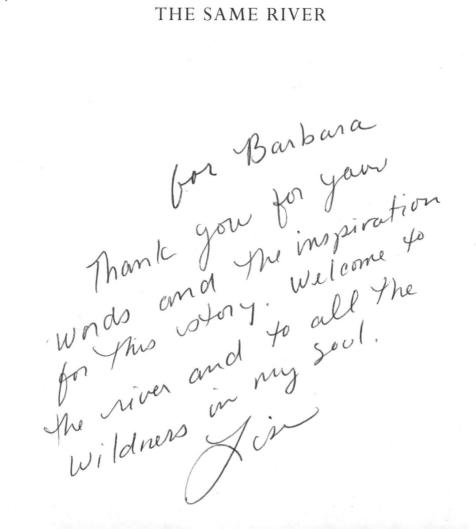

for Barbara

Thank you for your words and the inspiration for this story. Welcome to the river and to all the wildness in my soul.

Jim

THE
SAME
RIVER

A NOVEL

LISA REDDICK

SHE WRITES PRESS

Published October 9, 2018
Printed in the United States of America
Print ISBN: 978-1-63152-483-7
E-ISBN: 978-1-63152-484-4
Library of Congress Control Number: 2018942861

For information, address:
She Writes Press
1563 Solano Ave #546
Berkeley, CA 94707

Interior design by Tabitha Lahr

She Writes Press is a division of SparkPoint Studio, LLC.

This is a work of fiction. Names, characters, places, and incidents either are the product of the author's imagination or are used fictitiously. Any resemblance to actual persons, living or dead, is entirely coincidental.

For Robin
And the river

JESS

⟨◎⟩

This was the first time she had been alone in the house since the accident. Looking out the kitchen window, Jess watched a white-gray osprey tilt and plunge into the curve of the summer river. She could see the Nesika turning amid its green banks just down the low slope of lawn from the house, insistent and determined.

Her body felt unusually heavy as she bent over to place a glass in the top tray of the dishwasher. She was fourteen and used to the lightness and strength of her fast track-star form. Sometimes, when the heaviness of her grief became too much to bear, she would sink into it and let it hold her, wanting to understand why it was there and whether it would ever release her.

She stood and leaned against the sharp edge of the stained Formica counter. It was the middle of the afternoon, her parents were still at work, and she had just walked home from the school bus. Pushing away from the counter, Jess turned, made her way slowly down the dark hallway, and stood in front of the closed bedroom door.

Her hand seemed detached from her body as she reached out and grasped the brass doorknob. How could something so familiar, so normal, have become so painful? She opened the door tenderly. The room seemed frozen in time. Monica's bed was made perfectly, her lavender quilt folded, the lace edging the pillows soft and still. Her dolls were lined up patiently along the wall; a pink hairbrush waited on the dresser by her mirror. Monica's sweet girl smell seemed to reach out to Jess like an invisible hand as she stepped into the sun-filled room.

Lying down on the bed, Jess tried to remember her little sister. Monica's face and lanky arms had seemed to have an expressive life of their own. Jess let the weight of the memories pull her into the small bed and felt something hold her there, a presence, oppressive but not unwelcome, a knowing that had been braided into her flesh, shaping the life in her cells. She was bound to the river in a desperate way, Monica's death now dragging her through life like an inescapable undertow.

Jess's body broke into a sobbing cascade of release. Her tears felt like the currents of the river, and she followed them down into the torn chasms of her broken heart. Fighting them would only cause the river to swallow her; instead, Jess knew from swimming for years in the Nesika, she had to surrender, to flow with the current until the river released her back to the surface. She knew this was what had saved her that day.

She rolled onto her back and felt the sun warm her face. Its light—the light her sister would never see again, the light she had been born into and left too soon—felt cruel. She rolled to the edge of the bed and held on to her stomach. Monica's room, where Jess had held her sister during Monica's dark nightmares—maybe they had been of water, of drowning, of leaving this place too soon.

The dolls stared at her, daring her to play. They wanted Monica's hands and were mourning her loss, too, hating the river for taking her away. Jess was gripped by a desire to fling them around, mess them up, but she knew they were as lost and left behind as she was. They were misplaced, out of order, disoriented from being torn from the familiar, not knowing how or where to take the next step.

Jess wanted to touch her sister just one more time, wanted Monica to come into her room after a bad dream, begging her big sister to let her sleep in her bed. Her ears rang with the voices of the children singing at Monica's funeral, then, later, with the sobs of her family at the graveside, marked with flowers and white stones, the cold and desperate current of the river that day, and Monica's last cry.

She walked back down the hall, leaving the door to her sister's room open. She wanted her to come home now, to run through the door with her latest story. Jess looked out at the river through the glass doors that opened onto the backyard. She wanted to hate the river—she felt a flood of anger blending with fear rising in her tense back—but she also knew that the heaviness was a longing for her lost kinship with the river and with her own emerging wildness. It was a warm June afternoon; she should have been swimming almost every day in the river by now. The accident had been just over two months earlier—was that long enough?

She opened the door very slowly and deliberately. She knew she had to go back, and she had to go alone.

At this time of year, the Nesika's turquoise water tumbled around the rocks in a constant, pulsing rhythm. She waited. Her heart raced in her ears, and she braced for the sudden cold of the dive. She looked back up the hill to her house. Her parents would be home from work now. She wondered if her mom was watching, parting the heavy curtains in the house up from the river, just out of view, just enough to see Jess standing on the bank in her green bathing suit, waiting.

The Nesika had taken Monica's life as if it had been hers to give. Now Jess was an only child, holding the hand of her grief, hoping that by going back to the river she could go back to that part of herself that laughed, that ran along the green, sloping riverbank, trusting that the ground would hold her and never questioning the certainty of each day. She'd struck an unconscious deal with her parents after Monica died: that she could hold the place of both of their daughters. Filling that role at fourteen had shattered her identity—who was she without her sister? How would the world define her? She had hated and avoided social situations, constantly fearing the question "Do you have any brothers or sisters?" Her answer ranged from the lie "No, I'm an only child" to "Yes, I had a younger sister, but she died when she was eleven." If pressed, she reluctantly offered the story of her sister, who sometimes died, sometimes drowned, and sometimes was killed by the river.

She bent down and put her hand in the water, feeling its familiar tendrils flowing around each finger. She closed her eyes and felt for a moment as if she were reaching back through time to grab the hand of a lost friend.

It was so cold. She waded in just up to her knees, enough to feel a sharp edge cutting her skin. Then she dove in. She opened her eyes underwater and saw her sister's white tennis shoe bobbing up and down with the rhythm of the current. She knew it wasn't there, but it was. She broke up through the surface and swam easily to the opposite bank. It was the same river, the same flowing current, but now there was a white sneaker that hadn't been there before.

PIAH

The crash and roar of the falls numbed Piah's hearing as she
leaped down the slick, wet boulders to the base of the falls.
Closing her eyes, she lay back on the soft sponge of moss on the
gentle slope below the canyon wall. Water from the whirling mist
gathered on her skin and cooled where the sun had warmed her.
Reaching out toward a swaying stem of bright orange columbine,
Piah felt at home. It was finally the warm season, when all that
had sprung up during the surge of the growing season seemed to
rest. Piah loved this time of the cycle; she had been born fourteen
warm seasons earlier and celebrated her birth time by playing
in the wind and the comforting sunlight.

Looking up at the unbroken blue of the arching sky, Piah
stretched her strong back against the ground and let out a loud
cry. This was her home, her family, amid life-giving plants and
animals, and the constant song of the river bound them all
together. Runs of shining salmon pulsed with the rise and fall
of the seasons, feeding osprey, herons, and eagles, bears, mountain lions, wolves, and coyotes with their bodies, spent from
their journey to spawn.

Piah sang out the river's name: "Nesika, Nesika, Nesika!"
Then, standing up slowly, she brushed the water from her

clothing. Under her hands she could feel the changes in her body, no longer thin and willowy, her legs beginning to curve, her breasts starting to push out under her deerskin. Her long black hair hung in wet strands around her face.

Piah heard a rustling above her and turned quickly to see what or who it was. Tenas, her younger sister, had been watching her from the ledge above the river.

Piah yelled up at her, "Tenas, what are you doing? I told you not to follow me!"

Piah felt a sinking in her chest as Tenas turned and disappeared back into the forest. Tenas was Piah's only sister and followed her everywhere. Piah remembered the night of Tenas's birth. The birth dwelling was small, and Piah was given the task of tending the small fire. Piah focused on the lips of the flames as her mother began howling and crying out in her pain while the women chanted their low, growling birth song. The chanting got louder and stronger as the night dove into cold, blue darkness. Just as Piah thought she couldn't stay awake a moment longer, she had a sister.

Now, Piah sighed. She loved her sister fiercely and would give her life to keep her safe, even as Tenas was annoying her. Tenas looked more like their mother, softer and smaller, which made her seem more vulnerable. Piah was more like her father; her long legs and graceful stride hinted at being part of a hunting party, rather than in the women's hide-tanning circle.

Breathing in the cooling mist of the falls, sticking her tongue out to catch the spray, Piah closed her eyes and turned her face up to the caress of the sun. Then the roaring cadence of the falls consumed her, and, opening her eyes, she felt a summons to follow the river downstream through the warming forest.

The rushing water tumbled and slipped over the boulders, racing with Piah as she followed each turn. Eventually, the forest opened onto a clearing with a wide, still pool that looked like an open field, undulating in the bright sun.

Slipping easily out of her clothing, Piah walked to a rock ledge from which she could dive in. She stood for a moment, anticipating the strike of the chill water on her sun-warmed skin; then, holding her breath, she leaped off the rock and slipped through the water's surface. Held momentarily near the soft river bottom, Piah opened her eyes to see trout and other small fish darting away from her, and a crawdad reaching up to her in clawing protest.

Piah smiled and stroked back up to the surface. She floated for a while in the pool and felt the river hold her body. An osprey tilted in the arch of the sky and cried out, circling above her.

When Piah was young, she was taught the songs that came from the heart of the river, the pulse of the water matching the beat of her father's drum. Now, resting in the river's arms, Piah could hear the songs echoing through the stones in the riverbed as the river called to her people, letting them know when the salmon were moving through her body and when migrating eels wound up through her current to spawn in her gravel beds. It was a song of resting, of waiting, of nourishing the salmon eggs from fall and spring.

Climbing up out of the pool, Piah found a perfect place to rest. She lay naked on a large granite boulder on the soft moss, matching the curves of her body to the curves of the stone. She began humming the river song, as her heartbeat drummed along with the rhythm and the osprey's cries rang out within the canyon walls.

PART I

PIAH

⟨◎⟩

The smooth stones of her sister's grave were cool against Piah's cheek. It had been four seasons since Tenas had drowned in the rapids below.

She felt the loss of her younger sister rise in her chest, the clench in her lower stomach, and the surge of her tears. Piah could still hear her father's terrible cries as he carried Tenas's limp, lifeless body into camp. Piah ran to her father, and he held both of them while their mother's screams rang out through the surrounding forest. Piah sensed the rhythm of the day slide into something else. The animal sounds quieted, and the air seemed to still itself in response. Death was common to them, but this, a young woman just ready to marry, have children, and bring her family into the tribe was a deep wound.

Wiping her face, Piah leaned back against the familiar bark of the cedar next to her sister's grave. The Nesika fell from the cliffs below her into a cascade of white water. She could feel the force of the water's constant rush in her chest. The river hurt her.

Since Tenas had died, her father and mother had looked to her for something to fill the empty space left in their family, and Piah knew that the birth of her daughter, Libah, had helped them.

But ever since Libah had been born, Piah had been haunted by a dream that something like a horrible and dangerous storm was coming. Now she hoped that by calling to the spirit of her sister, she would receive a vision that would help her better understand what was happening to her.

Piah closed her eyes and let her awareness wander more carefully into the feeling, inviting the place of visions, invoking the place where she could be with her sister again. Following the path of her tears like a trail through a forest, Piah began to chant to the rhythm of the river's current.

Tenas.

Tenas.

Tenas.

Tenas.

Tenas seemed to be forming from the mist of the falls, her long hair streaming around her. Her spirit image looked the same way she had the day her father had carried her body into the camp.

"Tenas, I have a baby. I named her for the river—Libah. She is ours, Tenas. She is both of us."

"Piah, come closer. I miss you so much."

Piah felt the tear in her heart from the death of her sister. The wound still fresh, its edges bled red light into her vision.

"Piah, your baby is us; she will carry what we cannot." Piah kept her eyes closed, still seeing Tenas moved closer to her through the swirling vision. "There is much coming, Piah. She will be the one who will know the chanting, know the song. Libah will bring the medicine for so many, they will follow her even when you can no longer."

The earth under Piah began to tremble. The vision shifted, and the waterfall stopped flowing. Tenas became very clear, and Piah could see the fear and concern in her transparent eyes.

A spirit child of five or six ran up to Tenas, and Tenas stroked her long, dark hair, spoke to her, and placed a small beaded necklace around her neck. Piah realized it was Libah, grown into a young girl, and Piah's body leaped in response.

"Tenas, please keep us safe."

"I will do what I can."

The silence refilled with the sound of water. Tenas and the older Libah turned toward Piah. They gazed into each other until the mist dissolved the vision.

Piah slowly opened her eyes. She reached into the elk-skin medicine pouch she wore around her waist. The small beaded necklace from her vision was in there—clear blue beads interwoven with white crystals. She sensed the sweet power of protection emanating from them. Piah's grandmother had given her this necklace at her birth. She touched it carefully and knew it was now a gift for her baby, a sign from her sister in the spirit world that Libah would be protected and safe.

Piah's breasts ached, telling her it was time to get back to her daughter. She stood next to the stone pile for a moment longer. Large-bodied bears and other night animals around her were rustling through the undergrowth to begin their evening hunting. A female mountain lion jumped onto the granite boulder just below the falls. Piah could see the cat's tail whisk the air in response to sighting her. She stood still, and the cat turned away, bounding down the large boulder field along the Nesika into the shadows, leaving Piah alone with the rush of the current, insistent and indifferent.

JESS

⸙

The slow, cold autumn rain had not stopped all day. The clouds lay low in the forest around Jess, wandering with the swirling winds through the red tangle of vine maple, as she walked up the trail to the hot springs just up above the dam along the river.

She remembered stories that the Molalla people had bathed up here, and that they had created initiation ceremonies around the warmth of the springs. She was cold from having spent the day counting salmon, waiting for a pair to spawn so she could record their antics on her underwater video camera.

The hot spring was small, carved into the hillside by long years of water flowing from the spring. The familiar sulfur smell rose up to greet Jess, and she stood for a moment, remembering the many times she had come here to revive herself and to reconnect with the springs' healing warmth.

She heard him come up the trail behind her, felt excitement rise in her chest as he rounded the bend and saw her half-dressed and tired from a day's work. She had met him only several weeks earlier, while working a table at a conference. He had struck her with his quirky smile and intense stare. Something seemed to be hiding behind his eyes—something she found alluring and challenging.

She slipped easily from her jeans and stepped into the steam of the pool, sliding so her breasts were hidden just below the surface. He looked down at her and smiled. Jess breathed in the warm steam and, closing her eyes, felt the cool rain on her face and could hear the far-off pulse of the full Nesika.

He took off his clothing and stepped carefully into the hot spring next to her. Jeff was like the salmon Jess loved, moving in the air world the way they moved through the familiar currents of the river. He was confident in his body yet able to dart away with a flash when she got too close. She was wary of that now but believed after their day working together along the river that she had found a rhythm with him, similar to the synchronized sway of salmon bodies as they find their mate and begin to let go of the constant struggle and fight of their journey.

He moved closer, his hand sliding hesitantly across the back of her shoulders. Jess hadn't been close to anyone in a long time. She steadied herself and closed her eyes.

"Can I kiss you?"

She opened her eyes, smiling slightly, then pulled him toward her with the same certainty with which she'd stepped into the hot spring. She wanted him; she wanted to feel through him into the place where his love for salmon wound into his desire for her, a desire that moved toward life, toward connecting, sliding body to body in the fast curves of the river.

The rain fell harder, and the mist from the hot springs rose up around them. She looked up into his eyes, and he smiled. He slowly kissed her forehead, then her neck, then her shoulder. There was no one—just the two of them flowing together, abandoning themselves instinctively to the privacy of the water.

As he kissed her, her desire for him moved her closer. Her leg slid over his. His response was certain and careful. She felt the swaying of the river move through her body to his. He slid into her, and she opened to him. She came quickly, and her orgasm led her down the ancient path into the gravel of the spawning bed, her back pressing hard against the rock of the spring's bank. He came with her, and their cries soared out through the darkening forest.

BARBARA

⟨❦⟩

Turning from the plate-glass window, Barbara walked slowly across the living room to the worn plaid sofa. She sat heavily in the corner and ran her hand over the threadbare arm, the blues and greens once so alive in her once-so-alive world. Her hand rested there for a long time, and she let the weight of her body relax and press into the familiar softness of the cushion. Her heart was quiet, and she was glad for the peace, for the constant crying and terror to leave her alone. She looked out the living room window again, half expecting to see her two girls chasing each other around their backyard play set.

"Mooom," her daughter Jess would cry out in her lilting chant, "Monica won't let me use the swing, and it's been my turn for sooo long!"

Monica would smile back at her brightly, and Barbara would sigh and wipe her hands on her sunflower dishtowel before heading into the warmth of the summer morning.

"Now, honey, please take turns with your sister . . . Hey, you two—remember, your dad is coming home later to take you both fishing on the river. Let's make sure you have your lunch and are ready to go."

They had loved fishing with their dad and riding in the riverboat up and over the rapids around the bend from their house. The Nesika was famous for runs of summer steelhead, renowned for a mythical fight that fishermen craved. Barbara had once been happy raising her two daughters here, where they could swim and fight and play in the current of the fast-moving river behind their house. Moving here from Los Angeles had meant that she could protect them from the threats of the big city, from the drug deals going on in the schools there, and could try to preserve the gentle wonder in their surging young spirits. Jess had her beloved horse, and Monica had her sweet young friends and the adoration of her older sister. It had been almost perfect. Their days and nights had been filled with the constant chanting of the Nesika's current.

Barbara stood slowly. From her small kitchen window, she could see down to the Nesika and was surprised that it just looked the same—the river that had torn her open, taken her daughter Monica from her, a part of her heart that she could never get back. It was a physical tear, she was sure. Even now, eighteen years later, the healing felt only barely contained. She was able to go to the grocery store without collapsing in the cereal aisle when she saw Monica's favorite kind, but when she did the laundry and saw that Monica's clothes weren't there, it still felt like some sort of accident. They were just missing—just like Monica's smile, her laugh, her tears, and her sweet, open face. Gone. Into the river, into that river.

Barbara reached into the cupboard, remembering tea. She sighed and went through the motions of living and trying to make her life matter again. If it weren't for Jess . . . If it weren't for Jess.

Grief felt to her like an open, unexplored canyon with steep walls, unexpected storms, and beckoning, dark side canyons. She had spent years walking the trails and taking the unpredictable turns of unexpected loss. At first, it was always night. Then, after the local sheriff recovered Monica's body, Barbara felt like she was falling into the black fissures of grief and didn't even try to hold on—it wasn't possible. Her husband tried, her religion tried, but she just fell and held on to her falling. She wanted to cross over to where Monica was and had constant dreams of finding her, tangled in the bushes just across the river, along the bank, muddy and disoriented. In her dreams, Barbara would take Monica food and hold her again. Her sweet young body was still growing, still being, still loving.

Holding on to the edge of the Formica kitchen counter, Barbara closed her eyes, trying to stop the feeling that she was falling. In some ways, it hadn't changed. Taking a slow breath, she steadied herself and reached for her cup of tea. On the refrigerator was a picture of Jess and her big dog, Miko, standing proudly on the banks of the flashing blue-green river. Jess had become a scientist, and now she was studying, working for, and trying to save the same river that had taken her sister's life. Somehow Barbara took comfort in that, comfort in knowing that her daughters would stay close. Her brother, Robert, who had worked for many years for the Oregon Department of Wildlife, had inspired and supported Jess through her studies. Barbara was glad for that, as she knew she couldn't be the one to guide Jess. Science was too mysterious, too right about everything. Barbara wanted to know less, to rest in the mystery and simply trust in the process of everything. Mostly she knew now that she absolutely had no choice. There was nothing she could control, and so she spent her days getting through them, tending them as if they were a disabled child—hoping for progress but expecting none.

Her phone rang, startling Barbara back to the present moment.

"Hi, Mom!" Jess always sounded like she was in a hurry. "How are you doing?"

"I'm okay, just having some tea. How are you?" There was always a slight awkwardness to the beginning of their calls; then they evened out, became familiar—a simple way of checking in on each other without the tension, without the demands of anything unexpected.

"I'm good, Mom. Hey, I just met someone—well, I met him a while ago, but we're still getting to know each other—and I was wondering if you would like to meet him. Maybe next week? What about going out to dinner? His name is Jeff."

"Well . . . Jeff . . . I would love to meet him, of course. Dinner would be fun. Where did you meet him?"

"I met him at a conference a few weeks ago, and we just now, well, have been working on a project together. He works for PowerCorp—funny, huh? But he's really nice, cute, smart, you know . . . I think you'll like him. He's from Eugene but has been working here in Penden Valley for a few years."

Barbara smiled to herself—Jess had been a boy-crazy girl in her teens and had had a few close relationships in college. Although Barbara tried not to pry, she couldn't help but feel a constant tug of concern: After what Jess had been through, would she be okay?

Barbara sat back down on the couch and looked out the window. "Eugene is a nice place. Does he know your uncle Robert?"

A young doe walked across the front lawn as Barbara was talking; her movements were cautious, and her fur glistened in the morning sunlight. "Wow, a deer just walked into our yard. She's so beautiful, maybe not even a year old—so young to be on her own."

Just then, the doe looked up at her as if she knew she was being talked about. As Barbara paused to take in the young deer's eyes, Jess was quiet and Barbara sensed her daughter's worry. Jess tended to Barbara in between her words, her gestures. It was something Barbara loved about Jess—her complete certainty and her doting, devoted nature.

"If she's a year old, then she'll be okay. Remember the time Dad's friend brought home the albino fawn that he had shot? That was horrible. I never understood why people would do that! Men are so blind sometimes. Dad had some pretty clueless friends."

"Yeah, I remember when that happened. I made sure we made good use of that meat—poor thing. I was so mad at them.

How could they not have seen what a horrible thing that was? But sometimes the only thing they can see is what's right in front of them. Is Jeff a hunter?"

"His dad was—he was actually killed in a hunting accident when Jeff was just a boy. They were hunting elk in the coast range, and his gun just misfired. Jeff was twelve, an only child. The way he tells it, his mother never got over it. She still lives in Eugene, out in the country, in Jeff's childhood home. She's the same age as Uncle Robert—maybe they do know each other."

The deer walked slowly over to the blueberry bushes and began nibbling the last of the summer crop. Barbara wanted to shoo her away but just watched, imagining the horror of losing someone to a gunshot wound. Her heart took in the weight of this image, and for a moment, she loved Jeff, even though she didn't even know what he looked like yet.

"Oh my—that must have been so terrible for him. And his poor mother . . ."

Barbara paused. "Poor mother" was like a code when Barbara found herself in the rare company of mothers who had lost their children and wives who had lost their husbands. It was a strange country, filled with broken marriages and torn-open hearts.

The deer walked away, and Barbara sighed into the phone. "Well, I look forward to meeting him. Just let me know what night works for you two." She liked the sound of "you two" and imagined the "kids" coming for dinner. She smiled to herself. "I'm glad you found someone, sweetheart—you are so worth loving and having love."

"Okay, Mom—we'll talk soon? I love you."

"I love you, too."

Jeff and Jess, Barbara mused after she hung up. She imagined her daughter being drawn to the wounded boy, to his story and her story—the terrible threads that kept them strong, that perhaps helped them see more clearly the outcomes of their work together. Maybe they shared tenderness: for the young deer, for the panic in her eyes, for the gunshot that changed everything.

JESS

᪥

R ich looked expectantly around the room. "So, here we are.
It's good you could all make it today. We have our agenda.
Jess could you review some of your latest findings?"

She was in the room with the people who had the most
influence in what would happen to the Nesika. PowerCorp would
have to comply with whatever guidelines were required for it to
relicense the Nesika Power Project. There were seven dams on
the Nesika, and the largest—the Green Springs dam—was in
dire need of repairs and enhancements. Jess and others at the
Oregon Department of Fish and Wildlife had worked steadily
for two years, gathering data on the best options for the river
and the restoration of the decimated salmon and steelhead runs.
The best recommendation was removal of the Green Springs
dam and restoration of more than twenty-three miles of prime
spawning habitat. Jess's boss, Rich, had presented the findings to
PowerCorp and assured Jess that they had been accepted. This
meeting was a mere formality—the decision to remove the dam
had been made.

She sat up confidently and opened the report. "Sure. What
I have here—if you will look at page five of the Environmental

Impact Statement for the Nesika Watershed—are the sediment records for the reservoir behind the Green Springs dam. As you can see—"

"Just a second, Jess," Mack, one of the PowerCorp representatives, said, tapping his fingers nervously on the table. He leaned back in his chair, and the buttons on his red-and-orange-plaid shirt seemed to pull in protest. "I want you all to know how much we appreciate your hard work on this project. You've done some very fine research here. I know that it looks like taking the dam out is the best option, and we've been pursuing that idea for a while now." He cleared his throat and took a drink of his coffee. "However, unfortunately, something's come up: we just got word from our headquarters that they won't sign any settlement agreement that includes dam removal as an option."

Rich leaned forward. "Wait a minute—we've been working on this for years! How can you, how can they, make a statement like that after all this time?"

"Well, Rich, PowerCorp needs to keep this dam in place. It's just too expensive to take it down. There are too many changes we would have to make. We're going to have to look at our other options."

Jess couldn't be stopped. "What are you saying? I have the science right here." She pushed the phone book–size document toward him. "There's no way anyone can dispute what this says! We have findings based on our research and the independent research Greenbank did in Berkeley! Rich . . ." She turned to him as if she were trying to wake him up from a dream.

When he didn't respond, she felt her voice leap out of her throat. "There are no other sound scientific solutions. None. There is no question that the facts in this report support dam removal as the *only* solution that will allow us to even come close to accomplishing the directives of the Aquatic Conservation Strategy. Listen to what it says: 'Dam removal is the most effective option for both adult and juvenile fish passage at the Green Springs dam. The watershed analysis determined that the removal option was the only one that had high potential for restoring both habitat connectivity (upstream and downstream) and key physical processes.' You can't change this!" She slammed the report shut.

"Well, Jess, I of course see your point—but we just don't agree that taking the dam out is the only possibility. We need the Green Springs to run the rest of the system. Without that dam, we won't have any way of regulating everything that goes on above it. We've been working on a counterproposal that includes some fine mitigation for the salmon. You know, fish ladders and stuff."

"Wait—what? You can't tell me you have the ability or the desire to overturn this study. It's conclusive, Mack, not open for negotiation. We had PowerCorp's support on this. Today's meeting was about crafting the wording for the settlement agreement. You know we have to fight this." Jess felt heat in her chest and tightness grabbing at the small of her back.

"I've said all I came here to say." Mack looked over at Rich, then stood up and walked out.

Jess stared at Rich; why hadn't he pushed harder and defended the project? Instead, he was just gazing at the report and seemed to be thinking about something else. Then he said, in an even tone, "Hey, Jess, this has always been a long, somewhat uncertain road—we all knew that. I'm as surprised as you all are. I've been thinking this would be my legacy—you know, pictures of my accomplishment, the news . . ."

Jess stood, turning her back to Rich, and looked at a large photo of spawning salmon in the Nesika hanging on the wall of the conference room. She felt as if she were calling out to them, *We're trying to save you!*

"No, Rich," Jess said to the photo, "we *did* think this was a sure thing. We came a long way to this point." She put her hands on her head. "We were so close to having that thing signed, and they walked out on us. Just like that—like we were some kind of alien species . . . We can't let them do this. There's no way they can dispute the science. For God's sake, Jeff knows. He's their lead biologist!"

But does *he know?* Jess thought. They had just been at breakfast together—he had known the meeting was happening today; they had talked about it. Maybe he didn't know—he hadn't worked for PowerCorp long. Then again, he *was* the lead scientist on this project.

Rich rubbed his face and looked down at his hands. "I guess we need to go back to the drawing board."

Jess was still staring at the photo, the spawning salmon—now long dead and spent from their journey. *The ancestors,* she thought. She exhaled slowly and said, "Let me find out what I can from Jeff. He sure didn't say anything to me about this . . ." She let her voice trail off. "I need to use the restroom." She pushed back and gathered her papers.

"Fuck," she said to her reflection in the bathroom mirror. Her eyes looked clear and angry; her long, dark hair, draped over her shoulder, was evidence of a link back to her Native American ancestors on her father's side of the family. Her hands were shaking as she absentmindedly dried them and threw the paper towel into the garbage with a bit of force. She leaned on the doorframe before going out. Her throat caught, and she swallowed hard against the rage threatening to break through her.

Walking slowly back through the large, noble marble entryway of the federal building, Jess looked for Rich. He was leaning against a tall pillar, his lanky frame crumpled in sadness. She stopped and gathered herself. The anger in her throat and her swirling thoughts were not about him. She was sure he hadn't known anything like this would happen.

She approached him and said, "Hey, Rich, we can fight this, you know."

He looked up at her slowly, his large, light blue eyes seeking her out from under his thick, graying hair. "I don't know, Jess. Everything has changed so much in the last five years. The battles are different, and I'm just not sure how to fight them. I don't think we, as the agency, will have a legal fight. The environmental groups might. I guess we have to find a way to reemphasize how important this recommendation is, maybe get the media in on it somehow." He sounded so easily defeated, Jess couldn't help but wonder if he was telling her everything.

They walked silently out of the building and back to their bright green Oregon Department of Fish and Wildlife truck. Slowly opening the passenger door, Jess longed to be at home, sitting in the backyard with her dog, Miko, watching the slow fade of light in her garden. She wanted to ask Rich all kinds of questions, but the silent weight in the cab of the truck seemed to push at her chest, not giving her enough air to form words.

When she got back to her desk, she looked quickly at her email, but her attention was fractured. Six more hours left in the workday. She looked at her calendar, hoping that she had scheduled some field time for herself in the afternoon. She had: from one o'clock on, she would be up at the Nesika, making sure the fishermen were staying within the limits of their catches at the Corridor fishing area. In the fall, the coho were coming upstream in their dangerously small numbers, and Jess knew that if Power-Corp got its way, the fish population could continue to decline to the point where its slide into extinction was inevitable.

She imagined their slick bodies pushing upriver, silver flashing through the turbulent white water. The Corridor was a beautiful fishing spot, one that Jess had gone to with her family many times. It was a narrow place in the basalt canyon that forced the runs of salmon and steelhead to run a kind of fishing gauntlet. Jess had caught her first steelhead there when she was just nine. She longed for those days, but was that because she hadn't known the salmon were in decline back then? The only story she remembered was the tale of how, in the fall, when the salmon were running upriver, you could "walk across on their backs."

She thought back to when she had done her doctoral research in Alaska. She had kayaked by herself to a small island off Sitka. When she landed her kayak, she walked up toward a forested area in hopes of seeing a grizzly feeding on the salmon. She stood in the salmon stream where it entered the sound. Hundreds of salmon were making their way upstream, pushing against her rubber boots, being directed by the delicate shift in their hormones that signaled them to spawn . . .

Now, Jess looked up at the charts surrounding her desk. They looked like some kind of bizarre modern-art display in which the lines all went down, indicating loss of habitat and changes in the ocean currents, pointing to one thing: diving salmon populations. All the studies she had done with Jeff supported the one conclusion that would restore the spawning habitat above the dam: dam removal. They had put together an extensive evaluation of the habitat, showing that to simply provide fish with passage around the dam would put native salmon into a sedentary pond invaded by predatory species, like brown trout. This was not the salmons' habitat; their young would be eaten as trout food as they attempted to down-migrate through the reservoir behind the dam.

Jess wanted to call Jeff to talk all this through, but she wasn't sure who might be listening over the cubicle walls that created her artificial office, so instead she gathered her things and drove to her house for lunch.

"Hey, Miko!" she called, as she opened her front door. The love of her life came bounding out of the back room. He was big even for a male Akita, his black-masked face and strong, 135-pound, fawn-colored body moving toward her like a force of pure joy.

She knelt down and buried her face in his thick fur. "Damn, boy, how could it be like this? It seems like there's no logic working anymore." She absentmindedly pushed the PLAY button on her answering machine, and familiar voices rang through the room: someone selling carpet cleaning, a reminder call for her haircut . . . *Blah, blah,* thought Jess, and she punched the STOP button.

"Let's go, boy. Let's go see what's going on up the river." Miko spun in his "let's go" ritual, and Jess opened the door. The day was bright, the temperature high and unsettling for fall. She wondered if she should take some temperature measurements while she was upstream. The already too-warm river was enough to slow the coho from moving upstream in time to spawn.

As soon as she got into her truck, she called Jeff. She left him a message: "Hey, Jeff, it's me. I'm going upriver to do some work at Corridor. What the fuck happened today? Jesus—did you know about it? Anyway, you do now, don't you?" She heard her voice sharpening, and she took a breath. "If you're upriver today, give me a call, okay? If not, I guess we'll just catch up at dinner."

Jess ended the call and put her phone back in her pack. As she parked her truck near the fishing area, an osprey dove across the road in front of her, caught a thermal, and lifted up and over the Nesika. The hawklike bird's large white body stood out against the dark green river as it dove carefully into the deep resting pool below the falls of the Narrows. Ospreys always reminded Jess of the day of the accident: the quiet after the motor died on the boat, the rush of the water, her father shouting, and the high cry of the bird circling over them. It had been almost twenty years since then.

Pulling slowly to the side of the road, Jess looked out at the river and the families fishing along the Nesika's banks. She thought of the salmon, the importance of the fish to the river and to the people of Penden Valley, and the large concrete dam thirty-five miles upstream.

As she began to check the visitors' fishing licenses and salmon tags, she recognized an older man who was tying a neon green-and-orange plastic lure to his fishing line. He was an old family friend and father of one of her best friends growing up. Her heart tugged as she remembered her dad, bent over his tackle box, searching through a tangle of lures while trying to divine which one the salmon would go for. Jess used to help him; he would let her tie the lure on the end of the line using a special fishing knot. Then, almost five years ago, he had died suddenly of heart failure while working in his backyard garden. Attacked by his heart—a heart broken by the loss of his daughter—and by trying to love the fragments of his wife, who was so incredibly broken and wounded.

"Hey, Cliff." The man looked up at Jess with watery reddish-blue eyes, his graying hair sticking out from under his well-worn dark green Ducks Unlimited cap.

"Jess—hey! Good to see you!" He was like an old bear as he lumbered upright to face her. She longed to hug him but, realizing she was in uniform, simply reached out her hand in greeting.

"How's it going today? Catching anything?" Jess knew that fishing in the middle of the day was more of a meditation, a distraction, or practice for the times of day, like the early morning and late afternoon, when the fish were moving in the cool river, less likely to be spotted by predators with the sun shining on their silver backs. Cliff reached to take out his fishing license, and Jess gestured to him to put it away.

"Not getting much today," he said. "I caught one of those damn small-mouth bass, though. I didn't think they came this far upriver."

"Well, Cliff, the river's pretty warm this year. I'm not surprised the bass have come up this far. It's too bad—their favorite food is salmon and steelhead fingerlings. They don't belong in here."

"Yeah—someone told me they got in the river in sixty-four, when the big floods came. The Nesika flooded some fishing ponds up near the coast. The bass came into the river and have been doing great since the water's been heating up these years."

Looking out over the river, Jess sighed. "I remember going down to Ford's pond when I was a kid. It was full of bass and bluegill perch, remember? Dad would always fall in trying to walk out on the old pond logs. They love the warm water, these fish; if the river keeps getting warmer, there'll be a bigger bass fishery than salmon fishery on the Nesika."

"He was something, your dad." Cliff shook his head and bent down next to his fishing pole. "The river's sure changing these days. It's a lot different since you were a kid, huh?"

Jess nodded, and he continued, "How's your mom?"

"Mom's good. Busy with her knitting and begging me for grandkids. You know, you should call her sometime. I know she'd love to hear from you. I think she gets pretty lonely sometimes." Jess noticed that he got a faraway look and went back to tying on his lure, so she said, "Well, I'd better go. There's more folks up here than I expected."

"Okay. And I *will* give your mom a call. Good luck with what you're trying to do for these salmon," he said, gesturing toward the river.

The afternoon sun flashed in the folds and roll of the river. Jess walked downstream, toward the other people fishing, calling Miko to follow her. The whistling cry of the osprey caught her attention as it circled over the deep green pool below the white rush of the water moving through the basalt narrows. *Good luck*, she thought. And then she checked her phone to see if Jeff had called back.

JEFF

⟪◦⟫

The fluorescent lights buzzed loudly, and Jeff reached over and turned on the radio in his small trailer. Because he was new, they had given him a temporary office, down the gravel road just past the main offices for the Nesika Power Project. He was waiting to hear how the meeting had gone. Knowing that Jess was presenting their part of the research that had solidified the recommendation to remove the Green Springs dam, he imagined that evening, when he saw her again, would be charged with a powerful sense of accomplishment and that rush of Jess that he so loved. Jeff knew PowerCorp executives were uneasy about the possibility of removing the dam, but he also knew that they had other fights, bigger than the one over this little dam up in the high reaches of the Nesika. Jeff was even hoping there would be some publicity benefit to PowerCorp if it removed the dam—a new story told by an old, outdated corporate model—and he looked forward to working on the next phase of the restoration science that would be published and documented for other dam removal projects.

Jeff's phone buzzed, and Janice at the front desk called him in to see Stan and Mack. He felt uneasy; the meeting should have gone on longer than this.

Stan and Mack sat waiting for him in the small meeting office in the main building.

"Jeff, take a seat," Mack said, looking somewhere past Jeff, his large hands folded officially on the fake-wood tabletop. "We want to let you know how the meeting went. We had to deny the proposal to remove the dam. Just late yesterday, we got a fax from Mark Rey, the head of the US Forest Service, assuring us of their support to keep the Green Springs dam in the river. What this means is, that decision would override the proposal from the state agency and the environmental groups to remove the dam."

Jeff shifted in his seat. He remembered the camaraderie early in the negotiations, when Rich and the others, including Dave Rankin from the US Forest Service, had been convinced the dam would come out. It was like a win for the local boys, a legacy for the agency. But what meant more to PowerCorp than any of this was the amount of money it would cost it to remove the dam and restore the river. The actual science and what was best for the river didn't matter to the company at all.

"Great. Well, let's get on with it, then, shall we? Jeff, correct me if I'm wrong, but all we have left to do is to draft a memo that outlines what the Oregon Department of Fish and Wildlife needs from PowerCorp in order to support the new license." He paused and looked at Jeff. "We gotta make sure what we recommend won't be criticized too heavily by the science geeks at the agencies. That's why we need you, Jeff. Stan, what do we have so far? Did you see a copy of the memo that we had faxed down from Portland?" Mack shouted into the next room: "Hey, Janice, could you bring that folder on my desk that's marked 'Rey'?" Then he turned back to the others. "Hey, I heard a good one today. Do you know what a salmon says when it hits its head on a rock?" He paused. "Dam!"

Jeff smiled, but he felt as if he were in on plans to beat up a kid after school. He shook off his uneasiness when Janice came into the room and handed the folder to Mack.

The memo sat in front of him like a death warrant. Mark Rey assured the heads of PowerCorp that the Forest Service would not interfere in any negotiations over the new license. The Federal Energy Resource Commission was anxiously awaiting their recommendations, certain that the new license would be one that kept the Green Springs dam in place.

Jeff thought of Jess, her soft curves in the bed just hours before. He knew how much the dam closure meant to her, to Rich, and to the others from the environmental groups. Closing his eyes for a moment, he felt the familiar sinking in his stomach that he experienced whenever he faced something like this. He was grateful for his years of work and for his ability to stay out of the mainstream of major conflicts, but now he was faced with something that compromised more than him. He was the one who would have to craft a report that would provide the science to keep the Green Springs dam in place. He decided to let Mack react first.

Mack sat up and looked over the report in front of him. "Okay, one of the moves we can make is to set up what's called a mitigation fund. I have word from the office in Portland that we can put up to two million dollars into a fund that would support the various projects we recommend to mitigate the loss of habitat and other detrimental effects of the Green Springs dam. This looks good to the agencies, because who gets this money? Right, Jeff?" He nodded at Jeff.

Jeff was certain the money would be invested in the Nesika Power Project on an annual basis. And knowing that the fund would be allocated over a seven-year period would quiet Rich and the others. Of course, he knew most of this money would never actually be spent on restoration projects. Some of it would be used to upgrade the power station itself, and maybe the guy who ran it would get a raise for keeping a closer eye on regulating the downstream flows. The salmon would continue to be blocked from their spawning grounds, and the money would continue changing hands in the same way it had since the beginning of land management.

Pictures of the Green Springs and the Tahoma Power Station towered over them—a testament to development and to blind desperation for power, for energy to fuel a country bent on unlimited progress. The spill of the blue-green water and the web of power lines and blue sky over the granite canyon seemed like an irreversible part of the landscape. Jeff felt a stir in his groin, remembering Jess that morning, and a rising heat in his face at the knowledge that somehow this tangle of concrete and wire could stop what was happening between them, just as it had stopped the river and blocked the salmon while throwing electrons down wires—a mystery Jeff did not think he could ever completely understand.

"Okay," he said, "what I need to do is draft a new environmental assessment that will make recommendations to mitigate for the habitat loss, work to restore some of the downstream debris and gravel that's missing, and find a way to get the fish up and over the dam. I will take this directive back to Jess and Rich, and we'll put something together and let you know when we're ready to meet again."

Mack looked down at the memo in front of him as if it were a prize catch. "Sure, Jeff, sounds great. Why don't you take what you need from the documentation here?" He pointed to the large stack of documents on the table. "And let us know when you have a draft to show us. I'm hoping we can do this quickly so we can get going on some of those improvements we've been talking about. I hate it when negotiations drag on like this."

Jeff felt as if he were floating on an ice floe down an uncharted canyon. He and his report were about to discount everything he and Jess had worked for. He had fallen for her—for her wild and brilliant mind—and fallen for their science. Maybe that had clouded his judgment, but there was nothing he could do about that now.

◦◦◦

On the way upriver, he deliberately didn't check the message from Jess on his cell phone. Being with her, being able to hold her and listen to her, would be better than trading messages or having a tangled call that would end in arguing. He knew she would be taking this hard.

The radio played the dull sound of local country music, and Jeff stared down the road as he thought about his first day working with Jess, six months before. She wasn't tall, but she was strong and moved with a kind of determination. She reminded him of a wood elf, a hunter, aware of everything going on around her. Later, when she pulled off her damp wool cap, he could see her long, dark hair and a humorous glint in her crystal blue eyes. He liked her, that day, a lot. Then they had gone up to the hot springs and he had felt as if they had been transported back into a kind of ancient timelessness that transcended them both.

It was just getting dark, so he pulled into a small picnic area to spend some time by the river. The river curved around the bend under the darkening boughs of the old-growth Douglas firs that had survived in the steep river canyon. He wished he had brought his fly rod along. Impulsively, he decided to drop in on his old friends Fred and Janine. Fred had been a young boy when his family had settled in a small farmhouse on the outskirts of Penden Valley. He had married Janine, his high school sweetheart, and moved up on the Nesika, where he'd opened the Nesika Lodge. Fred was a powerful advocate of the river, and Jeff felt slightly nervous about telling him what was going on. They had started a fly-fishing organization twenty years earlier, the Nesika Fly Fishers, and Jeff had been a charter member.

He started his truck and drove up the long gravel drive into the hills above the Nesika where Fred and Janine had lived for more than forty years. The large wooden door slowly opened; Fred looked tired and resigned as he ushered Jeff into the dimly lit cabin.

"Hey, Jeff, what brings you around here?" Fred's lined face was lit with a familiarity that Jeff had grown to trust in the past years.

"Oh, just coming down from work and thought I'd stop in." Jeff had always appreciated Fred's special attention to him. Fred had been there for him when Jeff's father had died, teaching him how to tie flies and fish the deep holes of the Nesika River. As Jeff had gotten older, he'd realized that this friendship had become a cornerstone of his work and his devotion to protecting and caring for the river.

Fred's face dimmed with concern, and he looked over at Janine. "Yeah, I knew there was something going on. Rich was by the other day and said it looked like the dam was going to come down. I was surprised. Never thought PowerCorp would go along with that."

The silence fell around them, and Jeff let it rest for a moment, before he continued, "Actually, Fred, I just found out today that there's an agreement with the Forest Service assuring PowerCorp that the dam can stay in place and we can get by with building a fish ladder and other habitat enhancements. Of course, I'm the one who will have to come up with this plan and restructure the environmental-impact statement that Jess and I have been working on."

Leaning back into his worn leather armchair, Fred arched his wide eyebrows and looked sternly at Jeff. "Well, now, I can't say I'm surprised, given the priorities around here these days. But, Jeff, gosh, you and Jess have been working on this report for months. I saw parts of it just the other day, and it seemed clear that dam removal was the best option. What do you think is going to happen?"

Shifting his PowerCorp cap back onto his head, Jeff sighed. "Well, while it's true that dam removal is the best-case scenario, PowerCorp is convinced there are sound ways to move the salmon around the dam. But once they're there, the warm water that's sitting in the reservoir will be stuffed with brown trout, and we know their favorite food is baby salmon and steelhead, which would decimate the down-migrating fry. And Jess has taken this on as a kind of personal cause. She's so ardent and is convinced that this is the only way. I haven't talked to her about it yet, but I know she must be upset and ready to fight. You know, Fred, I haven't felt this way about someone in a long time. I just can't get enough of her. She's funny and smart and extremely passionate about this river. It's almost like she's never stopped trying to save her sister . . ."

"I know what you mean. What a sad story. She's always been so willful and so strong. We all love Jess and want to see her happy. I know this has been an important time for her, and I know she's pretty crazy about you, too. It's going to be rough—we both know that—but you two can work it out. Just stay steady." Fred looked over at Janine, who had just walked in from the kitchen. She was a vision of tenderness and nurturing, and Jeff felt for a moment the familiar tug of missing his own mother and put his hand on his heart.

Janine asked, "Jeff, would you like some coffee or something? The cobbler won't be ready for a while. Can you stay for dinner?"

"Thanks, Janine, but no, I have to get home. I would love some coffee though. You know, Fred, we all want what's best for the fish, for our own reasons. I think we can do this and have a win-win situation. The salmon and steelhead get their ladder, and Penden Valley gets to keep its lights on."

Fred looked at Jeff with a distrusting stare. "Shit, Jeff"—Jeff felt his stomach clench—"not one goddamn electron goes into the homes of Penden Valley. It all goes into some master grid in Utah, where it's bought and sold like cattle at auction. What Green Springs generates is a minuscule amount. You know that. Don't bullshit me. Just the other day, I was talking with the old guy who grows all those healing herbs up at Toketee Flat. He was telling me about an Indian friend of his who sees the bodies of salmon falling out of his lightbulbs."

Staring into the mug of coffee Janine had brought him, Jeff tried to steady himself. It took him a while to understand what Fred was trying to say, but he finally responded, "Fred, you and I know that power is profit. It's almost impossible to take the bone from the dog once he has it."

Sighing, Jeff looked down at the photos on the end table next to the couch, mostly of Fred and Janine's family—children and grandchildren. There was one of Jeff with Fred up on the Nesika the year before. He had caught a twenty-five-pound spring chinook on a very small fly rod. Before they'd released the fish, they'd had a passing tourist take their picture. Even then, Jeff thought to himself, he knew that the Green Springs dam would probably never come out.

While Jeff sipped his coffee, despite the now-tense atmosphere in the cabin, he felt the kinship of having lived in the same area as these people for such a long time. He could hear the Nesika flowing fast below the cabin, and he looked over at Fred in silence.

JESS

Why hadn't he called her? Jess pushed excuses around in her mind like old furniture. He knew what had happened today, knew she would be furious, and yet had slipped away, out of reach.

Just then, Miko's ears pricked and he huffed his low bark at the sound of Jeff's truck tires in the gravel driveway. Jess ran her hands through her hair, her heart racing in her chest, as she waited for the door to open.

When Jeff came in, Miko bounded over to him and she followed. She wanted tonight to be like all the others and sought out Jeff's eyes as he took off his PowerCorp cap and hung it on the coat hook just inside the door. She wanted to say something but let him pull her into his arms instead. She loved his familiar smell: sweat and machine oil from working in the power stations. In some ways, it was like any other night, and Jess wished that it could just be last night, when the meeting was the next day and they had assurance that the proposal to remove the Green Springs dam was still a possibility.

Jeff pushed back without looking at her. Stepping away from him, she sat in a chair across from the couch, where she knew he would sit out of habit.

"Jess, sorry about today. I should have known something like this might be coming down, but I really didn't know about it until just this morning. I would have called you—given you a heads-up—but I was feeling a little blindsided myself. The deal-breaker was a memo from the head of the Forest Service."

"I know who he is." Jess tried not to sound hostile.

"Basically, it guaranteed that the Forest Service would stamp any plan that PowerCorp comes up with. I didn't see the memo until after you were finished with the meeting. Now I'm supposed to come up with a proposal for you guys at the agency—one that you'll sign but that leaves Green Springs in the river."

"What the fuck, Jeff? You know their decision won't stand anyway. It can't, with all the scientific reports we have to back up our position."

"Well, I don't know, Jess. It's all very complicated—"

"Jeff, we both know the science, and it's *not* complicated." Jess felt the sharp stirrings of anger move through her stomach. "We did this research together! There's no other way to restore that habitat besides taking the dam out."

She got up and walked toward the kitchen, breathing in the stark light and focusing on her teal table stuffed into a too-small corner. *No, no, no*, she thought to herself. She opened the refrigerator and let the coolness calm her. "Do you want some wine?"

"Yeah, that would be great." Jeff had followed her into the kitchen and was leaning against the counter behind her. They were both silent while Jess filled two glasses. She looked up into Jeff's eyes; when she handed him his glass, he looked away and a heavy silence filled the room.

The phone rang, and Jess let the answering machine pick up.

"Hey, Jess. It's me, Suzie." The familiar, singsong voice of Jess's old friend rang in the room after the beep. "Holy fucking shit—Martin called me today and told me about that fucked-up meeting with PowerCorp. Fucking bastards." Jess looked up at Jeff and mock-grimaced. "Anyway, call me. He wants us all to get together on this—I guess at his house?—tomorrow around seven o'clock. Call me . . . Oh, God I bet Jeff is home. Shit—can't wait to hear how *that* goes!"

Jess sat down on the couch and looked into her wineglass, trying to divine what to say next. Suzie was a radical environmentalist involved in a fringe organization called Earth in Mind, whose tactics were sometimes questionable but seemed to fit Suzie's sense of style and attitude toward people making the decisions such as the one made today. Jess had chosen science as her brand of activism; Suzie's ways were just too erratic. Jess knew Jeff didn't like Suzie to begin with, but tonight she didn't feel like making excuses for her friend.

Conflicting feelings crashed in the room around them, like a cascade of whitewater rushing down a canyon during a storm. She reached out for Jeff's hand and pulled him onto the couch next to her.

She really liked Jeff. When she was alone and thinking of him, she thought she even loved him. They were a "good fit," people said to her, and she imagined their bodies—naked, tangled, fulfilled, and "fitting" so well. But now she sensed something new between them. Even though it was small, Jess could sense that the space between them was growing wider. Jeff moved back slightly and looked down at the floor in front of the couch. "So, you going to that meeting tomorrow?"

"Yeah, sure. Martin was really upset today when I called him. I don't know what he has in mind," she said, tucking Martin's "fucking lawyer" comment away in her secrets-from-Jeff file, "but I like the people who are working with the Nesika Watershed Council. They have their heads together, and maybe enough funding to figure out something that could make a difference. I just don't know how much I can be involved with them, since I work for the agency that's suddenly bowing to corporate interest, on the side of PowerCorp."

Jeff said, "Yeah, it would be good to be careful. I'm just not sure what can be done. It seems like this decision was made on a much higher level than the local groups can reach. But who knows? Maybe if they get someone good involved . . ."

"But, Jeff, you know they can't ask us to ignore our reports. They can't get away with this. And you don't want them to, right?" She leaned back to look at him. They'd been together for almost six months and hadn't had many fights, but now she felt her guard rearing up.

"Well, Jess, like I said, this is all complicated and we're just going to have to find our way through it. I know what the reports say, of course, and so do they. They may just . . . well, ask for another one—you know, an internal report that might have a different outcome."

"And who the *fuck* would do that? Jeff, you can't tell me you'd get involved in anything like that!" Jess jumped up and spilled her wine on the carpet in the process. Miko came over, looking worried, and she bolted into the kitchen.

"I might not have any choice," she heard Jeff say to her back.

Liar, she said to herself, as she came out with a dishcloth. She cleaned up the spilled wine in silence and then rushed back into the kitchen, taking too long to rinse out the towel in the sink. She glanced up and saw her reflection in the window, her dark hair pulled back and her eyes round with anger. Then Jeff slid into her view, and she looked up at him as if he were staring in at her from the darkness outside the glass.

"Jess, we're going to work this out. I know we will. There has to be a way that will work for all of us, especially us."

She turned and looked up into his dark brown eyes; they were sad and worried. But she just pushed past him, saying, "I'm going to take Miko for a walk. Want to come?"

Jess rattled Miko's leash, and he came crashing toward her, his big, bearlike body swaying in excitement, his black-masked face focused devotedly on her. Every evening they went on their walk up to the cemetery behind her house. Jess loved to be able to feel the roll of the seasons each day, moving into or out of one of their expressions. She liked to think of this as her way of staying related to her little sister, Monica, feeling as if Monica were still part of Jess's daily routine.

That Saturday morning, they had been playing along the

river together, fishing, throwing sticks for their small dog, Lappy, and splashing through the high, cold spring river. It was a beautiful day, and the sun was flashing on the water. Jess decided that they should try to swim to the rope swing across the river. It was early in the season, but the morning was so warm. They both jumped into the current, wearing their T-shirts and shorts. The fast current surprised Jess, but she made it to the other side easily. When she turned back to look for Monica, she was gone. Jess called out. She saw Monica pop up once, just before the fast whitewater downstream pulled her under. Jess jumped in after her, screaming her name. The rapids were high, too high for swimming, and Monica never made it back to the surface. Jess carried a wound that hurt her continuously and that she knew would never heal. Was it her fault? Could she have saved her sister?

She could never find an answer to these questions. Her sister was gone, out of Jess's reach forever, her once-lively and playful body resting in a grave on a small hill in the Catholic cemetery just a half mile from Jess's house.

"Sure, that would be nice," Jeff said, interrupting her thoughts, seeming to realize that Jess was struggling to reach him. And Jess was grateful when he reached for her, though she felt herself shaking, the memory of the trauma of losing her sister suddenly and viciously entangled with the possibility of losing Jeff, of losing the fight to save the Nesika. She couldn't bear it and let Jeff hold her. Finally, her trembling began to still and he kissed her. They fell onto the couch, knocking books and papers onto the floor. Jess moved toward him in an abandoned, urgent way, feeling his rising desire for her through the roughness of his jeans. This was a current that couldn't be stopped. The passion they had found in the hot springs that day flowed through every moment of their time together. They lived constantly on the edge between making love and not. And tonight there was a new fierceness underlying their attraction. Miko sighed and lay down heavily by the door.

"Be right back, buddy!" Jess called to him. They made their way onto their bed, throwing clothes around the house as they went. As Jess lay back on the bed, Jeff moved on top of her, looking into her eyes. He was certain with her, holding the small of her back in his hand, stroking the inside of her thigh and moving her strong legs around him. Jess let go completely into him, and they blended with the slow movement that always seemed certain and eternal to her.

They lay together, tangled and pleased, for a while. In those moments, Jess felt like the world was perfect, this world where she was warm and comforted, safe, and, for now, completely surrendered. Then she heard Miko rustling around in the other room and remembered their walk. "I've got to take Miko out. Still want to come with me?" Jess asked.

"Sure." He smiled, took her hand, and helped her out of the bed.

They dressed quickly, and their self-consciousness and the tension of their argument rushed back into the room. Jess watched Jeff's back as he methodically put on his jacket and hat. He always seemed to be moving slightly slowly, as if he were underwater. She loved that about him—he didn't ever seem to do anything unless it was deliberate, unless he wanted to. She wondered why suddenly he could just give up on the plan to remove the dam—give up on the science and certainty they both believed in.

As Miko charged ahead down the darkening sidewalk toward the cemetery, Jess moved to Jeff's side and he put his arm around her shoulder.

"Hey," he said, "we both know this is going to be hard for us. Everyone must be wondering—"

"Jeff, we both want the dam out. We aren't the only ones who know that removing it is the only solution. We don't have time to argue about it. Every season that goes by, we lose more and more of the wild populations that we need to keep the salmon going. You have to support us on this."

"I'll do what I can, Jess."

They walked in silence for a bit, then turned the corner toward the cemetery. Jess felt the familiar undulations of grief when she spotted the large golden cottonwood and the small white grave marker just below it. It was twilight, and the marker seemed to glow in the distance. Miko ran ahead, setting off the chirping alarms of the ground squirrels. *I'll do what I can*, Jess thought, and sighed as she looked down at the pavement.

When they got to the grave, she absentmindedly cleared away some of the brush around the headstone, slowly tracing her sister's name with her finger while Jeff rested his hand on her back. Jess sat on the ground next to the grave and thought of a time when they would have been joined by eagles soaring overhead, bears rumbling through the fields, wolves howling from the ridgetops, and mountain lions stalking smaller animals in the shadows. Would the salmon follow them? Or would their small families struggle to hold on, pushing against the current of human development, until the last of their kind slid to one side and let them pass?

The familiarity of her sister's grave gave Jess some comfort. Whatever happened, whether the dam came out or not, this place would be here, through the seasons.

She stood and called out, "Let's go, Miko! C'mon, boy!"

They walked back to the small house in silence. The air cooled quickly, and rain began to fall softly as they walked up the path to the door. The light glowed from inside, and Jess entered the comfort of her home.

PIAH

It was just beginning to get dark when Piah got back to camp. Lifting the damp, heavy elk skin that covered the door, Piah breathed in the scent of her home and knelt down on the musky deer fur next to her sleeping daughter. Piah cradled Libah and began to nurse her, feeling the warmth of her mother's knowing smile in the shifting light. Piah nuzzled Libah's hair, smelling the sweet, musky scent of her family, cedar smoke, and rain.

As Piah's mother began to stack the wood in the small fire pit in the center of their home, Piah was grateful for the certain warmth and light that the flames offered. She began to sing her fire song to Libah, and her mother joined in. It was a song of gratitude to the spirit of fire. Piah closed her eyes, remembering how her tribe had used big fires to burn the land and clear the way for gathering the seeds from the sticky tar plants in the valley down the river from their home. As she had grown older, she had worked with the women enthusiastically, swinging her willow branches in time with her companions, chanting songs of gratitude for the plants and seeds that gave them life. Last season, she had been pregnant and worked alongside her mother and grandmother. They had woven into their chanting lessons for Piah: how to be a mother, how to birth her baby and care for her body afterward.

Piah's husband, Maika, came in through the skin door and smiled when he saw Libah and Piah. She handed Libah to him and moved next to her mother to help her tend the fire and begin to prepare the evening meal.

It started to rain. Piah heard others moving into their homes and heard the Nesika filling with the steady fall rain that would call the salmon up from their ocean homes into the river's arms to nourish her family with their bodies. She wanted to tell her mother about her vision, about the necklace and the comfort of the promise from her spirit sister, and that she was concerned about what Tenas had said: "You don't know what is coming." She knew that her vision had been not just a protection blessing but something more.

Her father came in and sat next to her. Piah had the necklace in her lap and decided that she should share her vision with her family and trust her father to help her discern its meaning.

She held it out in her hands and saw the light from the fire reflected in the small, clear stones. "I went to see Tenas today— she came to me in a vision up near the falls. Tenas wants this necklace for Libah—to keep her safe. She said something was coming . . . I felt like she was warning me, but I don't know what about."

Piah's father carefully picked up the necklace from Piah's palms. It looked tiny in his large hands, and he gazed at it tenderly for a long time, before asking, "This is from Tenas?" His voice cracked with sadness, and Piah's mother moved closer to him. "It is a spirit necklace that is not from our kind of time. What did she say to you?"

"She said that Libah will be the one who will know the songs and chants, who will become the one that we can follow, who will know what to do. But she didn't say what was coming."

Her father shifted his weight and leaned against the fur-lined walls of their home. His dark eyes reflected the firelight and seemed to Piah to deepen with a blend of sadness and fear.

The rain grew lighter, and Piah heard the rustling of the night animals in the dark forest around them. The call of a male wolf rolled down the canyon near the river and was answered by his pack in the distance.

"This is an important message, and one we must tend to. In my own visions, there have been warnings as well—I can feel a tremble in the earth, a calling-out, a storm from an unknown horizon. It would have been a great effort for Tenas to come to you with this offering—it is a rare gift and one not to take lightly. It is for your baby, Libah, and a powerful blessing."

He began a slow chant that seemed to come from a time long before. Piah stood and carried Libah to his side. She held her while her father carefully placed the necklace over Libah's small head. He kissed her forehead, and Libah reached out to him in response. Piah smelled the river and her daughter's sweet, milk-washed skin. Her father's chant held them like a protective, certain hand in their home, around their small fire, in the center of a dark, uncertain place.

JESS

෧෨෯

As Jess drove through the rain to Martin's house, she remem-bered her first Nesika Watershed Council meeting, when she was a junior in high school. Martin and his wife, Maia, had been sitting near the front of the community meeting hall at the Unitarian church, trying to contain their roving two-year-old son. Jamie had wandered over to where Jess was sitting and crawled into her lap. She had been babysitting for him since he was an infant. It had been only three years since Monica had died, and holding Jamie always helped her feel connected again to the substance of life.

As she held him during the meeting, the present seemed to melt away and she heard a series of words ringing in her ears like an ancient chant:

Watershed
Nesika
Salmon
Fishing
Public
Interest

Public
Interest
Public
Land
Salmon
Salmon
Salmon

Martin came over to her and broke through her trance. She looked up at him and suddenly felt small, like his child. He squatted next to her and brushed his hand over Jamie's sweet blond curls. Jess leaned away from him and let her gaze take in father and son, continuous and flowing with each other, Jamie's body relaxing into his dad's.

"Thanks," Martin whispered. "Hope he isn't bothering you." Jess shook her head no and felt Martin's strength as he rested his hand on her shoulder.

When Martin left, Jess found her way into the back bathroom of the old church. She splashed her face with cold water and looked at herself in the mirror. She was small, and her short hair, neither curly nor straight, was a mousy, uninteresting brown. She was wearing her favorite earrings, dripping down her neck like water droplets, a blue-green stone that was the color of the deep pools of the Nesika.

After that meeting, Jess ran into Martin at the Saturday farmer's market. She noticed Jamie first, running determinedly through the booths of fresh, colorful produce. The air was balmy for early spring, and the flowers in white plastic buckets seemed to want to leap out into new owners' arms.

"Jamie," Martin called to his disappearing boy, "Jamie, come here a minute." Jamie came running back proudly, carrying an unpurchased bright pink peony high in the air like a small flag.

"He's . . . well, he's two. Hey, are you available next week to help us out with a project-planning meeting? We're going to look at the plans the Forest Service has put forward to redo the boat ramp facilities at Heather Bend. Jamie, sweetie, stay here a sec . . ."

"Um, yeah—when is it, again?"

"Next Thursday at three. It's going to be at my house—hopefully, Jamie will be napping and we can get something done."

The following Thursday, Jess walked up the uneven concrete steps to Martin's front door.

"Jess, come on in." Martin's house was strewn with papers and toys. A rocking horse with a crooked hat waited in the corner, and a fire truck was upside down in the middle of the floor. The living room smelled like a blend of garlic and nag champa, and a beautiful painting of Stonehenge hung behind the worn green-and-yellow floral couch.

"Maia's at work right now, and Jamie is sleeping, finally—I know he'll be happy to see you when he wakes up. Want some tea?"

"Love some—thanks. Ginger if you've got it."

Jess walked over and scanned the titles on the living room bookshelf: Edward Abbey; Barbara Kingsolver; books on Marxism, poetry, and tea making. She thought she could someday write a poem describing her friends by the titles of the books on their shelves. Martin handed her the tea and asked, "Have you read *Mermaid*, by Daniel Dennett?" He reached over her shoulder and pulled a volume from the shelf. "I loved it—here it is."

"We just read it in my Environmental Literature class."

The phone rang, and Martin went into the kitchen to answer it, calling behind him, "Come on in here, Jess—the plans are on the kitchen table."

Jess sat down at the table and ran her hand over the cool, smooth paper.

Martin came back and sat in the chair next to her. "The others can't make it. They just got a call from the daycare and they have to go pick up their sick kid—guess it's just you and me!" With that, he began talking about the plans, which recommended a thorough environmental assessment, including an impact study on the down-migration of the fingerling salmon trying to navigate the falls above the proposed boat ramp.

Jamie called out from the back room shortly, and Martin went to go settle the waking boy. Jess loved being in this house, where love and life moved to a familiar rhythm. Her home felt torn and wounded, filled with memories and the far-off sound of crying that never quite seemed to end.

⬥

The car behind her honked, startling her into noticing that the light had turned green. Her headlights reflected off the wet pavement, and Jess followed them like a path through the intersection. She drove slowly up the steep hill to Martin's house and his now-familiar driveway. She had learned a lot from Martin about how environmental groups worked and how she could use her love for the natural world for a good cause. To Jess, he would always be a warm refuge, a kind of love that she would hold dear and close to her heart.

Suzie's car was there already—a small gray Toyota with a worn, upside-down bumper sticker that said WHY BE NORMAL? on the back bumper. Jess waited in her car a few moments before going in. What was going to happen? Martin's anger and outrage when she had told him about the outcome of the meeting with PowerCorp would be mediated now, and Jess was certain he would have a plan.

An old Volkswagen bus she hadn't seen before pulled in behind her. Three young people got out and charged into the pool of light at Martin's door—probably kids from Earth in Mind who had come down from Eugene for the meeting. Jess began to worry; these were the kind of kids who were known to try radical things, like blowing up dams. In that case, why would Martin want them here?

Jess got out of the car, and as she got closer to them, she smelled marijuana and body odor wafting toward her.

"Hey, guys. I'm Jess." She reached out her hand.

"Mink."

"Remedy."

"Butterfly."

Jess kept herself from snickering. *These kids and their code names*, she thought. "Did you come down from Eugene?"

"Yeah," said Mink, a tall, lanky boy with long blond dreadlocks. "Just heard from Martin about the problems with PowerCorp and the Green Springs."

"Let's go in before we get soaked out here." The rain was pressing down harder, and Jess reached for the door and opened it into the living room.

Suzie stood up. "Hey, guys." She looked like she might lick her lips at the sight of three young, strong, and not-very-clean young men. Jess made eye contact with her friend—*back off, girl, they're too young for you*—and they both smiled.

"Come in." Martin gestured toward the couch. He brushed his hands along his gray-and-red flannel shirt, in a familiar nervous gesture, and Jess noticed that his eyes were downcast.

Introductions rang out. Maia came in with a pot of tea and a plate of some kind of bread. Jamie, who was now a lanky young teenager, loped into the living room and flopped into a soft chair in the corner. The house smelled nice, like family, and Jess felt a tugging sensation low in her abdomen.

Martin stood and poured some tea into a green-and-black MIND OVER MATTER ceramic mug. "This is great. Thanks, guys, for driving down on such a crappy night. We've fixed up the room in back if you want to stay over."

"Thanks, man, but we're going to crash after the meeting at our friend Gina's house. Do you know her? She works at the bagel shop here in town." Suzie nodded in their direction; Martin looked into his tea and didn't seem to be listening to the boy named Mink.

Instead, Martin continued with what he wanted to say: "Okay, right. We're getting together tonight to talk about what to do about the Green Springs dam removal project, as I like to call it. Those of us here at the Nesika Watershed Council have been working on this for a hell of a long time with the Nesika Fishermen, Trout Unlimited, and now you."

Jamie's cell phone made a sound like a car engine, and he jumped out of his chair and darted into the next room with a hushed "hello."

Jess smiled to herself—how cute. Martin sighed and looked over at Maia, who just shrugged. He continued, " But, like I told you in the email, we've run into a wall with these motherfuckers at PowerCorp. Even though some of the best scientists have concluded that the best action for the salmon is to take out the dam, these folks somehow think they have the authority to simply change everyone's mind. I guess what I would like to talk about is how we can get their attention. They claim they can't take out the Green Springs because it's what they call a reregulation facility, meaning it controls the flow from the whole fucking fluctuating system above it. Well, that's bullshit—Jess here can tell you more about that. We want PowerCorp to know that they can't bully us around, the way they do with the pansy-ass agencies. Sorry, Jess—you know what I mean."

"It's okay—kind of an insult to pansies, though . . . I'm so committed to getting this dam out. You know that. And the longer I work for the Department of Fish and Wildlife, the more I realize how ingrained it is in the pockets of PowerCorp. It seems like kind of a sad fantasy that I ever thought Mack and the others gave a rat's ass about the Nesika, when they're interested in only one thing. But I can't do anything illegal. As mad and crazy as I'm feeling right now, I also need to be really careful."

Martin paced across the living room and looked absently into the space where his son had vanished with his cell phone. "Sure, Jess, we get that. But, you guys, you were part of some plan up on the McKenzie River—am I right? Something about the Clark Dam?"

Remedy spoke up. "Yeah. We had a plan." He looked over at Mink and smiled. "We were going to blow it up. You know, we got the stuff together, with some help, and yeah—like, *boom!*" He gestured wildly with his hands, startling Jess. *Oh, fuck,* she thought. *This is exactly what I was afraid these kids would want to do. What twenty-year-old doesn't want to blow something up these days?*

Suzie laughed and put her wool-socked feet on the table. "Ha! *Boom!* I get it. Wouldn't that be freaking amazing? It's what those fuckers deserve." *Of course Suzie would be up for this*, Jess thought. Then Suzie added, "There's no way they would pay to rebuild it . . ."

Everyone shifted in their seats, as if a wave had washed through the room. Jess shook her head. Martin put his hands roughly into his jeans pockets and said, "Okay. We all know that's one option, and Jess is right. But, guys, we can't associate the Nesika Watershed Council with that kind of activity—it's too dangerous, and for lots of reasons. But we could find a way— maybe *act* like we're going to blow it up."

Remedy said, looking up at Martin from under his dark curls, "That won't fuckin' work—these pigs deserve to have this shit blow up. We'll do it. We just need the engineering specs—you know, the drawings that show how the dam was made. We know a guy who knows how to look at them and point out where the weaknesses are."

Jess felt the room fall away from her. Still hoping they weren't serious, she looked over at Suzie, who just smiled and shrugged her shoulders. Jess felt a shiver run down her back. Suzie was totally capable of inspiring a kind of renegade wildness in others.

Jess felt cornered. Jeff was at home, trying to convince her that he could somehow fix things, and now her best friends were getting involved with this radical group and their reckless ideas. This was not something she could do. She wanted to run away from being part of this. But then she remembered her fight with Jeff the night before and knew she had to do *something*.

"Wow. Well, Jess?" Martin looked over at her. "You'd be the one who could do that."

Jess stared at Suzie's socks. "Martin"—her voice sounded higher, less certain, to her—"it seems too quick. Didn't you hear what I just said? I could lose my job. Maybe we should give some other things time to work—"

"C'mon, Jess. Wouldn't that be so cool? God—that would fuck them up big-time. By the way, what's Jeff saying about all this?" Suzie turned to the Earth in Mind guys and said, "That's her boyfriend. He works for the power company." She said it in an almost taunting voice that confirmed for Jess what Suzie thought of their relationship. Jess stayed quiet for a moment, then said, "He read the memo and seems cowed by his boss right now. They've already asked him to start revising our report, in support of a fish ladder." Suzie let out a long sigh next to her. "And I don't know, Martin—I just can't see how this is going to work for any of us." She turned to Mink and asked, "Have you guys ever done anything like this before?"

"Nope. But we can—we almost did up on the McKenzie River, north of Eugene, but the company changed its mind and proposed a plan to decommission the Clark Dam. I sometimes wonder if they heard what we were about to do . . . But this time we have a solid plan. Don't worry, Jess—we won't let you get caught— but we really can't do anything without the engineering specs."

"Jesus . . . I think we'd better talk about something else. I just don't want to get involved with something like this. What if one of you got hurt? No. It's not a good idea," Jess said.

Martin looked down at the floor. "I know what you mean. But if we can make some threat, look like we really mean it . . . you know, kinda like you guys did up on the McKenzie. What do you think?"

Butterfly, who hadn't yet spoken, pushed back his rainbow-colored knit hat and cocked his head to the side like a large Labrador. "It only worked up there because we were really going to do it. We can stage something, but then they'll pile on the guards and there's no way anyone would get within a mile of that dam. So you just get us the specs, and we still have the stuff we got together to blow up the Clark."

"So, why don't we just plow ahead with this and see what happens?" Mink interrupted, an edge of excitement in his voice.

"I'm sorry. I can't help you. This is too dangerous. We were so close to the decision. I have the science, the reports. Martin, Suzie, please don't push ahead with this. It's too early." Jess looked from Martin to Suzie; they were staring at each other. She thought of Jeff again—the layers of deception she would have to be willing to endure, to cover him with.

"It's okay, Jess—we can take it from here. I don't want to jeopardize your job. You know that. And there's Jeff. I've known him for so long—I don't know how he survives working for those pricks," Martin said.

As he looked at her with concern, Jess stood up. "I should go. You guys just keep going. We all want the same thing, and I guess this is one way to go about it." She looked at the three boys, sitting like Rodin statues on the crazy floral couch. She remembered the time she, Suzie, and their friend Leslie, at sixteen, had all stood in front of a large, old oak tree some loggers wanted to cut down in the center of town. They had held hands and sung Joni Mitchell songs as loudly as they could, standing between the loggers and the beautiful old tree. They had been arrested and taken to juvenile hall, and the tree had been cut down. Jess still had a piece of its trunk on her desk. A relic.

"Thanks, guys—and good luck." She walked out to her car, the ground still damp from the hard rain. The moon had come out, and the air was fresh with the coming spring. She drove home slowly, rehearsing what she would tell Jeff about the meeting. It was like walking through a long valley up into another mountain range, weaving his point of view into hers. *How long will it last? This can't be right.*

⟡

"How'd the meeting go?" Jeff asked when she got home.

Jess patted Miko's head, avoiding eye contact with Jeff. "It was good. Some kids from Earth in Mind were there. Their names were Mink, Remedy, and Butterfly. God, I would love to be them, to be twenty, so convinced that what they're doing is the absolute right thing."

"Good, good. I took Miko for a walk. We missed you." He hugged her close, and Jess was grateful he didn't ask for more, though she had the layers ready to cover what had really happened: what she was willing to do or not, to say or not. She didn't want to fight with him—it was too hard, and she was too tired.

Jeff reached tenderly around her and slipped the hairband from her ponytail, running his fingers through her long hair.

She rested in his tenderness and felt the whole day fall away. If she could somehow just wish it all back, they could stay right where they had been these past months. He whispered into her hair, "I know we can work this out." Even as she felt herself melting toward him, she knew there was something else looming in the room, forcing itself up between them from the ground. It was cold and hard and smelled like damp concrete.

JESS

Jess pulled her small truck into her familiar parking spot in front of the hedge surrounding the dark brown walls of the Oregon Fish and Wildlife offices. She sat in silence for a moment, imagining what might be going on behind Rich's closed door or what might be waiting for her in her email inbox. It seemed impossible to her that something so certain could have changed so fast.

Her body was sore, and she hadn't slept well the night before. She walked slowly into the building's small, too-bright kitchen, where coffee was brewing, and stood watching the steady stream pour into the clear glass pot.

A hand on her shoulder startled her. "Jess."

She turned quickly around and looked up into Jeff's dark eyes. "What are you doing here? I thought you had to go take measurements in the reservoir above the dam."

"I thought I did, too, but I've been called into a meeting today, with the hydrologist and the fish guy—I think his name is Dave—from the Forest Service."

"What?" she said, shoving him into the corner. "Why wasn't I told about this meeting?"

"I don't know—maybe they're worried about you and me. Maybe they know about your involvement with the enviro groups—"

"I'm the lead fucking scientist for the state on this project! They can't have secret meetings without me!"

"Well, they're not exactly secret if I'm involved—they all know about us."

"Fucking shit. They *are* going around me, aren't they?" Jess turned and closed the sliding door into the kitchen, then continued, "Jeff, you have to help me. Rich won't stand for this, won't sign the agreement. I know that!"

"I don't know that for sure, Jess. I know you've known Rich a long time, but he has a family, he's going to retire soon, and he's done this work for years and knows when to choose his battles." Jeff looked nervous, and Jess wished they could just slip away. Instead, she pushed past him and slid the door open loudly, startling Emily, the receptionist, who was waiting outside, holding an empty PowerCorp coffee cup.

Shit, Jess thought, and she rushed down the dim, brown-paneled hall to the slightly open door of Rich's office. He was on the phone, but Jess didn't care. "Rich! Hey, what's going on? You can't have a meeting without me!"

Rich whispered, "Hold on" into the phone and cradled it against his chest to keep Jess's shouting from entering his conversation.

"Jess, let me finish this call and I'll come talk to you in your office."

"No. I'll wait right here." She flopped onto the green fake-leather couch and stared hard at her hands. She heard Rich saying softly, "I'll have to call you back. I'm sorry. Shouldn't be long."

When he hung up, he said, "Jess, I know—"

"You know! Of course you know! Why wasn't I told about this meeting today? Dave is here, Jeff is here, and I'm being sent out to check fishing licenses? I wasn't hired, I didn't get my PhD, to do that! What is going on?" Jess stood up and leaned on the front of Rich's desk, sliding his nameplate to one side: RICH HANSON, DEPARTMENT OF FISH AND WILDLIFE.

"Jess, please calm down. You have to understand what we're up against here. I know how hard you've worked on this, and your science is good, real good. Your results line up with everything we all know about what's best for the river. But you're too close to the project. You have too many . . . well, too many personal feelings about what's going on with the river."

"What! Oh my God, Rich, not you! I took this job because I trusted you and I respected you as a scientist. I know you and my dad were friends, and I know from him what a good job you've done for the state, for the fish, and for the river. I can't let you do this. I won't—"

"Please try to understand that there are a lot of sides to this story. There are the needs of the fish, that's for sure, and there are the needs of PowerCorp. It's about balancing all that out."

"Don't feed me that crap, Rich! You and I both know what's best here, in the long run, the short run, the *only* run, for the salmon and steelhead in this river! If this license is renewed, it will be another forty-five years before we get a chance at making any significant changes at all in this part of the river. How can you be okay with that?"

"Well, Jess, I guess my perspective is that we all have a different take on what will really help restore the salmon populations. I happen to believe that if we can put a ladder around the dam, we can at least partially restore the spawning grounds."

"But, Rich, you didn't believe that yesterday."

He just sat there. Jess looked at him and backed away from his desk, sitting back down on the couch. The room fell away as she recognized the familiar numbing of betrayal, and she suddenly didn't care to try to rescue Rich or her relationship with him. For some reason, because of some conversation that must have threatened his job or scared him in some other way, he was gone to her.

"I have to go to work." She stood up, and the silence between them felt like a dark, toxic haze that Jess couldn't quite see through. "But, Rich, you know I'm right."

He didn't say anything. He picked up his phone to redial his call.

Jess went back to her office and stared at her computer screen. She thought of the meeting at Martin's the night before and began to wonder if she shouldn't get more involved. *Jeff*, she sighed to herself, and looked up at the photo of the two of them on her desk. When they had first gotten together, it had all seemed simple enough. She had brought to him the current science and studies that she had done and been familiar with in graduate school, and he had brought to her his experience in working for years in this community, on this river. Now, now . . . Jess sighed and tried to think of what to do next. She felt alone, like she was a character in an old black-and-white Western, invisible to everyone in the office, even Jeff. How were they going to hold their relationship together through this?

Sitting at her desk, Jess felt small and powerless, wondering what her colleagues might be saying about her in front of Jeff. *It's just not right*, she thought. *None of this was supposed to happen.* She rearranged the reports on her desk; they all showed the continual decline of the coho, chinook, and steelhead that had lived in the Nesika for thousands of years. To her, it was simple: the salmon and steelhead were in a dangerous decline, and the best way to help them was to restore their spawning grounds by removing the old, worn-out Green Springs dam. She couldn't conceive of what they might be considering in the meeting down the hall. Anything they would think of would only create a false front for a failed project. *How can they ignore the science? It's not just some story someone made up.* It was as real to her as her hands and fingers.

Just let it go, she told herself, but Martin's comments from the night before rang in her ears. *What if . . .*

She grabbed her keys off her desk and hurried out to her truck. She wanted to check the migration monitoring station at Colliding Rivers station, where the Nesika ran headlong into the Toketee River upstream, creating a storm of white turbulence.

As she drove, Jess thought about calling her uncle Robert, her mother's older brother and a large, sweet presence at family events. After Monica's death, when Jess's parents, consumed by grief, hadn't seemed to have room for her and her loss, Robert had become a source of solace for her. And when the time had come for Jess to go to college, he had supported and championed her bright mind and tender wits and had inspired and encouraged her desire to follow him in his passion.

He, too, had been attacked by the agency he worked for. The Forest Service, where he was the director of one of the largest studies on salmon in the Columbia River, had disregarded and discarded his own findings. He had written a report concluding that the continued decline of salmon populations couldn't be offset by "manufacturing" the fish in hatcheries; the life cycle of the salmon was simply too complicated to be reproduced in an industrial environment. The wild salmon followed a story in their genetic code that was unique to their birth river. These genes shaped the physical growth of the salmon, which depended on the flows and currents of the river itself. To remove the eggs, to remove the bodies of the parents from the streams, was to degrade the environment and compromise the development of the salmon in a way that contributed to their demise and possible extinction. But the hatcheries were the tools of government agencies and justified the use of rivers for profit.

As Robert became more vocal in his criticism, his agency job became more difficult, until he had to "retire" early. He then started a private consulting company, built a large house on the Columbia River, and devoted his time to writing about salmon. His books and lectures became the fuel for young biologists and ecologists to fight for the wild fish.

Now, Jess knew, she needed him more than ever. She called him from the Colliding Rivers parking lot. "Uncle Robert!"

"Jess, hey—good to hear from you. I was just thinking about you. How's things going in the working world these days?"

"Well, I wish I could say great, everything's fine, but, to tell you the truth, I'm not exactly sure what to say to you about it. We had a meeting the other day with PowerCorp, and basically they just walked out of the meeting, declaring that they would not sign any settlement agreement that involves removing the Green Springs dam."

"What? But, Jess, I thought you said they were onboard with that."

"Yeah, I—well, *we*—did, too. But they got some directive from your old friend with the Forest Service Mark Rey, who we both know is a conservative ass, assuring PowerCorp that there would be no holdout on the Forest Service's part in regard to leaving in the Green Springs. It really sucks."

Jess felt as if she might start crying, and Robert was silent on the other side. She knew he was experiencing echoes of his own conflict with the Forest Service, how they cornered him when he proposed a new guideline to measure impacts of logging on salmon habitat. He had found himself defending his science against what he thought was a public institution—only no, it wasn't. The Forest Service had become just one more federal agency being run by corporations and serving only corporate interest.

"Damn, Jess, I really thought this would go through. I'm so sorry. I knew when you started working for the agency that there would be some hard times, but . . . I don't know—maybe I'm still too naive myself to realize how low they would go to get what they want. I just don't get it. There's no way there's a trade-off for anyone in this. One thing I can guarantee you: they're not telling you everything they know."

"That's just it. You know how I've been seeing this guy, Jeff? He's the head fish biologist for PowerCorp. We worked on all the reports together, he knows the science as well as I do, and he's back at the office at some private meeting that I wasn't invited to."

"I don't know what to tell you, Jess. There are matters of the heart and matters of work. Sometimes the two just don't always mix that well. Maybe this is one of those times, sweetheart. You're a good scientist. Your papers on sediment reduction and the relationship of water temperature to spawning rates are some of the best I've ever read. You're well respected and well published. If they know what's good for them, they won't ignore your science."

"Thanks. But they *are* ignoring it as we speak!" Jess gazed out the window of her truck. It was a clear day, and the golden leaves of the maples at Colliding Rivers station rocked in the light wind of the late morning. She looked out over the blending of the two rivers. She loved their force, rushing down from their high mountain sources and colliding headlong into each other, before rolling together into the same basalt riverbed.

"Jess, listen to me. They're going to do what they're going to do. These people are corporate hacks operating in an environment where facts don't matter. There is a really profound sense of invincibility among people who have corporate power. But you and I know that is only one kind of power. You have to wait. When the time is right, be ready with what you know."

Jess sat in silence for a moment. "I don't know if I can do that."

"I don't know if you have any choice."

"Yeah, I know what you mean. Uncle Robert, this is so hard."

"I'm not telling you to be a good girl—don't get me wrong about that. You know what happened to me. I'm just saying that it would better serve your career, and maybe the river in the long run, if you can stick to your science and not lose your job over this. I can tell you there's no way out. There's no way you can fight them. Not like you want to right now."

He paused, then asked, "How's your mom doing?"

"I think fine. I'm never in touch with her as much as I want to be. I've been so busy. She doesn't even know what's going on. I ran into my dad's friend Cliff the other day up at Corridor. You know, Uncle Robert, there was a time when all this seemed so simple: the fish just came back year after year. There were no questions, no concerns, no endangered-species listings. Now there's constant fighting while the populations just keep declining."

"Well, these are the days when change seems to be accelerating at an almost exponential speed. One thing changes, like the temperature readings you reported on last spring when you first started this project, and it affects other variables in unpredictable ways that continue their influence in even more unpredictable ways."

Jess looked out at the turbulent water as it crashed into itself and said, "It's like chaos theory. We've adopted this crazy motif of measuring and understanding, then behaving as if those measurements aren't true or don't matter. The system becomes chaotic, and the ability to predict an outcome more difficult. Like all the science around climate change—who knows how those weather changes will affect the ocean temperatures, which will have some effect on the ocean migration of all salmon species . . . Then what?"

"Then throw in human behavior, motivated by God knows what, mostly money, and there are times when it seems like we don't have a chance with the wild salmon."

"But, Uncle Robert, isn't there also the opposite effect? Could the changes become so extreme that the attempts at intervention produce a positive change and the system compensates in a good direction?"

"I know what you're saying, Jess. That's just it, in some ways: the closer we seem to get, the further away we become. Keep on doing your good work, girl, and you know there's a chance you'll find something irrefutable."

"But what I have is already irrefutable. They know that. They're just choosing to ignore it."

"I guess what I'm saying is that there will come a time when what you know about what's happening to the wild salmon populations in the Nesika will create an influence that will turn around what's happening right now."

"Thanks, Uncle Robert. Your support in this means a lot to me. I'm going out to check the fish counts for the past few days. There should be a lot more coho in the river this year than there are. I'm going to do some temperature readings up above the dam later in the day, when the surface temperature is highest. It's late October. The water should be cooling after all this rain we've been having."

"Yeah, sweetheart. Again, I'm so, so sorry. I know how hard this is, believe me. Please stay in touch with me and let me know how it's going. Actually, it looks like I might be down your way to give a talk at Nesika Community College in a month or so. I'll let you know, okay?"

"It would be so good to see you. I'll be in touch soon. Promise."

"Take care of yourself, kiddo, and pat that enormous dog for me, will ya?"

"Sure will. You take care, too."

Jess let in what he was saying and looked out over the rivers through mist that swirled and gathered on her windshield. She rolled down her car window so she could hear the rhythm of the white water drumming on the boulders in the rapids.

In a calm back eddy, a great blue heron was carefully picking its way through the shallows just in front of her truck. Its snakelike neck jutted out in front of it as if it were following something. It struck the surface of the water with an almost imperceptible splash and came up with a small fingerling, holding it in the flash of the sun for a moment.

PIAH

ᘓ

Mist from the two rivers swirled into the sun-warmed air around Piah. Standing on the large boulders near where the Nesika crashed headlong into the Tokatee River, she held her hands over her head, sending a blessing from her heart down into the mingled rivers.

This was where her family made their winter home. Standing along the banks, Piah remembered the many times she had been here with them. She remembered her younger days, when she had played along the bank even when the elders warned her to stay out of the cold, racing water of the colliding rivers.

This was a sacred place, a place of force and reconciliation, of resistance and resolve. The water here had a strong voice and taught her and her people much about strength. When Piah became an adult, the river spoke to her here, showing her how the relationship between the waters could be invoked and resolved: the force, the release, the joy of coming together, the kinship, the water's inseparability from itself, and the way the blending of the water and the sky carried snow back and forth from the ocean. Like the beating of her heart and the breath in her chest. The flow of blood and birth and death.

A vision of the night Libah was born, a year earlier, rose up in the mist by the crashing rivers. It had been a late night in the beginning of the winter season. The moon had been full, and the silver light had seemed to keep the forest still and the night animals somehow quiet.

The elder women who helped with birth tended a small fire and massaged Piah's back and rolling stomach as the waves of labor broke through and over her. They sang to her the old songs of the birthing time and encouraged Piah to give a voice to her pain. Piah trusted them but was still afraid of hurting. She had tended births before but didn't know about the pressure, the force of separating from one she had been so close to. Then, like a wind from all the women who had birthed before her, Piah released Libah into the arms of her grandmother. The women's voices blended together to welcome the new girl into their family. Piah knew by their song that she had a daughter. Libah, named for the river, had come.

Now, Piah felt, in the misty, crashing current of the rivers, the coming and going of life. Her sister, taken so young, and now her daughter, given by the same force, had done the same sacred dance of living and dying. Piah had learned this from the animals and plants they lived with. Their lives wove together into a kind of fabric that reflected the time of year, the need for food, and the power and beauty of living. She imagined the softness of that blanket around her now, holding her and her family, protecting them, keeping them safe from harm, and teaching them how to take care of each other.

She saw a blue heron feeding in the shallows. She watched it picking along, staring hard at the still surface of the pool. It darted into the water and came up with a flashing catch. Piah smiled.

Suddenly, she felt as if someone were watching her. Her skin rang with alarm, and she turned to look behind her. No one was there. She put down her basket and stood tall, letting her long, dark hair fall over her shoulders and back. It wasn't an animal—Piah could sense them—but this presence was one she didn't know. She walked slowly away from the water's edge, toward the camp at the intersection of the rivers, but still there was no one. She reached her hand out into the air as if trying to touch something or someone invisible. She could feel a presence reaching toward her. It needed help, it was in pain, and somehow, as Piah felt that pain echoing her own suffering from the death of her sister, Tenas, she wanted to help.

JESS

Jess sat at her desk, reflecting on what Uncle Robert had said. Her cell phone rang, startling her. It was Suzie. She thought of not answering but was too curious not to.

"Hey, Suzie, what's up? I'm not sure you should be calling me at work . . ."

"Oh, yeah—whatever. I really need to talk to you about something. Can you come by after work?"

Jess hesitated. "Okay, just for a bit. I'll have to stop by my place and get Miko."

She felt sick knowing what Suzie was going to ask her for. Her mind twisted around the possibilities, and she knew she just needed to focus on her work for the day. Thinking of Jeff, she looked at the pictures on her desk: Miko and Jeff from last summer, up on the Nesika. They had gone backpacking, in the Boulder Creek Wilderness that bordered the land just along the river, before the power project began. It had been a beautiful weekend, their newish relationship starting to take hold and the soaring in her heart as they fell more and more in love. Leaning back in her gray plastic office chair, she thought of the meeting the night before, of the dam, of the decision, and now of the betrayal by so many . . .

Just then, Rich knocked lightly, looking down on her over her cubicle wall. "Hey, Jess, how's it going? I was wondering if you could meet with me later today to talk more about what's going on. I know this is such a shock to both of us. Do you have time around one thirty this afternoon?"

"Sure, Rich. And I want you to know that I did go to the Nesika Watershed Council meeting last night. There are some pretty upset people who were as sure as I was about the dam coming down. I'm hoping that's news that will mean something to you." Jess realized she sounded snarly, but she didn't care. This was affecting too many layers of her, professional and personal.

As she turned back to her computer, she began to sense the precarious edge of her place in the ODFW. This new landscape in which she found herself could be dangerous. She wanted guidance, she wanted assurance, and she missed her dad. He had always been her champion, his life, like hers, torn open by Monica's death. Even though the shadow of this loss sometimes consumed his heart, he always supported her, challenged her, and cheered her across the finish lines of her life. She looked over at the pictures of him and remembered all the hours she had spent fishing with him and just being close to him and to the river.

⁂

"Why don't we go for a walk, Jess?" Rich said. He held open the back door of the building, and she felt the afternoon sun warming her as they walked down the familiar dirt path through the brown grass field next to their office. The oak trees were rustling, sending leaves drifting into the breeze. The world as she knew it was falling away from her with each step. She could hear Rich walking on the path behind her, what was left of summer drifting in the gold light around them.

There was an old bench under a myrtlewood tree on the bank of the Nesika. They sat there together for a moment in silence. Then, leaning forward onto his knees, Rich sighed and looked over at her. "I know this is rough for you, but we really need to find a way to make it work. One of the things I've learned is that plans don't always play out like you expect them to, and you sometimes just have to take what's best and go from there."

Jess tensed and took a minute, before responding, "And sometimes you don't. Rich, don't patronize me. You know as well as I do that the only reason this is now the plan is that some corporation has lobbied some politician who called Mark Rey and told him what the plan was. This is so shortsighted and so ridiculous that there's no way you can tell me that somehow this has become the right thing to do!" Her hands were shaking, and her heart pounded in her chest. She stared hard into the folding light of the afternoon river and tried to steady her breathing.

"You know, Jess, this is really like a game, and we have to figure out what the next move is. They didn't say they would do nothing for the salmon, for the dam. There will be changes—just not the ones we wanted. I want you to know, Jess, that I wanted this as much as you did. Taking out that dam would set a precedent for other decisions all over the country. It sucks. It really does."

Jess imagined the salmon and steelhead that had once migrated through the murky green depths of the river in front of them, glistening as they let themselves go with the current, trusting their birth waters to take them downstream into the unfamiliar, salty world of the ocean.

She stood up quickly and started walking back to the office, with Rich close behind her. Just before they got to the front door, he stopped, turned to Jess, and said, "Just promise me you won't do anything stupid."

⚬

When Jess stopped by her house after work, she hoped Jeff wouldn't be home. He wasn't there. She grabbed Miko's leash and left quickly. She pulled into Suzie's cluttered driveway and sat still in her car, breathing and clearing her mind. Then Jess got out, walked to Suzie's front door, and, without knocking, opened it.

Miko bounded into the kitchen in front of her. Suzie was waiting at the kitchen table. The house smelled like old coffee and pot smoke.

"Jess, honey, come in! How was work today, dear?"

"Ha ha. You know how work was today—don't even go there. I'm so sick of all this game playing and indecision. It makes me completely crazy." Jess sat down heavily in the red kitchen chair across from her friend.

Suzie smiled. "It's all just so fucking nuts. It must be crazy for you and Jeff. I mean, really, Jess, what a guy to pick!"

"It's rough. Mostly we avoid talking about it. I'm just so mad at him—at everyone—and I really do want to help you and Martin and those kids, but I'm just not sure what I can do."

"I guess it depends on how much you like your job, and why."

"Suzie, you're asking me not only to lose my job but also to break the law. How can you do that? I'm not like that—I'm just not. You already know that about me."

"Okay, okay. I do know that, and I'm sorry. These kids are crazy and probably not reliable at all. But, you know, when you make a list of all the possibilities, you have to admit that this could be one of them. Maybe not the safest or the wisest, but damn, Jess, it could certainly be the coolest!"

Miko whined at the back door to be let out. Jess got up to let him out.

"All I need is your password." Suzie let that drop in the air behind Jess, as Miko barked madly at the squirrels, both real and imagined, in the backyard. Jess followed him out and shut the door behind her.

The sun was beginning to set behind the low hills that lined Penden Valley. Miko's fur seemed to blend with the fawn-colored grass that covered the slope behind Suzie's house. His bark echoed down the hillside as Jess sat down in the shade of one of the oaks.

Her thoughts sank into a kind of vortex. How hard she had worked on this issue—with Jeff, with the others—and how assured she had been going into the meeting that it would be a simple settlement procedure to fund the removal of the Green Springs dam. It was all she could think about: what the restoration projects would be like; the media coverage; and her own role in restoring the Nesika and saving the salmon, steelhead, and trout from their inevitable slide into extinction.

She felt as if she were entering a maze with no clear instructions. It was a treacherous and dangerous place, and she glared into the possibility of it. Her fury leaped up in her, and she clenched her hands tightly in her pockets and closed her eyes against the bright intensity of the setting sun in her eyes. Maybe she *could* get away with it—if the kids could get it done and clear out of there, no one needed to know they even had the engineering specs.

With that, she turned a corner in the maze and found her way to an opening, with a kind of clarity that surprised her. It was as if she could suddenly see that the systems she had always depended on were failing. Her throat tightened, and she fought back tears, feeling more kinship with the oak than with anyone around her.

Leaning back against the trunk of the old tree, she opened her eyes. The alarm calls of the squirrels and Miko's excited barking echoed off the hillside. She sank into the softness of the brown summer grass and the familiar scent of the lowland black oaks. They had no idea what she had been through, what she knew about this river. She had seen it in her dreams, in her research, and in her restless quest for what was right for the river, the salmon, and the lives that depended on them. If she couldn't save her sister, she would save them.

"Miko!" Jess called out, and he came bounding over to her. They walked back inside, into the kitchen. Suzie was still sitting at the table.

Jess sat down across from her and said, "It's 'miko1220'—all lowercase."

Suzie smiled. "Just a sec—let me write it down. This is going to work, you know." But the glint in her friend's eyes made Jess uneasy. Knowing what she had just done and considering the possibility of being caught caused her to imagine Jeff as a weak part of corporate greed and injustice. Her love for him and her commitment to the river twisted inside her. She took Miko and left.

PIAH

⟨◦⟩

The smoke from the campfire floated through the trees like an early-morning mist. It was time for Piah to be initiated as a woman. She sat in the comfort of the small ceremonial lodge where many women before her had sat and chanted the songs that called the spirits to guide them on this part of the journey.

The drumming of the elder women grew louder, and Piah braced herself for what was going to come next. It was midsummer, and the air was still and bright. The Nesika flowed freely and lively through the canyon below their summer camp. The birdsong had quieted, and the only sound coming from the forest was the low hum of insects.

Piah had looked forward to this day when she was younger. The older women of her family all had tattoos of three lines from their mouth down to their lower chin area. These marks were made after the birth of the women's first child. Each tattoo represented three spirits: the spirit of the sky, to help them with their vision and to be able to recognize the changing seasons and the cycles of the moon; the spirit of the earth, to teach them about gathering food from the plants that grew above- and below-ground, and to be able to communicate with the animals that gave them their bodies for food; and the spirit of the underground, the unseen world, where the spirits offered visions and guidance for their families.

Piah waited with her feathers and her newly tanned elk-skin clothing, bracing for the pain and listening for the song that would call her into the circle of women. She could tell through the small smoke hole that the light was shifting toward the end of the day when she finally heard it. She stepped slowly from the small house and into the arms and cries of the women in her family. They had prepared a small space for her to sit, a large stone covered with cedar branches and fur. She recognized her mother; Lamoro, the healer; and the shaman, who was wearing the mask of the bear and making low, growling-humming sounds behind a nearby tree. Piah sat carefully in her place and joined the chanting.

The tools were laid out on a bed of flowers gathered from the fields surrounding their camp. One was a sharp shell that had been traded from the coastal tribe. It was marked with the blood of her mother. There was a bowl of ash from burned willow branches that Lamoro had prepared. Piah shivered when she saw them. She had heard stories that the pain could be intense but would ease in a few days. Piah closed her eyes and lay back on the furs and branches that covered the stone. She steadied her breathing and held very still. Smoking cedar branches were waved above her, and the cedar's heavy, sacred essence filled her lungs and made her eyes water. She braced herself and clenched her fists. She would not cry.

The first nick of the blade was surprising; it felt like a bite. The women's singing grew louder still, and Piah felt their hands on her shoulders and legs. Each nick of the blade caused more pain, and Piah had to fight the urge to cry out. She connected to the power in her, the power of the lineage of women who had been marked in exactly this way, as silent tears ran down her face. As they worked on the first tattoo, Piah called the sky spirits. A large bird came to her—a bird she knew, that lived near the Nesika. It was an osprey and landed in the tree above her. The osprey cried out, and Piah felt welcomed by the spirits in the sky.

When the first line was done, Lamoro spread the ash of the willow into the wound. She held her hand over the mark and cried out, in a high-pitched song, to the sky spirits to enter Piah's body and guide her through her life. The ash burned into her, becoming part of her for the rest of her life.

Piah was learning from the pain. As each mark was made on her face, images floated around her and accompanied her on this journey. What was happening to her was initiating her as one of the women in her tribe who was ready to take on the responsibilities of children and caring for the elders. An image of a white flowering plant, a sacred plant used for both medicine and food, rose up in a mark from the earth. The elderberry would become a teacher for Piah, and she would spend days learning about the healing and nourishing properties of her plant teacher. Soon, her face became numb to the cutting, and Piah felt as if she were floating above the circle of women.

But when Lamoro started on the final chin mark, Piah became afraid. She wasn't as familiar with the underworld spirits and didn't know what would come to her. Her eyes began to water, and her pain mingled with a kind of sadness. Like a large hand, the underworld spirits pinned her to the ground. The singing shifted, and Piah opened to who or what would be her guide from that world. Her sister, Tenas, appeared before her. With Tenas was another being, someone older, with a large staff and long, braided hair. Tenas stopped in front of Piah, and the spirit guide stepped forward. She looked over Piah, put her hand on Piah's heart, and said, "I will be your teacher and your guide. I am bound to you by this mark." Piah felt a strong desire to be with Tenas, to run to her, but her sister faded into the dark underworld forest. Her guide sat next to her.

Piah's eyes were uncovered, and she felt the light slide into her awareness. Her chin burned, and she tried to steady her breathing. Lamoro and her mother were at her side, and the singing and drumming began to fade. Lamoro handed her a bowl of water and helped her stand. Piah turned and went back into the ceremonial lodge, where she would spend the night getting to know her guides and learning even more from the pain and the healing. She was excited to have been marked this way, to finally be a woman; she would now look to become part of the circles of women providing nourishment, healing, children, and teaching. She set her bowl of water in the middle of the lodge, curled up on the elk fur, and slept.

JESS

The lilt of Jess's cell phone ring startled her. She was up at
Eagle Rock, checking licenses and fish tags. The early spring
river was high and full, new dogwood blooms laced the dark
understory of the forest, and the cries of returning buzzards
meant the fish were in the river. Six months had gone by since
the meeting at Martin's house and Suzie's crazy request. Jess had
been kept out of the negotiations for the settlement agreement
with PowerCorp and had focused her time on other projects that
could have an impact on salmon. The environmental groups
continued to meet, and she heard from Suzie now and then that
they did have a plan and were going to bring a lawsuit against
PowerCorp and Jess's employer, the Oregon Department of Fish
and Wildlife.

When she answered her phone, it was Rich. "Jess, I just got
word that there's police action up at the Green Springs dam. I
need you to check it out. Sounds a little crazy—could be dangerous. Be careful."

"Sure, Rich." Jess felt her stomach drop and almost said
the Earth in Mind kids' names out loud. She had been hoping
they had dropped their plan to actually blow up the dam. Even

though she was determined to try to undermine PowerCorp any way she could, she still could not support such a criminal action.

"I'll head right up there. Is anyone hurt?"

"Yes, I'm afraid so, but I don't know how badly. Call me and let me know as soon as you get there."

Miko was wandering down by the edge of the river, and Jess called to him in a frantic, high voice. He turned quickly and ran for the truck.

Jess parked in the gravel parking lot near the dam. A sheriff's car and a PowerCorp truck were already there. The whipping sound of an ambulance echoed off the canyon walls as it made its way up from Penden Valley. She slipped on the gravel as she ran down the road to a clump of brown-and-red jackets and looked down at Mink's crumpled body, twisted into the forest loam.

"Oh my God. What happened?" Jeff appeared at her side then, and she was glad he was there. He put his arm carefully over her shoulder and moved her away from the injured boy.

"It looks like he was trying to secure some rope and he fell from a cedar. Stupid kid. We found a radio and other supplies that make this look like a pretty sophisticated attempt at blowing up the dam. There's some stuff in his pack that says he's from the Earth in Mind group that was at the meeting with you and Martin. Jess, please tell me you had nothing to do with this."

Jess pushed away from Jeff and walked toward the dam. There was nothing she could do to help Mink. She wondered where the other boys were. The sounds of the sirens grew louder and bounced off the stained, wet concrete into the canyon below. She heard Jeff turn and walk away. Jess reached out and held on to one of the old stones from the river like a hand. She sat down on the cool, wet bank and started to cry. The sirens stopped, and she could hear the hum of the turbines from the power station like a steady growl across the water.

PIAH

ᚽᚬᚽ

Piah stood on the top of the cliff edge overlooking the river
valley below. A pair of osprey whistled their cries to each
other as they circled in the uplifts of air currents from the basalt
cliffs. The dark green of the fir forest below her filled in the crev-
ices of the ancient valley. She could smell the water gathered into
the careful folds of the watershed. Her hand rested on the trunk
of a sinewy, hundred-year-old cedar next to her. She closed her
eyes and caressed the tree, feeling into its slow expansion, its
tender reaching for the sky. The bark furrows reflected the land
around the tree and the meandering furrows of river canyons
and streambeds. The cedar blended with the land around it, rose
up from the basalt cliffs like an expression of the woven, turning
river in the canyon below. Piah could feel the rhythm of the river's current in the bark of the tree and felt her own pulse blending
with the same current.

Moving away from the tree, she came close to the edge
of the cliff. The osprey had flown off, chasing something they
had spied farther downriver. Piah heard something coming up
behind her, moving heavily and deliberately through the brush.
She moved back from the cliff edge and leaned once again

against the tree, sliding to sit in a soft area beneath it. Through the forest, she recognized Mian, a young boy from her tribe. He had just come down the mountain behind the cliff and had with him some stones he was going to use to set up a vision-quest site.

This cliff side was where her people came when it was time to begin a vision quest for a rite of passage into adulthood. They brought stones from a place high above the tree line and made a circle where they remained alone, still, without food or water, for as many days as the number of stones they had brought down from the hills. The elders of the tribe, the spirit woman and man, guided the boy or girl in the ceremonies they would need to pass through one kind of life into another.

Piah sat looking at Mian, with his rocks and his slightly surprised expression. She knew his mother and family well and knew that they were pleased with his severance time. His hair had grown long and was blowing wildly around his face. She was amused by the sight and covered her smile with her hand. As they regarded each other in silence, Piah could see in the depths of his dark eyes a kind of knowing curiosity. Slowly standing, she turned to leave, giving him a small, quiet bow for his journey. It was his time to communicate with the spirits, ride waves of hunger, and struggle with tempting dreams and the flood of visions that would overcome him.

Piah remembered her own time on the cliffs and carried the mark of that time tattooed on her face. The women in her tribe quested in the same way as the men, their visions valued with the same intensity and focus. Her spirit guide was the river; she was the riverkeeper of the tribe and would spend her life listening to the stories of the water and taking them back to her people.

She walked back to the oak grove, where the medicine wheel was laid out in a clearing. She felt moved to leave Mian an offering from the river that he would find when his quest had ended. He seemed unusual, easily startled and fearful in ways she was not used to seeing. What she saw in Mian's eyes seemed to reflect the message or warning from Tenas: "There is much coming . . ."

Piah felt uneasy and afraid. She trusted that Mian would return to his people and tell them of his visions, which would give them guidance and power. And she knew he would need the river in some way. She found a small stone and some sticks to make her symbol. She sat in the circle of the medicine-wheel stones and let herself drop into a familiar visionary place. She closed her eyes and waited.

She felt the cool pull of the river like a friend coming to ask her to play. She dove off the cliff of her spirit place and let the images rise around her. The blue light of the river spirit became a vortex of swirling visions around her: people she knew, animals playing, the sunlight flashing on the river itself.

Then she said, "River, I come to you with questions. I am leaving an offering for the boy questing here. Is there a guiding spirit or image I can call for him?"

The river spiraled blue in front of her and opened into a cave. She walked in carefully because she was walking into total darkness. The cave was just large enough for her to stand in, and she felt carefully along the walls to make her way through the passage. She called to her power animal, a river otter, to be with her and felt its sleek fur brush by. The cave wound opened to a luminous pool of water that was the color of pearl or moonlight. Her power animal dove slickly into the pool and disappeared. She did the same, and the water felt thick and smooth, like diving through the fur of an animal.

She landed on her feet in another chamber, one that looked like a building she had never seen before. Her power animal looked up at her, urging her to follow. The shapes of what looked like trees made by humans amazed her. There were stone people, larger than life, holding strange things and staring down at her. She wanted to stay and explore this very strange place, but she felt the impatient demand of her power animal beckoning her to move on.

They entered another large room. This one was even stranger than the first. The walls seemed to glow from within, and a slight haze hovered just above the damp floor. She stopped for a moment, gathering herself. In the center of the space was a bright silver bowl. She walked over to it and reached through the haze to touch its cool edge. Her hand looked odd to her, as if she were wearing a robe made of soft white skins, unlike anything she had ever felt or seen.

The fog in the room began to swirl in low spirals, and she stood close enough to the bowl to see what was happening on the inside. The bowl reflected back her image, then shifted into an opening that seemed to appear beneath the floor of the room. She watched and waited for what was coming to her. There was an image of a man—though not a man she had ever seen before. He had hair on his face, and his skin was light colored. He turned his head quickly to face her, and a sharp burn of fear shot through her.

She brought herself back to where she was sitting, in the tall spring grass in the center of the stone medicine wheel. Her breathing was rapid, and she felt dizzy. *Who was that man, and what did he have to do with Mian's quest?* she asked herself. She shuddered and stood to leave, without making an offering for Mian. She decided to keep to herself what she had just experienced—it was incomprehensible.

She walked slowly down the mountain to the river, gathering wood for the evening fire as she went. She felt the familiar hum of life moving around her, the day ending, and the shift toward night just beginning. She was haunted by the image of the man, the room she'd been in, and the sense that something in the fabric of her life was beginning to tear.

JESS

Jess had heard from Martin that Mink hadn't said anything that would incriminate her, but they had found his pack, and in it copies of the engineering specs from the ODFW office. She was glad that Martin could be with Mink at the hospital while he healed from a serious fracture in his leg and a broken arm. Martin had told Jess how the police had started questioning Mink as soon as he regained consciousness.

When she got to work after hearing from Martin, she knew there would be accusations. She flopped into her chair and turned on her computer, her back stiff with apprehension. She knew she had crossed the line, and she waited for Rich to call her into his office.

"Jess." Rich's low voice echoed through her phone intercom. She picked up without answering. "I need you to come to my office." Each word was like a steady, sad order.

She stopped off at the restroom on her way to Rich's office. Her face in the mirror looked shocked and weary. Dark circles shadowed her eyes, dimming their brightness. She was giving up, getting out, being thrown out. She ran her damp hands through her hair and thought of cutting it short, to reflect these changes that meant the end of everything. Jeff would be finding out now, just as Rich had. She knew it would ruin their relationship. Her chest felt as if a piece of metal had pierced it, and she had no way to remove it. Not now. She didn't want to.

Everything in Rich's office seemed brighter, surreal, as if she were in a place she had never been before. For a moment, she felt panicked, but she also hoped that, in some obscure way, maybe Rich didn't know or suspect her.

His face was pale, and he stared into the glow of his computer screen, not looking at her. Jess felt something like shame rise in her, and she sat quickly, looking down at her hands.

"I got a call this morning. There was a police investigation, and, Jess, they found engineering specs that came from this office in their materials. Jess, you're the only one who could have given those drawings to them. Someone almost died there—this was about as stupid as it gets. I'm really surprised you would have had anything to do with this."

It was almost a question. Jess sat silent and looked at him.

"I know this is still at the investigation level, but the evidence is, well, strong enough that I have to ask you to pack up your office."

His voice cracked when he finished, and Jess felt a little sorry for him.

She answered, "Okay, I get it. I'm sorry, Rich. You know how much this work means to me." The instant she had seen Mink's body lying on the ground, she had known that this moment would be next for her.

Rich turned away to his computer screen, and for a second she felt like lying, telling him that she hadn't done it, but she felt cornered and protective of her friends, of the beauty and importance of what they were trying to protect, and understood the burden of her choice.

When she got back to her desk, she found she was locked out of the office data files. Her work would be confiscated and her email files handed over to the investigators. They wouldn't find anything incriminating—she knew that. Whoever had gotten into her computer would have been good enough to make sure there were no tracks left. Still, she was the logical source by association, and she felt that accusation draping over her shoulders like an old cloak.

Her cell phone rang loudly, and she saw Jeff's number. She let it go to voice mail. She took a long, deep breath, holding it in until the message tone on her phone finally chimed. Then she went to the copy room to find some empty boxes.

She left with her photos, some papers, old highlighters, and a tangle of paper clips. Why was it called getting fired? *Fired*—as if she were being kilned like pottery, melted like glass, changed into something else, hardened.

Rain was pouring from the deep-gray sky as she got into her truck. The engine came to life slowly. She turned to look behind her as she backed up, and the twisting motion seemed to wring tears from her—gripping her with loss, the river again taking away a part of her, pulling it into the swirl of its dark downstream current.

She dug into her pocket for her cell phone and called Suzie. "It's me. I'm coming over." She knew her friend would be home, though still asleep. Her body ached for Jeff—she knew what his message to her would say without even checking it. She also knew he would leave.

The rain stopped, and she rolled down her window. The fall air rushed into the cab of her truck and cooled her face. As she waited at a red light, she felt as if she were crossing a threshold. This would be a different kind of time—there was no doubt about that. Then the light changed, and she paused for a moment, before driving through the intersection and making a left turn up the road to the hill, to Suzie's house.

JEFF

In the conference room at PowerCorp, Jeff sat back heavily in his hard plastic chair. Mack looked over at Jeff and said, with an accusatory sigh, "Hey, guys, I just got the report about those kids who tried to blow up the Green Springs dam. They were some eco-terrorist group—I think you know about them, Jeff—called Earth in Mind. Bunch of radical hippies from Eugene. God—, stupid kids."

Jeff tried to mask his concern that Jess might have been involved "Yeah I know about Earth in Mind... What does the report say?"

"Well, as far as I can tell, based on a search of the Earth in Mind office, Jess was most likely the one providing them with confidential engineering specs on the construction of the dam. Or at least we know that the specs came from the Oregon Department of Fish and Wildlife offices. Someone's computer..."

"Yeah, I'm not sure what to make of it. I know Jess loved working with those kids and helped them out in the past. I absolutely did *not* know what she was up to with this . . . *shit*."

"Well, Jeff, I'm sure someone will have a few questions for you. Too bad—I hear she's a good at her job."

Jeff shifted in his chair and looked over at Mack, noticing the rugged lines in Mack's face furrowing with concern. Jeff wondered how much to say right now; if he revealed too much, he could put Jess at risk.

⚬⟡⟿

Jeff rubbed his eyes, and an image of Jess, sitting on the riverbank alone while paramedics hustled to fight for the boy's life, rose up in his mind. He felt sure that she was worried about more than the boy. "No, the kid fell from a tree, that big cedar up on the hill above the dam. God, if they had been able to blow it up, what a fucked-up mess that would have been. Shit."

Mack looked over at Jeff. "This could be good press for our side—do ya think?"

"Well, the timing is interesting, for sure. It'll be easier to raise the public against a radicalized enviro position, but we'll have to be sensitive to the hurt kid at the same time."

"I'll let you work on that, Jeff. Thanks. Get in touch with Sally in PR—she'll be in contact with the sheriff's office for the details."

Jeff looked out the window. He thought of calling Jess, finding out for sure that she'd had nothing to do with this, but part of him didn't want to know. He stood and walked out into the afternoon sun. He sat in the cab of his truck and felt as if he had fallen into the space between two entirely different worlds. What this could do to him, to his career, to his love and respect for Jess . . . The thought of losing her almost caused him to gasp. His love for her was raw, seamless, and fueled with a kind of desire he had never known. But this Jess, this reckless shadow of her, was someone he didn't know.

Holy fuck. The woman he had been living with—sharing intense lovemaking, breakfast, and walks—wasn't who he thought she was. He fell into a chasm of shock and anger. Jess had, according to the reports, been more involved with Earth in Mind than anyone had thought. When the kid, Mink, had been hurt and the explosives confiscated, the investigation had revealed myriad plans—mostly sloppy-kid plans, but they had the necessary engineering specs, which could have come only from the ODFW. And, most likely, only from Jess. How could she have been so careless? He knew she hated what was going on, and they had spent hours arguing over what to do, what was best for the river and the salmon. He had been hoping that they could find a way through this. But now . . .

Jeff got back to his office and called Jess's cell phone. He knew she wouldn't answer, but his hands shook anyway while he constructed a message. He looked down at the photo of the two of them on his desk, then left his voice mail: "Jess, I need to talk to you. I just heard from Mack about the accusations . . ." He paused "Is it true? Call me. I need to know what's going on."

JESS

❦

Opening the door to Suzie's bedroom, Jess stepped quietly through the mess of clothes on the floor and sat heavily on the side of the bed, shaking her friend's arm, knowing that it would take a lot to wake her. She didn't care that she might startle Suzie, not now.

Suzie rolled over slowly and squinted. "Oh, hey, Jess." She pulled the covers more tightly around her.

"I called. You didn't get it."

"No, I was sleeping. What's going on? Why aren't you at work?"

"They found the engineering specs for the dam in Mink's backpack, and I got fired."

"Oh my God—are you okay?"

"No. Shit, Suzie, do you know what this means?"

"Not really—not all the way." She rolled onto her side and grabbed a T-shirt off the floor. "I thought you wanted out—away from the bullshit of the settlement agreement. I need some coffee. Want some?"

"No, thanks. This is the end of my career, my relationship . . . Fuck." She turned and walked into the mess of Suzie's kitchen, where she turned on the electric teakettle. She looked out the window. The sun had come out, and the wet trees glistened in a surreal, animated way. Jess wanted to walk out among them, to float above them and vanish into an arc of sunlight.

Her cell phone vibrated in the pocket of her jeans, and she didn't look at it. Maybe Jeff again, maybe the investigator, maybe her mother.

Suzie came in, buttoning the top button of her jeans. She looked ruffled, her short, dark hair sticking out at sharp angles, as if she had just been really scared. "Hey, Jess, I know this is some kind of weird trip for you, and it will feel shitty for a while, that's for sure, but I really believe you're going to be okay." Suzie absentmindedly picked up her marijuana pipe, then put it back down. Jess just stared at her, suddenly feeling small and vulnerable. She knew that it would be a long time before the pain would dissipate.

There was a knock at the door, and Suzie looked up. "God—who could *that* be?"

Jess knew and looked over at Suzie's marijuana pipe. For a moment, she just wanted relief, a way to escape.

Suzie opened the door. "Hey, Jeff."

Jeff stood there, backlit by the morning sun and looking comically angelic. Suzie turned to one side, and Jeff pushed into the room without looking at her.

"Jess." His eyes looked surprised and confused. Jess thought of a salmon caught in a net—or running into the concrete wall of a dam.

"What the fuck is going on here? I just heard from Mack."

"I just got fired. I've been involved with Earth in Mind—"

"Did you give them the specs? Your career is ruined. For *what*?"

"You know what for." The bathroom door closed, and she could hear the shower running.

"But, sweetheart, my God . . ." Jeff stopped himself, and she knew the old argument they had had so many times was beginning.

"Jeff, I really don't want to talk about it right now. You should just go. Maybe someday we can talk about it." She felt herself fading in his eyes as he looked over her body—they had enjoyed each other so much that even now Jess felt the warm push of her desire for him.

"Why don't you come by later and get your stuff? I'll go for a walk up the river. I really want some time to myself anyway."

Jeff looked down, and the space between them filled with a weird uncertainty that she hadn't expected.

"Okay, I guess I can do that, but I don't know . . ."

"Jeff, don't. I'm on the other side now—actually, I've been there all along, and we both know that. This is all just too much right now."

For an awkward moment, Jess thought they might hug goodbye, but then she turned and sat back down at the small table in the dusty corner of Suzie's kitchen.

"I'll leave the key in the kitchen," Jeff said.

"Fine."

She put her head in her hands and listened until she heard his footsteps turn heavily and recede through the still-open door.

When it clicked shut, Jess let gravity pull her into the chair. It was cold, so cold, and she wrapped herself in her jacket, against a wind blowing from deep inside her, from a time very long ago.

"How'd that go?" Suzie asked, as she came into the kitchen, drying her hair roughly with a towel.

"Not well." Jess was having a hard time breathing, as she felt the familiar hand of betrayal take the blade in her chest and turn it, hard. "I can't believe this is all happening. It seems like my first day at work was just last week. How can so much happen in such a short time?" Closing her eyes, she sensed all of her publications, predictions, studies, plans for the future dissolving into a haze.

Suzie sat down next to her with her coffee and said, "Hey, I told you, it's going to be okay. We didn't try to blow up the dam. We just gave some people some information. They aren't going to send us to jail, I don't think. I hope Martin's okay. I'll call him later. Too bad we live in such a paranoid time—goddamn government stealing people's cell phone data. Jesus, you would think someone would get fired over *that* one."

"Yeah, I know. It's just that right now, I'm feeling so many things. I think I'm going to get Miko and go up the river today. I need to figure out what to do."

"Sure, Jess."

Jess thought she saw Suzie smiling and wondered what was up.

"I'm just going to go. Sorry I woke you."

"Naw, it's good. Call me later, though, and let me know how you are."

"Sure. See ya."

As she stood to leave Suzie's, her body felt heavy and stiff. It was the weight of grief, a sensation born of love torn away and left just out of reach. The only refuge she had was her dog, and she longed for his simple, uncomplicated presence. Her mind kept trying to construct what to do next, but all the familiar structures of her work and her future were falling apart, and she couldn't imagine how to hold it all together anymore. Her *work*. She was a scientist who had been violated by the system she trusted most. She was also a scientist who had made a bad decision.

Earth in Mind was such a tenacious, renegade group of young people. She had been one once. And now, as she thought of Mink's crumpled body—he had seemed so small—a shadow of her sister washed over his image, like a passing cloud.

JEFF

Walking up to the small blue-and-white house, Jeff felt the weight of what he had to do in each step up the gravel driveway. He took a breath before using his key, a key he knew he would leave without. He expected stillness when he opened the door, but Miko came out from the back bedroom, his large woof nearly sending Jeff jumping off the ground. Jeff's throat caught at the thought of a world without this dog and his girl.

"Hey, buddy." Jeff roughed up Miko's head and scratched behind his soft black ears.

Miko twirled and loped into the other room to get his ball to play. Jeff stood up and scanned the living room. Where to begin? "Damn," he said, under his breath. He went over to Jess's desk and picked up a photo of the two of them on the Nesika just above the Green Springs dam, their arms around each other, blended like the lovers he had imagined they would always be. Holding the photo, he sat down in Jess's chair, gazing into the picture, the feelings from that day mingling with the floral-incense smell in the house. He put it back in a different place on her desk, with an awkward sense that maybe she would notice. The report on the Nesika Watershed study that they had worked on sat squarely in the center of her desk, their names as coauthors something that would not change.

There wasn't a lot for him to pack; he had moved in from his own place, bringing just what he needed and putting the rest in storage until they could get a larger house. He grabbed his old gray duffel from his side of the bed and threw in his clothes and books from the nightstand. Miko watched from the doorway like a sentinel. Jess's jeans and one of his favorite light green T-shirts lay crumpled by her side of the bed. Tears rose in his eyes, and he felt his heart breaking for her, for them.

Why had she done this? It was so hard to imagine that she would have compromised her work, her career. Suzie—Jeff knew that she had talked Jess into it. Not Martin—he wouldn't have pressured her—but Suzie cared only about Suzie's agenda. He had never liked her; she was too shifty for him to trust her.

He moved from the bedroom into the bathroom to get his few things. Jess's earrings, blue-gray stones set in silver that he had given her for her last birthday, were sitting on the edge of the sink. He picked them up and held them for a moment, remembering her delight, her sincere, grateful smile as she put them on without even looking in a mirror. And later that night, they'd been all she had on in the dim light, and her back had undulated under his hands as she'd taken them off and rolled over to put them on the nightstand. He felt a stirring in his groin as he remembered her softness, her body rising to meet him, her hand guiding him into her. She was always so ready to make love, with a mixture of desperation and delight that Jeff craved constantly.

Yet now he was unweaving his life from hers, unraveling the small threads of him that ran from room to room in this house. Miko followed him expectantly as he packed, and, when Jeff had finished, looked up at him with what seemed like a question.

"Okay, boy, I'm going now," Jeff said to him in a seeming answer. "You take care of Jess for me, okay?" Miko's curled tail swirled in response. He would—Jeff knew that. He patted the dog's broad head, left his key on the kitchen table, and walked out.

JESS

Jess startled awake. She reached over to the other side of the bed and found only the vacant space where Jeff had been for the past year.

"Miko!" she called out into the dark. Miko came shuffling in from where he had been sleeping, next to the cooling woodstove, and climbed onto the bed.

"Hey, how's my boy?"

Miko thumped his tail and curled up next to her. The darkness seemed wider, more open, without Jeff, and their fights these past weeks kept echoing in her mind. She had come home that evening to find his key on the kitchen table and all his stuff cleared out.

Jeff was gone, her job was gone, and tonight her life felt like an open bowl holding her in its dark curves. She turned to Miko, holding on to him. He wouldn't leave. His breathing was steady, and she could feel the drumming of his heart just below her hand. Her throat tightened, and grief took her like an undertow into its swirling depths, where she cried.

A memory of her mom the night of the accident came flooding back. It was dark then, too. Jess was in her room with her friend Leslie, still shivering from shock, from the cold terror of seeing her sister's small blond head slipping beneath the river's surface. Because the search party hadn't found her body yet, they claimed there was still hope. Jess knew there was none, but the people around her were still waiting. She remembered someone shouting, "Someone saw something moving across the river!" There were search dogs running along the tangled banks, divers swimming slowly through the current, and a man in a boat with a large hook, which he kept throwing again and again . . .

Jess shuddered, recalling her mom curled up on the couch, the Catholic priest stoically petting her arm, calming her. Then, later, when it got dark and Monica still hadn't come home, her mother started screaming.

It took them twenty-one days to find her body. Jess went back to school, feeling like someone from another planet. In ninth grade, her social life had been stratified according to carefully drawn social lines; now, those lines were blurred and in some cases disregarded. She walked through the halls, and kids who had once ignored her or shunned her socially were suddenly smiling and acknowledging her with obvious sad looks. Jess felt self-conscious and wondered whom they saw her as, so freshly and deeply torn and wounded. Even the teachers who had once made her feel invisible now asked her questions.

When they found Monica, Jess took more time off from school for the funeral. She could only imagine what her sister must have looked like after those three weeks, what the river had done to her eleven-year-old body. Her mother insisted on seeing Monica; she needed to touch her daughter's body one last time. Jess knew why, and remembered the hysterical crying when her mom came home that day—a wrenching, horrible sound.

After the funeral, Jess tucked her grief inside her chest and hid it there, refusing to share it with her friends, her parents, or even herself. Now, the memory of that day was coming up again, and it was impossible to ignore the grief echoing within her. As the searing pain from her old wounds began to surface, for a moment all she could see were bodies lying by the river: her sister, her dad, Mink, the doomed salmon.

Miko stretched out next to her, and the images of dying fish, the impenetrable dam, and the corporate smirk of Mack from PowerCorp spun in the darkness around her. It was several hours until morning. She would wait for the certain light that would come, while the uncertainty of the next day waited like a wild animal in the corner of the room.

⬥

Jess got up stiffly after having fallen asleep for what seemed like only a few minutes. Miko jumped off the bed and trotted into the kitchen to drink noisily from his water bowl. Jess made tea, then sat down at her desk and held her mug against her chest, allowing the warmth and the sweet smell, familiar and unchanged, to ease the tightness within her. She hadn't checked her email since she had left her job the day before. And she should call her mother—but what would she tell her? *Hey, Mom, I got busted, I lost my job, and Jeff left. At least the dog is still alive . . .*

Miko came in and curled up on his bed next to her chair. She noticed the rearranged photos on her desk; Jeff's cell phone charger was gone, his computer. She put her tea down next to the glowing screen of her past life. "Fuck," she said out loud in the room. She tried to piece together the memories of everything that had gone on, but the meetings, the fights, the reports all seemed to tangle like fishing line backed up on a reel.

Her back tensed as she reached forward to open her email. The first one was from her uncle Robert:

Jess,

I'm forwarding along some reports from the Union for Concerned Scientists. I think you might be very interested in what they have to say about the falsification of scientific reports. It looks like you aren't the only one! One interesting thing that I'm including a link to is a memo to the Forest Service directing

*them not to respond to the survey the union sent out
to them, asking about falsifying reports. Damn, girl,
this is something! I hope it helps you out. You know
you're fighting the good fight, and I'm sure they'll come
around. There's no way they'll get away with asking
you to change your results.*

Love you,
R

Jess clicked on the highlighted link and read aloud to herself:

"When scientific knowledge has been found to be in conflict with its political goals, the administration has often manipulated the process through which science enters into its decisions. This has been done by placing people who are professionally unqualified or who have clear conflicts of interest in official posts or on scientific advisory committees, by censoring and suppressing reports by the government's own scientists, and by simply not seeking independent scientific advice."

Damn, she thought. Reading this helped her feel less alone. The certainty she worked from, the care with which she used to document her research, had meant nothing. The only important thing was the resulting agreement with the power company. And now that she was seeing this email from her uncle, a part of her knew she had never been safe. Her naive beliefs that scientific answers were really what were important, really mattered, had been destroyed by that decision—which had also almost murdered a young boy.

Jess read through her other emails, mostly from political organizations clamoring to get her attention. She sat there for a moment and tried to find her focus. She thought of calling Martin but felt protective of him, of his family. Her throat was sore from crying, and part of her wanted to go back to bed, to the safe covers where she could tend her pain and find ways to let it slide from her body. But she had to know.

"Okay, Miko, I'm going to take my shower now. Then let's go wake up Suzie."

Jess pushed open the door to Suzie's house, and Miko bolted in ahead of her.

"Suzie, you here?" There was no answer, and Jess moved slowly through the house. Suzie's car wasn't out front, but Jess figured she must've loaned it to someone—Suzie would never have been out this early in the morning. Miko went to his water bowl—they spent so much time here that he had his own space. Jess walked quietly into her bedroom, but the sheets were pulled back and Suzie was not there. Jess opened the closet—Suzie's clothes were gone. She opened the drawers to the dresser—no clothes. In the kitchen, the refrigerator had been cleaned out, its contents thrown into the garbage can outside the back door. There was no note.

Jess called out one more time: "Suzie! You here?"

No answer came. Suzie was gone.

PIAH

Piah was breathless when she got back to her home. She crouched down, leaned against the cool mud wall, and closed her eyes. The man's face seemed to be waiting for her behind her closed eyes. *What does he want?* She wondered. The image pressed into her, and she opened her eyes. She knew she needed to tell someone, share this terrible vision and have it interpreted. Her visions had always given her solace; they were steady and predictable. Who these spirits were and what they were trying to say to her seemed frightening.

The evening was cooling, and the others were beginning to emerge from the forest with their wood for the community fire. Piah moved away from her home and toward the low-lying lodge where they would gather for the evening meal and stories of the day. Was she prepared to share her story? She wasn't even sure her language had the words to tell it. But maybe there were others who were familiar with this spirit, who had also seen it?

She heard coughing coming from inside the small home of her brother. Some of her people were beginning to cough and seem sick in a new way. Somehow she knew this was connected with her vision, and her fear expanded. She placed her hand on the curve of the small mud-and-wood roof that covered her brother's low, earthen home. *Go away*, it seemed to say. She could feel the heat of the disease rise up under her hand, and she yanked her hand away. This was something so powerful, so foreign, that she was sure she wasn't the only one receiving these visions, having these feelings.

The community house was quiet and felt to Piah like being in a large earth bowl. Familiar faces blended with the dark walls, and deer and elk hides lined the floors and walls. The smoke curled slowly toward the small opening, and the women were beginning to bring in dried salmon and fresh elk for the meal. Small children rolled on the floor, continuous with the family that surrounded them. For a moment, Piah forgot the images that swirled around her and settled into her place near the fire.

Someone behind her started coughing and startled her. It wasn't a familiar cough to her—there was a low rattle, almost like a hum, to it that wasn't right. She looked over and saw her brother's wife bending over, caring for her newborn son. Then an elder uncle in the far corner started coughing—the same cough. Piah reached out and started tending the fire; the image of the man's face seemed to dance in the rising smoke. She waited for her father to come in. She would seek his counsel, let him know what had come to her. Since she had seen the vision, she had felt a new, inexplicable kind of impatience, as if something were pushing her from behind—not pulling her toward it in the benevolent way the slope of a mountain, the call of a bird, or the high, sweet singing of the Nesika would.

Her husband, Maika, came in with Libah. She was happy to see them but felt haunted by the visions and suddenly very protective of them. Maika moved toward her, and they embraced. His long hair smelled like a bear pelt. Her baby reached for her, and Piah's heart filled with a leaping recognition and love for her daughter. Her breasts were taut with milk, and she sat in a corner to nurse and melt into her child. Next to Libah and Maika, she felt the strands of family travel through her to the land and the crying animals in the dying evening light.

Piah's father came in, and she could tell by the strain in his face, his mouth pulled tight with concern, that something was wrong. One of his sisters had come down with the strange rash. The shaman would journey that night, he announced, to find out what spirit had come into their camp, what guest had landed in the chests of the people who were getting sick, and how they could make it leave them alone. Outside the wind was rolling through the forest and up into the river canyon. Piah switched Libah to her other breast and leaned into the sure back of her husband. He stroked the blue tattoo on her chin and smiled. Piah rested in her place; she knew the shaman would help them. The elders were preparing the smoke and drum for the night's ceremony. A tingling coursed through her—the presences of the spirits were beginning to gather. The soft fur of an otter brushed the outside of her leg. Food was passed in silence. An old woman began humming her power song in the corner. The low tones of the night river blended into her singing, and the circle of people who had gathered began to swell with anticipation. Someone had come and was waiting to be seen.

When the meal finished, the drumming grew louder as others joined in with their drums and began chanting their part of the power song. When Piah had gone on her vision quest, she had received her part of the power song to share with her people. The song had lived for many generations, and each member of her tribe had been gifted his or her part. The song was like a member of their tribe, a living being that changed and grew, reflecting the times they lived in. Piah felt her song rise and catch the others. It wove around them like a nest, holding them in their home, assuring them.

The shaman in the corner rose in her mask. It was the prized mask of Raven, a trade made with the Lower Nesika tribe. Raven would look over the land for them, seeking the intruder, naming it and calling it into the circle to be addressed and questioned. Often, Piah remembered, some of the spirits who seemed to want to do them harm were the spirits trying most to get their attention, and when their message had been received, they slunk away into the dark places they'd come from.

Piah pulled Libah close to her as the ceremony began. The swirling of the song seemed to build like an active volcano around them; it held them in its molten belly while the shaman slipped into her trance. The eyes of the mask gleamed in the firelight, and Piah felt herself slipping into the place of visions. She stopped herself by opening her eyes and focusing on the dance. Smoke from burning green cedar branches filled the room, and Piah's eyes watered. She covered Libah's face and kept singing.

After a long time, Piah sensed the singing shifting, the volcano dissolving, and the molten cauldron spilling forth, carrying the shaman back to her people.

The shaman lay on the ground next to the fire. Piah's father lifted the heavy mask from her head. The eyes no longer gleamed, and the final humming of the song slowed and stopped. The shaman retched and vomited on the dirt floor. Piah was afraid. Had the spirit possessed the shaman and ridden Raven back into their home?

When she stopped, Piah's father began asking questions in a low, rolling voice. When he was finished, he stood up and described the shaman's vision for the people. She had seen a strange village and a man who had light skin and a rough gray beard. Piah's heart skipped. She felt sick from the vomit smell and the smoke. There was no question that this was the same man she had seen in her vision. She thought of Mian, questing on the mountain above them. The sound of an avalanche roared in her ears, drowning out the familiar song of the Nesika.

JESS

The fury of the environmental groups mirrored the smugness of the agencies and PowerCorp. Meetings held in homes and living rooms were more subdued after the accident with the Earth in Mind kids. Mink was still recovering in the hospital, and Remedy had been arrested in neighboring Wyoming while hiding out on a sheep ranch with his friends.

Jess had tried to stay out of it after giving Suzie her password. She had kept her head down at work, fulfilling her daily tasks with a kind of dedication and silence that kept her superiors blind to the action organizing against them.

Now, she found herself in a clearing with no job and no relationship, and filled with a new kind of purpose that would require her energy, her passion, and her calculating savvy to transform her work into a meaningful mosaic that would sustain the steady pressure on PowerCorp to change.

She knew she needed to get away, to find time to reconnect with what really mattered to her, what inspired her, and what was at the core of her work. She decided to go to the Nesika and spend time on its banks, listen for her voice there. Jess had done this when she was in high school. She used to take off and spend days and nights alone along the river, tending to the complexity of her feelings, her visions, and her teenage passion for the world and for life. Now, her questions were different, but her desire to be close to the river, and her trust in it, assured her that this would still be the best thing to do.

Jess dropped Miko off at her mom's house and drove her small truck up the winding highway along the Nesika. She wanted to be above the dams, above the PowerCorp offices near the source, the clear, translucent spring high in the mountain valley that fed the Nesika. She had enough supplies with her for three or four days and could already feel solitude calling to her like an old friend.

The logging road was rough, and her truck bounced slowly through the potholes and tire tracks. When she got to the end, she turned off the engine and just sat in the silence of the forest, the Nesika a gentle hush of current like a soft wind through the trees.

It was quiet, so quiet. The shrill call of a flicker rang around her, and she opened the door of her truck. The stillness struck her, and she missed her dog, but she knew that if he had been here he would have been a distraction from her work, from her goal to go deeper, to be still and let the river, plants, and other animals be her companions.

Her pack was heavy as she swung it over her shoulders, but she liked the weight of it and cinched the waist belt tight enough to keep the shoulder straps from cutting into her back. As she headed down the road to the river, a small gray squirrel cried out an alarm, announcing to the woods that an intruder had arrived. Jess smiled to herself and rested in the cadence of her walking, enjoying the sturdiness of her boots, the strength of her body, the definition of her edges already emerging in this solitude.

After hiking for a few hours, she found a clearing next to the small, young Nesika for her camp. She put down her pack and rested near the water. It was shallow and wide here and made a high-pitched sound as it fell over the rocks lining its bed. Jess sighed; the stillness of the forest and the movement of the river seemed so simple to her, pure in some ways and vulnerable, childlike, in others. Her mind raced, and she looked forward to the time when it would begin to quiet and match the rhythm of time here in the forest—a slow, steady kind of time in which light and dark rose and fell in a dance, in which the river was a constant, steady presence, rising and falling in its own cadence, responding to seasons and weather and, up here, free from human touch.

She set up her camp and her small two-person tent and made a fire ring of river stones. She put her food into a bright red bear canister and stored it away from her camp. The damp chill of the coming evening graced the slanted light of the forest. Jess walked down to the riverbank and sat, resting her back against a downed cedar. The current sounded like a small drum as it wound over stones and ran toward the sea. She wondered what it was like for the water to suddenly encounter the dams and flumes of the power system.

For a moment, she thought she heard a voice in the river, a young woman singing, chanting in an old way. Jess listened harder, trying to tune in to the voice, as if it were a distant radio signal. The song seemed to come from the river itself, from the trees along the bank swaying in the early-evening breeze.

Jess had brought a book with her, *The Water Walker*, about a group of Native American women who were creating ceremonies to bless and heal rivers. She read about the women who carried water from each of the four oceans—the Mother Earth Water Walkers—and poured them into Lake Superior. They were offering the water to the center of Turtle Island so it could have a conversation and return to their home oceans. In another ceremony, a group of women and men carried water from the source of the Mississippi river to the delta, wanting to give the river "a taste of herself."

A kingfisher called out from a small lodgepole pine just above the current of the river. Jess thought about what these people did, about their intention to offer a prayer to the water, and she decided that, in the spirit of that ceremony, she would carry water from the source of the Nesika to the place just below the Green

Springs dam. From where she was, the walk would take about two days. She was grateful that the old Nesika trail had been restored and would carry her close to the riverbank for most of the way.

She got up and began to look for wood for her evening fire. Everything that had happened to her felt far away, down in Penden Valley. People there were watching the news, preparing dinner, searching the Internet, hanging on to the distractions of daily life, while she was alone with her river and ready to weave together whatever strands of meaning were left for her.

⤢◎⤣

The next morning, a blue jay woke her up just as it was getting light. She slipped out of her sleeping bag and zipped open her tent door. The Nesika looked sweet to her in the early morning. A gentle mist rested on its surface, and the song from the day before seemed to glow within it.

Jess pulled on strong leather boots over rough wool socks. She wished she had some sacred special vessel to carry the water in, but she had only the water bottles she had brought for drinking. She felt a little clumsy when she went down to gather the water for her walk. She sat for a while on the bank and tried to summon a prayer, a song, something that would be like a blessing. She thought of the old, clumsy prayers from her Catholic childhood and smiled. She wanted to find another way to pray, to open herself to the spirits of the land and the river.

She stood up and walked to the edge of the water and watched the stream and the light in the water run over and around the stones of the riverbed. She thought of her sister, of how losing her to the river had created a kind of kinship, as if Jess and it were now related somehow. That was why she was here, then, why she had been called to do this work. She reached her hand into the water and held it there, waiting. The water seemed to pull away the anger, the tension, and the fury that she had been feeling. It was just the two of them, and she let go. *Okay, river, tell me what to do.*

She filled her red water bottle and stood up. She held the bottle next to her heart and let out a strong breath. She packed up her camp and put on her pack, carrying the water with her like a young child.

As she walked, she recited to herself the names of the plants and animals along the trail:

Mountain laurel
Salmonberry
Devil's club
Salal
Mourning dove
Chickadee
Dark-eyed junco
Crow
Trillium
Skunk
Elderberry
Raven
Trout

The walk took two days, and each step made Jess feel lighter, more determined, and part of something very important. She looked for signs from the Native people who had lived in this river valley hundreds of years before. The Molalla people—the wild ones. They were shy, and not much was known about them; by the time traders encountered them, two waves of smallpox had decimated most of them. The only people left were herded out of the valley, to the Cow Creek reservation, more than a hundred miles away.

Sharp sadness seized Jess's chest then. Their home, where they had lived for thousands of years, was gone to them forever. Like her sister.

The Green Springs dam looked to her like a granite fist holding back the wild flow of the Nesika. She was careful to stay out of sight of any PowerCorp workers who might be nearby that day. She found a clearing just below the dam that she was sure was hidden from the highway or anyone other than fishermen and hikers. She set up her camp and gathered her evening wood. An osprey whistled overhead and dove into the clear blue-green water just below her camp. She could see the large flumes running along the ridgetops and dropping down the hillsides into the power station. The river was fed into almost forty miles of flumes and through four power stations before it even reached the Green Springs dam. It looked like a formidable opponent.

Jess stood up and carried the water bottle down to the riverbank. The only thing she could think to do was make a promise. She held the water to her heart and closed her eyes.

Hey, river, it's me, Jess. I am bringing you yourself, a taste of yourself from above the dams we have laid across your back. I am so sorry. I will work for you, try to give you back what is yours. In the spirit of the Water Walkers, I bless you with this gift.

She could smell the decaying body of a salmon just downstream, and an image of her young sister rose up in her again. *The river gives life and takes life.* She opened the top of her bottle and poured the river water back into itself, inseparable now from its own wildness.

Sitting at the water's edge in the fading light, Jess made another promise: *I offer you my life, in a new way. I will work for you and for the life in you. For coho, steelhead, chum, and chinook. I will be your Water Walker, your protector.*

That night, she heard what sounded like a mountain lion's cry not far from her camp. And in the cadence of the night river, a song rose up and was matched by distant drumming.

PART II

JESS

A year later, Water Walkers had become a lively nonprofit and Jess had become skilled at researching and finding grant money to keep her going. It was a good blend of her passion and tenacity to get the work done for the river. One of her first projects had been to hire a professional photographer to take pictures of the Nesika, both above and below the dams. She put the photos together in a beautiful book called *The River's Cry* that she hoped would help people better understand the need to completely restore the spawning grounds above the Green Springs dam. She had just finished packaging another shipment that would go to the Riverkeepers' annual conference in New Mexico later that month. Knowing that the story of the Nesika was true for many rivers all over the world, she had dedicated the book to the Water Walkers, then and now.

Her phone rang, and she jumped, remembering that she had forgotten to return her mom's call from the day before.

"Hi, Mom. How are you? Sorry I didn't call back yesterday. I had kind of a weird day."

"That's okay, sweetheart. Is everything all right? I've been thinking about you so much lately. How are things with your work? I think you told me that the grant came through finally, the one that you asked for from . . . what was the name of that foundation?"

"Smitherton. They give out grants to environmental organizations thinking of pursuing legal action against corporations. I should know by the end of next week." Jess let the silence rest between them, trying to coax out of her mother her real reason for calling.

"I was thinking of inviting Uncle Robert and his new wife, Jody, down for Thanksgiving, and I wanted to check with you about your schedule. Do you have anything going on next month?"

Jess thought of the photocopied notes she had on her desk and her desire to keep moving ahead with the lawsuit. But that shouldn't interfere with her plans for the holidays. Her closest friends were all in other places, and she hadn't heard from Suzie in over a year.

"That would be fine, Mom. I'd love to see Uncle Robert. And I like Jody."

"Great. I'll call them later today. Is everything all right with you?"

"Well, I had a strange thing happen yesterday. Rich from the agency called and said he had something he wanted to show me. I went over there, and for some reason he gave me the copies of the meeting notes that were used to write the report that justified everything they needed to let PowerCorp keep the Green Springs dam in place. I'm not really sure why. Maybe he feels guilty, or maybe now that he's retiring he just doesn't care."

"Gosh, sweetie, how hard it must have been for you to go back. I heard from Cliff that he was having a tough time with retirement. Cliff also told me Jeff is back in town. Have you heard anything from him?"

Jess felt a rush of heat in her face. "No. I didn't even know he was back."

"Well, maybe you should call him. He might be able to help you out with some of this, especially if Rich is willing to talk to you now."

"Right now I just want to go upriver and take Miko fly-fishing. There's a strong run of summer steelhead moving up the Nesika, and I feel like it would be fun to go and bother them."

"Well, sweetheart, you be careful. I'll let you know what I hear from Uncle Robert. I love you." Jess took in everything she could. *Enough for both*, she thought.

"I love you, too, Mom. Bye."

She stared at her phone for a moment, mulling over her mom's advice, and thought about calling Jeff. She was struggling with her work and longing for the meaning it had once held for her. But she knew her mom was right—Jeff had been part of those meetings, and Jess had a dim feeling that he might be able to help her now.

Jeff. She wished she didn't miss him so much. She leaned back in her chair, toying again with her feelings about calling him. Maybe an email would be a better idea. She looked up at the picture of a Molalla woman carrying her small child down to the river. This was a copy of the only documented photo of a Molalla and had been a gift to her from the chair of her doctoral committee. The woman in the picture was walking through a ray of sunlight down to the Nesika, her baby bound to her back. The child was looking straight at the camera, across time, into Jess's eyes—like the river itself peering out, seeking something, beckoning.

She reached out, grabbed her phone, and dialed his number.

⊙

The neon-orange fly-fishing line drifted in a slow arc on the surface of the deep pool. The sun was warm, and a kingfisher trilled from the branch of a fir tree hanging over the river just upstream. Jess played the line downstream, then whipped it up and over her head, laying it back down in the upstream current with the flair and ease born of many years of fishing.

Reeling in her line, Jess carefully walked upstream and called to Miko, who had found an interesting downed tree to sniff through. The sun had just come over the ridge and begun drying the forest; the rising steam lay over the still, opaque green depths of the pool. Jess breathed in the cool fall air and let herself rest for a moment, before heading back to her truck. She hoped Jeff was upriver today, available, willing to talk with her.

She had a message from him waiting for her. "Hey, Jess, good to hear from you! I'm working on a highway project up on the Nesika. Try to call me. I'll keep my phone on, and hopefully I'll be able to hear it above the noise of the trucks."

Jess looked down at her cell phone as if it were an injured animal. She was surprised at how good it felt to hear his voice, how deeply she had let herself fall both toward and away from him. She played the message one more time and noticed her hands shaking and her heart beating more quickly. *What do I want?* she wondered. After what had happened to Mink, after they had found the plans, she had never had a chance to talk with Jeff, to hear more from him about what was happening, to get answers to the questions she had been afraid to ask him.

She took a moment to drink some tea from her metal thermos before returning Jeff's call. *Maybe we could have lunch at the lodge. Maybe he won't answer. Maybe . . .*

"Hey, Jeff, it's me, Jess." She paused, as a small but vast silence overtook their conversation.

"Jess, what's up?"

"Thanks for calling back. Look, some stuff has come up about what happened last year, and I think it would be helpful if I could talk with you about it. I'm upriver today."

He said, "Sure—I can meet with you later today. I'll be done here around two or so. We could meet at the lodge for some coffee. Will that work for you?"

"Yeah, that's perfect. See you at two o'clock. Thanks, Jeff."

Gathering her fishing gear, Jess called Miko into the cab of her truck. Petting his sweet head, she looked into his brown eyes. They were so certain, so constant; they seemed like the one thing in her life she could depend on.

"Let's go, boy."

She waited at the intersection while log trucks whipped by

with their latest quarry from the timber sale up Blanch Creek. She played the conversation with Jeff over and over in her mind. He had sounded good, like himself, maybe even happy to hear from her. In less than four hours, she would be meeting him. Her body trembled with nervousness and curiosity.

Pulling into a gap in the log-truck traffic, Jess decided to distract herself by going to see whether Martin and his crew were ground-truthing the Blanch Creek logging area. "Ground-truthing." Jess had always liked the sound of that—telling the truth of the ground. It really meant that because you couldn't count on the timber companies to follow the rules of an environmental impact statement, someone had to become parental and check on their work. Martin's organization, the Nesika Watershed Council, was ground-truthing the latest logging operation on Blanch Creek, a major tributary of the Nesika. It wasn't easy, and no one paid them for it, but if the rules weren't followed, there would be another landslide like the one two years before, which had suffocated all of the developing salmon redds in Gold Creek, another tributary of the Nesika.

Turning onto the small logging road, she could see the dust and hear the grating sound of chain saws screeching through the woods. Swinging her truck around the bend, she parked in a wide pull-off in the road and decided to walk up the hill the rest of the way. Miko bounded ahead of her, leaping noisily into the underbrush. She shouldered her old green daypack and started up the road. Not far off, Jess could hear the familiar sounds of the logging camp: the compression brakes of logging trucks huffing through the trees; the constant wail of chain saws and shouting loggers. She stopped and watched them in the distance and imagined maybe they felt a kind of closeness to the land, the open heartwood of trees, and the sweet smell of sun reaching the forest loam for the first time in a century.

The road was damp from the morning rain, and a robin bounced along with her through the red lace of vine maples. Although bright flashes of sun danced on the road, she could sense the small shift toward winter beginning. Jess longed for the comfort of a turn in time that would happen no matter what was going on around her.

She saw the clearing up ahead and hoped that she would find Martin working in the new clear-cut of the forest sale. Miko bounded ahead and met Martin before she did. Other members of Martin's ground-truthing team wandered slowly in the forest around them, as if people from an ancient time, measuring the girth of trees, shouting numbers and slope percentages like incantations.

Jess saw the top of Martin's shaggy, multicolored wool hat disappear into the underbrush, and she called out, "Hey, Martin! It's me, Jess!"

"Jess!" he called out from within the damp, sun-filled forest. "What are you doing up here? I was thinking of calling you the other day and asking some advice about this stream and how it became classified as a level two when there's no question there are salmon just downstream from here. It should be a level three, at the very least. Did you see that show on TV last week? I was going to email you about it. Jess, it's so good to see you! How have you been? Have you heard anything from Suzie? Someone heard from her not long ago—can't remember who . . ."

Jess pushed her fists deep in her pockets. *Suzie.* "No, after she left, I just kind of gave up on her. It was just so crazy, and so much was going on for me, reaching out to her or trying to find her didn't make sense."

Jess bent over and patted Miko's head. "I did just talk with Jeff, and we're going to meet up later at the lodge. I had some time to kill before then, so I thought I would come up and see how things are going."

Martin got very still. "Whoa, Jess . . . That . . . Wow. Still slutting around for PowerCorp. Actually, Deb, his girlfriend from Alaska—don't know if you know about her—well, she's right over there." Martin gestured toward a woman bending over and hammering in a survey stake. She stood, and Jess noticed that she was tall and slim, with a long, dark ponytail flowing out from under her black wool hat.

A girlfriend. Well, what did you expect? she chided herself. Jeff hadn't lived the monastic life of a woman starting her own nonprofit. He lived his passionate life with someone else . . .

"Oh, wow. I didn't know he had a girlfriend. He met her up in Alaska?"

"I guess so. C'mon, Jess." He put his arm around her, and Jess leaned affectionately into the side of his damp wool coat. He smelled good, like the forest—like damp, open earth just after a hard rain.

However, a clear-cut always felt like a kind of war zone to Jess. She knew there could be violations all over the place and slipped out from under Martin's arm and turned to look behind them at the scarred landscape. Martin walked over and sat heavily on a damp, decaying nurse log, the young saplings swaying as he jostled their ground. "I was just reading the other day some letter from the head of the Department of Natural Resources and the Environment. They're really framing their move to destroy any protection the forest has by turning it into some kind of monster. What they say is that the whole fucking forest is going to explode if we don't go in and remove the dangerous woody biomass that's choking our forests and creating a potential disaster. Jesus, Jess, it's unbelievable! They've reframed the whole thing as some kind of warped horror movie. 'Beware! The forest is going to get you!' The terrorists are now the trees!"

Jess knew that "woody biomass" meant trees, and that to remove the "woody biomass" meant cutting the forest. She looked down at her boots and kicked a small stone into a clump of grass. Her focus had been so much on getting the Green Springs dam removed that she had lost track of the Healthy Forest Initiative to clear-cut forests that would otherwise be protected. The administration's ability to manipulate language and say the opposite of what it was proposing to do was almost laughable.

"My God, Martin," she said, "you would think they were having enough fun demonizing the Arab people and turning the world into a pit of terrorism waiting to explode. You're right—this *is* some kind of nightmare we're living in, when the administration can demonize a forest, ignoring science and ramming the whole thing down the throats of the public."

Martin stood up. "Come here. I want to show you something."

He leaped easily over the log and down a gentle slope into a clearing. The cut had taken place only a few days before. "This is a new version of abuse, called a stewardship contract. The motherfucking DNR has found a way to bypass all the typical procedures and open up land to logging and clear-cutting in a big hurry, because if they don't, well, all this 'woody biomass' is going to explode any minute, and you know we have to keep the public and—get this—the *firefighters* safe! Can you believe they went so far as to say, 'We have to clear-cut this hillside, because if we don't, you and the firefighters are going to be in terrible danger'? Jess, these hills are one of the only remnants of the natural ecosystem of this river valley. Other than the care the Native Americans gave it for thousands of years, this land, the very place where we are standing, was untouched, rolling through the cycles of time, seasons, storms, life and death . . . And now look at it.

"You know what I think? This is a time when people are too scared, too easily swayed to see only what they are shown and not to question it. I feel overwhelmed. Jess. I've never in all my years of working in the woods felt so desperate, so helpless."

Jess looked over the clearing and let the weight of what he was saying set in. She knew he was right.

Martin looked at her and let out a sigh of resignation. "With all the fucking media spin these days, who knows what they'll say about us? PowerCorp is like some predatory animal that stalks and kills whatever it wants, as long as the innards are money. I don't know, and mostly I don't care, what people think about me and my work these days. As someone said the other day, my only goal is to be a really good ancestor."

The area they stood in looked very much like a war zone indeed. Downed trees, scraggly undergrowth suddenly ripped from its natural place, exposed seasonal streambeds, and ever-present stumps all waited like soldiers in a minefield.

"I like that—imagine anyone in the timber industry even thinking about himself as an ancestor. But they don't and they won't unless something fundamentally changes. In the meantime, we do what we can—and you know what, Martin? I have so much respect for you and the others working here," Jess said, looking out at the scraping backhoe, watching a tree fall and the logger leaping to set the cable choker. She walked over to Martin and leaned into his shoulder. They stood like that for a long time, their blended gaze gathering the wounded image and storing it with the many others they held from their past years of activism.

"Thanks. I think of Jamie and the world I'm leaving to him, and I think of the salmon and steelhead that depend on a clear path to their spawning grounds. Then I think of the dumb-ass politicians and it makes me want to scream." He pulled Jess in even closer to his side. "Actually, sometimes I *do* scream."

He walked out into the clearing and called to Miko, who was being overly social with the logging crew. Jess shook herself from her numbness and walked back to the day-camp area that Martin and his crew had set up. She sat on a log and pulled an apple from her pack. Miko came back to her and flopped in the wet grass at her feet. Her body felt heavy and unused to being in the presence of so much destruction. She longed to feel a sense of belonging to something—to a way of changing, to a bearer of wisdom—like the elders and medicine people of the old times. She wished someone could teach her an old song she could sing to the logging crew and Martin's workers, something that would heal what was wounded and stop everything that was happening.

"C'mon, Miko, let's go give them a hand." Jess stood slowly, checked the time, and walked over to the area where two women were taking measurements, using a long orange cord. One woman was in the stream, wearing hip waders and hidden under a hat, and the other was someone from the yoga class that Jess had started taking at the local YMCA. They were measuring the stream buffer, making sure that the logging crew had left enough vegetation to keep the stream shaded and cool once the Oregon summer sun bore down on the now mostly barren hillside.

"Miranda, it's me, Jess, from yoga! I'm a good friend of Martin's and came up here to see if you needed some help with ground-truthing this project. Is there something I can do?"

"Jess! Good to see you. Sure. If you can record our measurements, we can call them out to you from down by the stream. The slope gets pretty tricky up here around the bend. This is Deb. She's been working with Martin for the last few months."

Deb looked up at Jess from under her black wool hat. She had striking blue eyes that looked both a little startled and amused at the same time. She smiled at Jess and walked down toward the stream, holding the measuring tape. Miko was ready for a new game and plunged through the brush after Deb. The water was low for this time of year but flowing with a gentle, flashing, folding current. Jess smiled, secure in her understanding of the regulations being fought for so that the little stream could have the protection it needed and deserved to carry the cool water into the salmon stream below. This was where she found a precious little stone of hope—here in this cool, shaded bend, and in the hearts and courage of the people making careful measurements, taking time away from their families and jobs to work on behalf of a life other than their own.

"Damn!" Deb shouted. "This looks like they left only a seventy-two-foot buffer where they were supposed to leave a hundred."

"Yeah, God, it looks like there was a beautiful stand of cedars right here that would have been within the hundred-foot buffer zone," Miranda said. "I think we should call Martin over here."

Jess looked up from her clipboard and made eye contact with Deb. She was standing tall by the stream, blending with the trees, in defiance against the rage of the timber companies striking just outside the small claim that the stream had staked.

They stood like that for a moment. Then, breaking the weighty silence, Deb said to Jess, "I haven't seen you up here before. Are you from around here?"

Jess's stomach gripped, and she had to hold on to her composure. *Not good timing*, she thought. Breathing out slowly, she said, "Yeah, I live in town. I'm Jess." She hesitated as she saw the recognition dawning in Deb's eyes. "I run Water Walkers, so I come up here to help now and then."

"Oh, you're Jess, Jeff's ex. Right."

"Yeah, I am."

Just then, Miranda and Martin came striding through the forest, talking loudly and exclaiming how messed up the land was and what level of reporting he was going to file and apply for.

Jess and Deb broke their eye contact and refocused on the work.

"What were the measurements again?" Jess lovingly touched the newly exposed heartwood of the cedar stumps. It was almost as if she could feel the dying pulse, the pain of the cut, of her own inability to protect them, even when there were agreements, even when there were laws.

Deb said, "The buffer is seventy-two feet here and only sixty-one feet downstream. Aren't they supposed to survey and flag this area before they cut?"

Martin measured the buffer himself. Sighing, he said, "Why don't we move farther upstream and make sure they were consistent in their inconsistencies?" Jess watched him look down at his feet and move slowly up along the small stream, Miranda following close behind. Jess called for Miko and walked up to Deb, not sure what she wanted to say but feeling as if she needed to say something, connect with her in some way. But Deb turned away and walked down to the streambed.

Jess had thought she was finished with schoolyard battles and crushes. She walked over to the cedar stumps and traced the edges of the new cut with her fingers, wishing there were some way to end the struggles she constantly felt and to relax for just a moment in a clear place, where the splash of spawning salmon and the roll and rise of a free-flowing river could wash through her, cleansing her and assuring her that she was home.

She walked back to her pack. Deb had gone off to another group, and Martin was way upstream now, working on the buffer measurements with Miranda. It was almost one thirty. Calling to Miko, Jess walked to her car, the sun washing over the small valley, illuminating the torn hillsides with the special, fresh light that fills the air in late fall. Miko charged by her to the truck, ready for whatever was next.

PIAH

⟨◑∽⟩

The dark current pooled behind the boulder where Piah was waiting for Lamoro to bring the herbs for their sick people. Libah, nestled against Piah's back in her elk-skin wrap, moved in her sleep. A pair of spawning salmon splashed in the shallows just downstream from where Piah was waiting, and she started. The fall rains had come again in time to call the salmon from their ocean homes up into the arms of the Nesika and the lives of the animals and humans who depended on their return. Piah stood up slowly and looked out into the dimming light for Lamoro.

Lamoro was one of the medicine women who tended Piah's people. She was the one to whom the spirits had come with the remedy for the fire illness that was sweeping through the small family tribe in the high mountains near the headwaters of the Nesika. The other tribes that lived in the valleys below were also getting the strange disease. The spirits had told Lamoro to gather willows from the low-lying areas and bring them to Piah's people. These were what Piah was waiting for now.

She heard rustling on the forest floor and turned to see Lamoro struggling up the hill with a large bundle of willow branches lashed to her back. Piah went silently to her side and lifted the bundle off Lamoro.

"These will help," Lamoro said, more to the willow than to Piah. Piah could see she was shaking from her effort and put her hand on Lamoro's shoulder to steady her.

"Thank you." Piah shouldered the bundle next to her baby on her back and helped Lamoro over the large stones up the mountain to where their people were waiting.

Their camp had grown sullen with so many ill. Smoke rose from the fire that the elders made each night for the sweat lodge. Piah could hear their songs vibrating through the stones around her as they chanted to the spirits, pleading with them for healing.

Lamoro sat with the women near the cooking shelter and began to show the others how the spirits had instructed her to strip the bark from the willows and pound it into a paste. Piah tasted the paste. It was bitter and seemed to suck all the moisture from her mouth. It was a familiar taste from her childhood, when her mother tried to sweeten the willow tea with dried elderberry.

The women worked into the dark, peeling and pounding the paste with the stones they used to grind berries and dried salmon into their food. Piah took some of the paste to the shelter where the sick ones were drying off after the sweat lodges. She carefully covered her mouth with a cedar cloth as she entered the low-lying earthen home and gave each of them a small amount of the willow paste in water. Some spat it to the ground, others swallowed, and some, too weak to open their mouths, slept and would get their medication in the morning.

Piah looked around her at the disfigured faces in the low flames of the evening fire. Some were swollen, with weeping sores; the ones whose sores had scabbed over were the most sick. She looked over at one of the old women. It was Piah's aunt. She was slumped over, not moving, and Piah knew she had died. She slowly backed out of the shelter and stood looking into the dark arms of the cedar trees that surrounded their home.

In the distance, Piah could see a hovering light. In the center of the light was the face of the man she had seen in her vision when she was at the stone circle, praying for Mian and his journey. He was laughing. Piah clenched her hands and wanted to shout at the strange man to leave, leave and take the disease with him. Then he was gone and Piah turned to find her father.

Piah sat in the doorway of her family's home and watched as the men carried the body from the healing shelter. Lamoro stood next to her and placed a welcoming hand on Piah's head. Piah drew closer to her.

"The willow bark is helping those with the fever. Others seem more restful. Can you go with me tomorrow to get some more? It grows only in the lower valley and is very far. If we can gather enough, we won't have to go back down there for many days."

"Yes, Lamoro." Piah shifted her nursing baby to the other breast and carefully petted her soft black hair. She felt the healing power of Lamoro pulse through her and into Libah. They would be safe from the disease, from the spirit that laughed at her from the arms of the dark trees.

The next morning, Piah fed Libah and left with Lamoro to go down into the lower valleys. Usually they went down there only in the winter, when the other tribes were gone. Now, it was dangerous for them to go. The lower tribes had been known to kidnap and enslave the men and women from Piah's tribe. Especially now, when so many were dying, kidnapping was becoming a way to replace the lost relatives. Piah heard others call this the Mourning Wars.

Watching Lamoro flow gracefully over the large river boulders, Piah could see her strength and her power carry her to the medicine she needed for her people, her role as healer seeming to be a kind of weight and strength she was giving herself and her life over to. The basalt canyon narrowed sharply before opening into the wide river valley below. Piah knew they would have to go almost as far as the colliding rivers before they found the willow. She worried that going so far would keep her away from Libah for too long, and that her own breasts would begin spilling unused milk before she would be with her baby again, but she knew other mothers would feed her daughter. She looked into the billowing white water pouring down the canyon. The Nesika, which nourished Piah's family much as the milk of Piah's body nourished Libah. The bodies of the spent salmon and eels that the river pulled from the faraway sea layered its banks, feeding the plants, the willows they were seeking now to help Piah's people.

JESS

The Nesika Lodge was an old, familiar, wood-stained struc-
ture. Jess had been here for her high school senior prom
dinner with her date, a tall, awkward boy named Dale. The sun
was slanting through the trees, just catching the edge of the river
as it turned behind the hundred-year-old log building. She sat in
her truck for a minute, absentmindedly brushing Miko's ears. He
put his head down on his large paws and looked up into her eyes.

"Well, Miko, here it goes. I just need to remember why I'm
doing this."

Miko answered with his watery, hopeful gaze and thumped
his tail.

As she opened the heavy, carved-wood door, her arm felt
weak and her hand shook. Jeff was sitting at the corner table,
playing with the bill of his dark green hat. He looked up, pushing
his dark brown, curly hair away from his face. He stood a little
too quickly and walked toward her. It was so good to see him.
Jess wanted to run into his arms, like in the old love story, but she
could smell the damp concrete between them and backed away.

"Jeff, hi. Thanks for meeting me."

"It's okay. Yeah, I know. It's good to see you, Jess. Really good." He sat back down in his chair and almost missed his seat.

Behind him on the lodge wall was a beautiful, large photo of Tom McCall, a well-liked former Oregon governor who loved to fly-fish on the river. There were fly rods hanging overhead and a large glass display case showing the many hundreds of hand-tied feather flies that could be used to seduce the fish of the Nesika. Jess was familiar with most of them; she had collected many of the more exotic "species" and learned how to tie some of the flies on her own.

"How was Alaska?" Jess asked.

Their waitress interrupted them. Jess asked for coffee with cream and a glass of water with no ice. Jeff asked for decaf coffee and a slice of apple-blueberry pie. Smiling absently, the waitress took their menus and they refocused on the table in front of them.

Jeff shifted continuously in his seat. She noticed his hands, streaked with mud, nails broken from working with equipment like the underwater cameras they had used the first day they'd met. Jess could almost smell the forest from that day, the damp, insistent rain, the ease of their quiet moments, and the warmth of their intimacy and passion.

"Alaska was good. The project was pretty clear-cut—to use an apt metaphor for that area. The Tongass is a really big place, so much bigger than the patchwork forests we have here. We saw a lot of bears and eagles, and the streams were choked with salmon. You ever been up there?"

"Yeah, remember, I told you about the summer I crewed on an old fishing boat for a seminar on whales?" Jess said. "We went up into Frederick Sound and listened to the humpbacks sing to each other and scoop the krill from the water. I loved it—it's amazing yet unexplainable."

"It really is." Jeff looked up into her eyes, and for a moment Jess let his gaze rest in hers. "I didn't get a chance to go out into the sound. We mostly took flow measurements up on the Brooks River. You would have loved it, Jess. The rivers up there have to get down to sea level in a hurry, so they really move. The rapids are crazy, almost like a steady waterfall."

Looking up at him across the table, Jess liked the mental image of Jeff sitting next to the Brooks, thinking of her, feeling their connection pulling him, the flow of a fast, high Alaskan river reminding him of his love and care for her. She looked up into his brown eyes and saw the hurt and the shimmer of recognition that she had expected.

Jess took in the familiar light in his eyes. He was so smart; she loved the lucidity of his mind. She half listened to what he was saying but mostly focused on her feelings rising up in response to his opening up to her. At the same time, she felt her ideals, like a pillar that stood inside her, beginning to deflect her sensitivity to her memories.

For a moment, Jess imagined that even though they had been apart, separated by oceans, they might have been communicating in an old way. She remembered a time when they had sat in the sun along the Nesika, a time when their bodies had seemed continuous and she was certain in love. "Remember that Marge Piercy poem I read when we were camping in the hills above the Nesika last spring—'Perpetual Migration'?" Jess closed her eyes and recited, "The salmon hurtling upstream seeks the taste of the waters of its birth but the seabird on its four-thousand-mile trek follows charts mapped on its genes."

Jess caught herself and looked down at her hands in her lap. Her throat tightened, and she felt like apologizing, for wandering into this memory, this tender, private place of connection that she so missed, so longed for in her life. She knew that this sense of connection, of something from an older time, was holding her to her work, to her vision, and to her desire to save the river.

"Hey, Jeff, sorry. I miss you. You know that right?"

How could I have just said that? She wanted to run from the café. She gripped the edge of her chair. Suddenly, the clatter of the café sounds around her grew louder. She knew she had to hold herself— the flight instinct gripping her felt as strong as the steady migration toward her desire that she had experienced moments before.

Jeff reached his hand quickly toward hers across the table. "Jess, it's all right. I miss you, too—of course I do. When we broke up, you have no idea how much I wanted to follow you, try to save you somehow, but I knew I couldn't. I was so sorry about your job and what they did to you. You must know that. I kind of just put my head down, kept doing my job . . ." Jess noticed he stopped himself before he headed over that cliff. "You know I can't help you right now. I have my job, and I know that if the dam had come down, it would have been amazing, for us, for the salmon. But it didn't and it isn't. Maybe Rich is just trying to show you why."

They sat together in silence. Jess felt her breath high in her chest and her heart beating a strange, strong pattern. Playing with the curved handle of her coffee cup, Jess relaxed into the vortex of feelings swirling around her.

"More coffee?" the waitress asked, almost on cue.

"Sure, that would be great," Jess said.

Just outside the window from their table was the old apple tree that had been there as long as the lodge had. The branches were bare, and a few small apples clung to the higher limbs. Jess watched a small chickadee bounce from branch to branch, and she longed for a moment of similar innocence.

"He seems to be pretending that he just discovered the whole thing, like he had nothing to do with the wording that was changed in the watershed analysis. Damn, he makes me so mad. He's like you. It's like trying to work with a Gumby doll that gets bent into whatever shape the people in authority want him to be in. You know how I felt about all that." Jess felt the heat rise in her as she leaned against her wooden chair back. "So what he did was somehow 'find' these notes in his office and give them to me. Why would he have done that?"

Jeff looked down at his half-eaten pie and didn't answer.

"You know what I think? I think you believe that because they're paying you to believe that. Our science was sound and conclusive. The report was created, and I, a state employee, and you, a scientist for a private corporation, based the conclusions in the report on our findings. I'm going to meet with Planet Justice lawyers, and we are most likely going to bring a lawsuit."

Now he spoke: "Oh, Jess, that's going to be a waste of your time. I really doubt PowerCorp is very concerned about a lawsuit . . ." Jeff stopped himself and looked out the window.

Jess kept her eyes locked on her coffee cup, her hands clenched under the table. She didn't enjoy feeling like some peon being lectured to. She was the one with the PhD. "Jeff, I know that we're now living in very different worlds, but I also know we both want what's best for the salmon, for the river." Her anger balled up inside her chest, and her face flushed with heat. She didn't want to cry, to lose herself in front of him. Pinching the skin on the back of her hand, she avoided his eyes so he wouldn't see the fury of the storm raging in her heart. "And I know you know what is wrong, too."

"We *do* want the same thing. I envy your tenacity. I see the sacrifices you've made, and they're impressive. And I'm sorry. I absolutely understand what you're doing, and mostly I think I understand why. It's one of the things I've always loved about you."

Loved about me. Jess let silence surround them and the voices of the other diners take over. Her body raced with confusion and something like desire, and she choked back the impulse to say, *Come home.* It was as if she were looking at Jeff across a great chasm, the river flowing steadily in the canyon below them. Shaking herself, she refocused on why she was here, what she was trying to get from him.

"They never formally charged me with anything, you know."

"I heard they couldn't find enough evidence to, but that your computer was the source of the file and that Suzie went missing not long after you were fired from the agency."

"Yeah, she did—I heard she's somewhere in Florida. I feel bad for those boys. Mink is doing better, thank God. It could have been so much worse than it was. They'll do their time, and that's a drag, I just wish their time meant something. That's one of the reasons I'm going ahead with the lawsuit—and that's why I'm asking for your help. You were at those meetings, and you know the details of how those decisions were made. You became the main scientist for the new watershed analysis—"

"Well, as far as I'm concerned, the changes that Power-Corp is proposing should give the salmon access to the spawning grounds that the dam has blocked. The best lawsuit will never change their minds."

"Okay, I get it." Jess pushed back her chair. "Want to see Miko? He's out in the truck. We've been hanging out with Martin at the ground-truthing they're doing up at Blanch Creek. Miko loves ground-truthing . . ." Jess darted a knowing look at Jeff and watched his body stiffen. She wanted to ask him about the truth—if that mattered to him.

"Did you meet Deb?" he asked.

The feeling between them plunged.

"Yeah, she was there. We didn't talk much, and she wasn't too interested in getting to know me, but that's okay."

Jess scanned the books near the door while Jeff paid the check at the cash register. Mark Twain and other river books, fishing manuals, and a small collection of nature essays lined the crooked shelves. They walked out to the truck in silence. The river was lined with golden alders and cottonwood, and the late-afternoon air was cooling quickly. Miko jumped up in the front seat, wagging with pure dog exuberance at seeing Jeff.

"Hey, boy, how are ya?"

Miko jumped from the truck and twirled in excitement.

"C'mon, Miko," Jess called out, walking toward the trail behind the lodge, down to the long slope of the Nesika's west bank.

Miko bounded ahead, and Jess instinctively moved close to Jeff's side. She could feel the tingle of his presence, and body memories of their lovemaking surged through her. Remembering the lace of the vine maples on the fall day they had made love in the hot springs made Jess feel weak and vulnerable. She pushed her hands hard into her pockets to stop from reaching out to him. The brush of his slick black PowerCorp jacket against her arm sent a charge through her torn heart.

The river was high, even for fall, and the familiar rush of

the rapids led into the calm pool of the Tent Hole where she had caught a winter steelhead just over a year ago.

Jess looked out at the rapids pouring through the river canyon into the pool. She remembered the first time she had gone down into a hatchery, on a river in southern Idaho. The adult spring chinook had been captured and were being held in horrible concrete pens. The water was murky, and they moved together like one dying organism swaying in the flaccid current of the pool. When the females were ripe, the hatchery workers pulled them out, clubbed them over the head, and took their eggs. They then pulled a male and physically squeezed his sperm onto the eggs, clubbed him over the head, too, and tossed him on a pile of bodies that would decompose or be shipped off for pet food. These eggs would then be incubated until they hatched, and then raised until they were fingerlings that could be artificially pumped back into the river.

It had sickened Jess to see the bodies of the fish lying in the heat of the sun, having been robbed of their dying crescendo in the shallow rock beds of their high mountain birthplace. And she knew from her uncle Robert that the hatcheries didn't work the way they were supposed to.

The light was fading quickly, the sun long dipped behind the high canyon walls. Jess breathed in the familiar scent of the river, a musky coolness mingled with the tang of decaying apples from the old tree near the lodge. Reaching into the water, she felt as if she were holding the hand of an old friend, unable to tell where the boundaries of her skin left off and the river began.

Opening her eyes, she watched the water swirling in eddies around the small granite islands that seemed to have broken from the bank and were making their way into the full, strong current. These grass-tufted rocks offered miniature refuges for people fishing, herons, osprey, and leaping children when the water warmed in summer.

Standing up, she turned to Jeff, who was looking down at his feet and kicking distractedly at some exposed gravel. "This all really sucks. No one seems to care about anything or anyone other than themselves—how much money is spent, what it's worth. How about what it's worth to the salmon, to the forests, to the basic needs of all of life? Dammit, Jeff, I wish there were some way to convince you—I know you know this, and now we could have another chance to try to have the dam removed. I'm sure Planet Justice wouldn't be wasting their time on a project that wasn't worth pursuing."

Jess wanted all this to be so much simpler than it was. There had to be a way she could convince him; she needed him, wanted him, to change. Moving toward him, she felt the force of their passion crying out from each other's bodies.

"It really sucks, Jess. I know how much you care for this river . . ." Jess noticed that he didn't finish his sentence, and she waited for more, but Jeff averted his eyes.

"You know, Jeff, unlike you, I do believe there is a path through this, and you and I may both be missing something really important about what we think is right for the river. And yes, it does suck. C'mon, Miko!"

Miko rushed back to them along the trail, his tongue lagging and his curled tail waving. Jess and Jeff walked in silence back to the parking lot, and, after a quick hug, she got into her truck and left.

The log trucks huffed across in front of Jess as she waited at the intersection. She suddenly felt lonely, alone. The tension and sadness rolled up through her body, and she cried onto her steering wheel. There was nothing around her but the continual loss of what she loved.

Drying her face on the sleeve of her jacket, she pulled into the evening traffic and headed for the Green Springs dam. She knew it would be cold there, but she wanted the cold, wanted to struggle against something familiar, wanted the falling light to wrap around her like a piercing velvet blanket. She wanted to fade into the darkness.

$$\sim$$

It was quiet at the dam. Jess knew Miko must be hungry, she made him stay in the truck, worried that he might take off into the night after some awakened creature. She pulled her fleece jacket around her and put on another wool sweater, which she found on the floor of the truck. The air was crisp, the river still, the sound of the turbines a constant, restless hum.

Walking over to the dam, Jess felt the mud pulling at her boots and bunched her hands in her pockets against the cold. She looked down at the road where all day large trucks had carried in loads of gravel to be dumped into the river. She sighed, remembering Jeff's excited phone call to tell her PowerCorp had agreed to add the spawning gravel back into the river. The pile of gravel had washed down the river in that winter's flood and had been distributed in the natural eddies and pools of the spawning grounds. The trouble with machines was that they sometimes broke. After the redds were restored, the dam shut down and the eggs in the spawning beds were destroyed.

In the twilight, Jess could see the pile of this year's gravel. She walked to it and sat down on the riverbank, watching the rippling folds of the current. Looking upstream, she could just make out the gray-black wall of the dam, standing guard-like and forbidding. She wondered what it was like for the salmon, steelhead, and other fish of the river to continuously meet this obstruction. Something must confuse them in the certainty of their migration, the old story of the Nesika that they carried in their genetic material. Of course, then would come the confusion of the hatchery fish finding themselves in the wrong river, listening to the stories of their own genes saying something very different about the migratory path they were trying to follow.

Jess sat and closed her eyes. Her head ached, and she tried to steady her breathing by inhaling and exhaling in time with the river. She imagined diving in, sliding along the slick basalt bed, like moving through a birth canal, toward her death, pulled to completion by the stories being told to her, carried through many lives on the simple protein ladders of her DNA. Like the salmon, she shaped her life according to this story, watching her dreams, listening to the river, and pacing the migration of her desire.

There was a sudden rustling in the darkness behind her. Jess opened her eyes and shifted her attention toward the sound. She stood up slowly, trying not to fall on the pile of gravel, her body gripped by fear. She waited to hear the noise again, but all was quiet. Wondering if she had imagined it, she sat back down by the river, her attention focusing on each sound. Then she heard it again, this time much closer.

"Hello!" she called out, thinking it might be a PowerCorp worker who had stayed late to do some fishing. No one answered. She stood up and started toward her truck, stumbling over the rocks in the dark. Suddenly, a dark shape leaped in front of her. Her body stiffened. In the dim light between her and the truck was a large mountain lion. Jess started shouting, frantically trying to make herself large and intimidating to the cat, as it moved through the brush near her truck. Miko had started barking frantically, and Jess was glad at least he was safe.

"Hey, big cat! Get *away*!"

Her throat was dry with fear, and her wavering voice rang with terror. She looked around and, seeing a large stick, she stepped slowly toward it as the cat moved between her and the river. She bent down and reached for the downed limb, taking her eyes off the cat. Then she felt the weight, like a large boulder falling from a hill, knocking into her and throwing her against the gravel. Her head cracked on one of the river stones, and her teeth cut the inside of her mouth. She could taste her own blood and felt a pressure burning in her leg. She reached up and started hitting the cat with the stick. The cat grabbed at her head, and she felt a searing force at the back of her skull. Then she was being dragged across the pile of gravel. She tried to cry out, hoping someone would be along the river. No one was going to help her. Her body went limp. The last thing she heard was Miko's desperate yelping and the constant drone of the powerhouse turbines.

BARBARA

B arbara set down her coffee cup and newspaper when the phone rang. When she answered, Barbara heard a low, cautious voice ask, "Is this Barbara Jensen, mother of Jessica Jensen?"

Barbara's heart fell, her nerves following the same path of panic they had eighteen years ago when Monica had died.

"Yes, this is she. Is Jessica all right?" Barbara surprised herself at her protective formality.

"Ma'am, I'm sorry to have to tell you this, but Jessica was severely injured in a mountain lion attack last night. PowerCorp workers found her early this morning along the river. She has lost a lot of blood and is unconscious. She is down here in intensive care at the Penden Valley Community Hospital. Is there someone I can call to help you?"

Her stomach turned, and she felt the room dip and spin around her.

"No, I'll come right over. Oh my God, oh my God . . ."

Weeping and choking, she thought vaguely that she should call someone, but she couldn't form a clear thought and her instinct was to get to the hospital as soon as possible. She pulled on her clothes, found her keys, stumbled to her car, and made her way in blind terror toward the ICU. The red of the Texaco sign seemed luminescent and strange as she turned onto the highway. She passed a playground full of children and thought she saw her two young daughters swinging in unison on the bright orange play set. She almost stopped the car. *Maybe this is a dream—maybe they're all right.* But she kept going, her heart drumming her down the familiar streets. She knew she needed help, but couldn't put the thoughts together who to go to, where to start. She needed to be with Jess, help her find a way to hold on to her life. To lose both daughters would destroy her.

The hospital room was like a glaring, fluorescent light–filled cave. Wires and tubes hung down to Jess, who had been intubated and was breathing with the help of a respirator. She was pale, her hair matted with leaves and mud. Weeping uncontrollably, Barbara stumbled through the nurses to her side.

There was a strange, feral scent in the room, and she guessed it was from the cat. It evoked the times her husband had brought home deer and other game and she had helped to skin and clean the bodies. Here was her baby, her little one, who had grown up wild and certain. Now, under the lights and the washed-out white sheets, her body was lying torn open and broken by a savage animal, as instinctive and earth-bound as the will to survive.

The doctor, a gentle-looking, middle-aged woman, came in and carefully placed her hand on Barbara's shaking shoulder.

"Are you Jess's mom? My name is Dr. Sheldon, and I've been working with Jess these past few hours. May I have a word with you in the hall?"

"Yes, of course."

Dr. Sheldon helped her to stand and supported her out into the low light of the waiting room. They sat in the rough blue cloth chairs near the nurses' station. Barbara noticed how time seemed to be moving slowly, the details too dreamlike . . .

"Ms. Jensen, I'm afraid your daughter has some very serious injuries. She was attacked by the mountain lion and dragged for some distance before the cat, for some reason, apparently was startled and ran away. That saved Jessica's life. However, the cat inflicted a very deep wound to the lower part of her left leg, and she has abrasions on her back and neck, which seem to have come from the initial attack. Because of the loss of blood and her exposure to the cold last night, she's in shock. Right now we're trying to stabilize her blood pressure and body temperature with IV fluids and antibiotics, and we have her on the respirator. Even though her condition is very serious, unless her heart gives out, she will recover. As far as her injuries go, we will assess what kind of initial reconstruction we can try. Right now, we must get her on solid ground before moving forward. I am so sorry. The last time we treated anyone for a mountain lion attack was twenty-three years ago. It doesn't happen often. I think she was just in the wrong place at the wrong time. They're trying to track the cat now. The Oregon State Fish and Wildlife people will most likely be able to trap and kill the cat, at which time they will do an autopsy to determine whether it had rabies or any other diseases."

Barbara looked at her hands the whole time, focusing on them as a way of keeping herself from screaming, as a way of holding on so she could take in what the doctor was saying. She felt like she was choking.

"So," she said, taking a breath between each word, "she is going to live." Barbara said it more as an announcement than as a question.

"Yes, the chances are in her favor. It's early, but she's young and in very good shape. Why don't we go see how we're doing on raising her body temperature? Can I get you anything? Water or juice?"

"No, no, thank you. I'm fine. I do need to use the restroom, though."

"Right over here, second door on the left. I'll be in the room with Jess. Just come back in when you're ready. Again, I am so sorry."

She squeezed Barbara's hand and walked away. Her white jacket looked crisp and unreal, angelic, almost, thought Barbara, who headed down the hall into the bathroom. Sitting in the stall, she felt a breaking inside her, like an ice floe that had been holding back the terror and the searing grief she carried from losing Monica. Sobbing, she lay across her knees and let her tears wash through her hands and onto her legs.

She washed her face in the sink. In the mirror, her eyes looked stunned, filled with terror, desperate and lost. She brushed her hands through her short gray hair, breathing in the antiseptic smell of the hospital soaps. She made her way to the nurses' station and wrote down a number for them to call, her brother, Robert, in Portland. On the precipice of breaking, Barbara wanted family, the kind of support that came from the depths of relationship, of kinship. She hoped he was home.

⧉

Barbara sat waiting like a small boat drifting on an uncertain and dangerous current. She wanted to let go, let what was happening sail away from her, unimaginable and unreal. When Dr. Sheldon walked up to her, she jumped and didn't recognize her at first.

"What's happening? Is Jess okay?"

"Well, unfortunately, we just discovered a puncture wound on the back of her head. Because her hair was so matted with blood and saliva, we didn't notice it at first. There's a possibility that there's some damage to her brain. We're scheduling her for X-rays and an MRI, which will show us the effects of the wound."

Barbara felt the room fall away around her. She heard only the words "brain" and "damage." She imagined her beautiful, strong daughter confined to a wheelchair, unable to speak. She felt rising in her a certainty and conviction that she would be there to care for Jess, no matter what, no matter how high the expense or how lasting the damage to her body. She closed her eyes and took a deep breath, quieting a cry that was trying to resurface.

"I'm so sorry, Ms. Jensen, it's just too early to be able to give you a clear prognosis. Your daughter is strong and is responding to the fluids and medications we're giving her. We will know much more once we run the tests this afternoon. In the meantime, you can stay in the room with her if you'd like. Has someone contacted any other relatives and friends?"

"Yes, yes, I think my brother is on his way down from Portland—I guess it's about two hours from here. I'm not sure who else to call. Do you know where her dog is?"

"Yes, there was a dog in the cab of her truck. He was very upset when the paramedics got up there. They had to call animal control, who gave him a tranquilizer and took him to the Penden Valley Veterinary Clinic. He's okay there for now, I'm sure. Is there anything I can get you?"

Barbara thought of Jess and Miko, how they seemed to move together through the world like a little unit. Miko had been such a cute puppy, all fluff and tufted ears, like a small bear. Barbara had wondered if having a large dog while she was still in school was a good idea, but Jess had had her heart set on him, and her stubbornness and love for the furball had won over Barbara. Now, whenever they came over to visit, she looked forward to his large bright eyes and the certainty he brought to Jess's life.

"If he's okay there, I'll wait until my brother gets here to decide what to do about him," she replied in a vacant, hollow voice, sounding to herself as if she were speaking in a tunnel.

"Well, if you need me for anything, let me know. I'll be on call until two o'clock this afternoon. We hope to have Jess's MRI results before then. The nurses on this floor know where to find me."

"Thanks, Dr. Sheldon. I think I'll just stay here."

Barbara turned and walked into Jess's room. Ducking under the tubes that strung across, she settled into the cold plastic chair, found her daughter's hand, and held on to it, repeating her name, assuring her she was close by, chanting to her like prayer, like an incantation, calling her back, urging the medications and the fluids to help her. For a moment, Barbara could sense Monica's presence trying to push Jess back into her arms.

JESS

⸺

"Jess, can you hear me?"

Her eyes opened, and she stared hard at the sound coming toward her. It seemed so far away, like wind blowing through the trees near the river. Winter. She could hear winter in the voice—that's what she named it. She tried to form the word "winter."

"Jess, sweetheart, it's me, your mom."

Jess could hear other sounds and named those "walking" and "wonder." *Wwww*—the sound of *w* was floating around her. She imitated the sound for the person, her winter.

"W-w-w-winter."

She closed her eyes and fell back into the whirl of sound, the swirl of light and dark holding her like water, lifting her to the surface so she could breathe like a newborn. Something was grasping for her; she resisted, then let herself rise to the surface. She opened her eyes again and cried out in pain as sharp fragments of light began to pierce her underwater world. She could see them, drifting around in the room with her: *w*'s made of plastic, the sound coming from winter, her winter.

She tried to move toward the winter, but the weight of the dark water pulled her back under. She let the *w*'s pull her up like a net. It was so hard here.

BARBARA

B arbara glanced over at Dr. Sheldon for assurance. She was looking down at her charts, making notes.

"She said 'winter.' Did you hear her?" Barbara was holding on to what little movement Jess had made in the last several days. Traumatic brain injury. TBI. Barbara had spent nights and mornings on her computer, trying to learn what the doctors wouldn't tell her. Jess had experienced a stroke as a result of the damage and now was diagnosed with Broca's aphasia, a speech disorder that resulted in her being able to speak only in short, startled sentences, as if her language were balled up inside her and only small strands could come to the surface.

It was winter. A light, early-January snow had fallen the night before and was dripping in small rivulets off the roof just outside Jess's window in the hospital room. Ever since Jess had arrived in the hospital, she had kept her face turned toward the natural light. Barbara knew her daughter would come back to whatever that meant for her.

Dr. Sheldon appeared next to Barbara. "Her reactions are consistent with the results of the CT scan we did a few days ago. Now that she has become more responsive, I will order some more tests for her, including an electroencephalogram." Barbara looked at her blankly.

"It's called an EEG. What we will do is attach electrodes to Jess's scalp and get a more detailed measurement of her brain activity level. I will talk to the neurologist and find out what the schedule looks like for the next few days. Once we get a sense of her brain activity, we can begin to plan her therapy schedule."

Barbara stood unblinking next to Jess. "Will my daughter ever be the same, Dr. Sheldon?"

"It's too early to answer that. I'm so sorry. Her symptoms have stabilized, so her body is doing what it needs to do to heal from the injuries. It's going to be a long road back for her, but we know so many ways to help patients who have had the kind of trauma she's had."

Jess's eyes flew open, and she said, "Winter! Come winter!" She looked frantically toward her mother.

"Jess, I'm here. Oh, please don't be afraid. It's going to be okay."

The rhythmic sounds of the monitors increased in their tempo as Jess's heart rate and breathing rate rose.

"Dr. Sheldon, she's so scared!"

"It's okay—she's just disoriented, and the next few days will be a dance between waking and a dream state that will be kind of haunting for her. It will be up to all of us to help lend meaning to what's happening to her."

"Bird coming! White bird is coming?" Jess looked wide-eyed toward the window.

"Sweetheart, there is no bird coming. I'm your mother. You are in the hospital. You have had a terrible accident."

"Bird! Mother! Winter bird coming mother!" Jess closed her eyes, and the rage of the increased beeps calmed to a slower rhythm.

JESS

Her wheelchair felt like a kind of harness holding her up to the hospital window so she could see out to the court-yard below her room. The book in her lap, recommended by her speech therapist, was like a children's book, with pictures and words that would help her bridge her thoughts and words to images. Now-familiar shooting pains ran up her left leg, and the vision in her right eye was still blurred and, according to her doctors, "of concern."

Jess wanted to get up and walk away. She had never been good at waiting, at healing, but now she had to give herself time to let her scar tissue develop gradually, so it wouldn't be hard, protective, and unmoving. Because of the attack, she had missed winter turning into spring and it seemed to her that the trees had suddenly blossomed, the birds had arrived overnight, and the sun had leaped up into the center of the sky from the low winter place on the horizon. Just below her was a small grove of alder and maple trees that had shed their early-spring catkins and were fully leafed out and shimmering in the spring morning sun. Kids were making their way to school, laughing and charging ahead to meet up with friends. She could hear the subtle edge of their voices, the high-end murmur blending with the spring birdsong. Jess closed her eyes and shifted her weight, letting the book fall closed. Time surrounded and waited, taunting her, reminding her that there was something missing—or was it that there was suddenly something there?

She shook her head and wheeled herself around so she could see the too-large face of the hospital clock. Another twenty minutes until her first round of physical therapy for the day. The nurses, doctors, and therapists all encouraged her, cheering her toward the finish line: full use of her leg. Right now it felt foreign to her, as if someone had popped it out like a Barbie doll's leg and popped back in a leg belonging to the wrong doll. She rubbed her thigh, and a swirling mist of memory gathered in her mind. She was young and could hear the TV in the other room. Her Breyer horses were placed on the floor around her in her bedroom. She had one of Monica's Barbies, which would be the rider. Her leg popped out as Jess forced her onto the wide back of the plastic horse. Jess tried to put it back. She just couldn't get it right.

In the last three and a half weeks, she had gotten really good at maneuvering her wheelchair, but she had to be careful—moving too quickly would cause her headaches to come back, feeling like nails driven into the side of her head, and she would stop, catch her breath, and wait for the pain and the flashing red light show in her mind to calm.

"Hey, Jess!"

Jess swung her chair around to see Leslie coming toward her with a wide smile. She was carrying flowers draped across her arms like loose bunny ears.

"Oh, Les, I forgot it was you coming today!" Jess exclaimed in a slow, careful voice.

Les put the flowers down on the nurses' counter and kneeled in front of Jess. Her black hair had been cut boy-close, and her deep-blue eyes shone with both concern and delight. She had lost weight, Jess noticed, which was a sure sign Les was in a new relationship. The image of a priestess came to Jess's mind: tall, regal, in a flowing gown . . .

"Oh, sweetie, you look like shit. I know so many people must come to see you and say, 'Oh my God, Jess, you look *so* much better.' But you were practically killed, torn open and left on the riverbank like a spent salmon. Damn, I am so sorry this happened to you. I wish I could have come sooner, of course. But word has it you've been pretty out of it these past months."

"I'm glad you are here," Jess said slowly, while wondering whether it was true or not. "It's good to see you, Les." Les held her hand, and Jess closed her eyes, letting the good feelings and positive images from their long friendship ride up on waves of recognition.

Her speech lulled, and she knew that, as hard as she tried, Les would be able to see that she had been damaged, that there was a chance she would not fully recover her speech abilities. The right upper fang of the mountain lion had pierced her skull and torn her brain. She was partially paralyzed on the right side of her face, and she couldn't tell whether her mind was okay. She tried to find a way to tell, a reference point from a time before. She looked up at Les, her eyes focusing, trying to order her words in a way that would make sense. It was as if she suddenly had to pay attention to something that was unconscious and taken for granted. A crevasse had opened up in her mind, and she was trying to rebuild the bridge from one side to the other.

Les looked at her sadly. "I'm going to be here for a few days, Jess. I handed off one of my projects to Jamie, my assistant, and I can work from here by email and cell phone. But you have to promise me that you'll let me know what you need from me, how I can help you."

"Thanks, Les. It's so good you are here. I have a few minutes before physical therapy." Jess looked up at the large face of the clock on the wall above her. She tried to focus on the letters—no, numbers—the idea of time forming in her mind like a small storm. "Where are you staying?"

"Oh, I have a room at the Riverside Hotel in town. It's not bad—at least I hear the sounds of the Nesika blending with the freeway traffic at night."

"My place. Haven't been there. You could stay?" Jess closed her eyes, picturing her front door and Miko, like a sentinel waiting for her, taking care of her little house. Thoughts of her boy wrapped around her like a cloak. She missed him so much.

"Mom has Miko."

"I hope he's okay. Wow, that would be great if I could stay at your place. Thanks, Jess. I don't have a lot of extra money lying around these days."

"I can't remember how I left it." Jess looked down and thought hard. There were clear places—she recalled seeing Martin; the cedar trees that had been cut, the pungent, open wood; and the rough, hard edges of the fresh stumps. From there her mind slid down a ramp into disorder. There was the dam, Miko barking, Jeff's embrace, the chords of the river, the salty, blood smell, the saliva on her skin, and the sound of a woman's voice shouting in a strange language . . .

"Hey, Jess, you okay?"

"Yeah. I . . . I need some fresh air. Let's go this way." She wheeled herself over to the elevators and pushed the down arrow. They waited in silence and she rolled her chair quickly through the open doors and faced the back of the elevator. Les stood beside her and put her hand gently on Jess's shoulder. Jess folded forward and began sobbing. She felt like something was breaking open now that Les was here. She reached up to her friend, and Les put the flowers in her lap and knelt down beside her. When they reached the floor, Les stood up and wheeled her chair through the too-bright hallway and out the automatic doors.

Jess leaned back in her wheelchair and felt the soft, cool rain of early spring on her already wet face. Les stayed close and quiet near her, and Jess could sense her protectiveness and steady concern. She felt the first strand of her healing begin to cross the divide in her mind. It created a path for a current of grief and terror to ride out, and for her connection to who she had been before the attack to return.

"When they ask me how I feel, I know they want answers. Something else going on for me, Les." She stopped and she tried to slow her mind, breathe into it, and find the tangible strands of thinking that she was beginning to put together.

"Something old has happened to me. From another time, but not now, not like this." A pair of robins swooped in front of her, and as she watched their curved flight up into the welcoming branches of the alder, she shuddered, as if she were beginning to wake from a dream.

JEFF

Jeff had been calling Jess's house for the past few weeks. He wasn't sure how to reach her, since the attack had happened so soon after they had awkwardly reconnected. He had decided that leaving messages at her house was better than seeing her at the hospital or talking to her while she was still there. Imagining her body, so torn and suddenly out of her control, was something Jeff couldn't or didn't want to do. He had heard that Jess's friend Leslie had come to town, and he hoped she might get a message to Jess. He had thought about Jess a lot, more than he had expected to, after their meeting and the next day at work, when they had told him where they had found Jess and how dangerously injured she was.

The ring of his cell phone startled him. Jeff flipped it open. "Hi, it's Jeff."

"Jeff, it's me, Jess." Her voice sounded slower, more deliberate, and Jeff steadied himself by leaning against the side of his truck.

"Les said you called, and I wanted to talk with you."

"Yeah, I've been calling your house. I don't know, I guess I just wanted to wait until you got home. How are you doing?"

"I'm doing better. My brain is messed up, and my leg is trying to mend itself as best it can. But, according to the experts, with the right kind of therapy and time, I should be all right enough." Her voice was different, but Jess was there; she would find her way back. *She's going to be fine*, he thought.

The silence held them for a moment. The twisted conflict of his feelings stuck in his throat at first, but then he told himself, *She has suffered enough*.

"Do you know I tried to track the cat with Dale?"

She didn't respond; he felt her pull back, ready to pounce.

"I didn't know what to do with myself when I heard what happened to you. I wanted to see you, do something, but . . . so I called Dale and asked if I could help. Work was slow, and I thought I could be useful. It felt good to be in the forest, to be hunting." He wanted to say, "To be helping you," but he stopped.

"Thanks, Jeff." He could hear her breathing slowly and felt her taking time to sort through what she wanted to say.

"Leslie brought my laptop and work over from the house. I know this sounds strange, but could we meet? She's trying to get me going again. I need to get back to work."

Jeff had a hard time understanding her. Her words were clear but out of sync—like a new rhythm, a drumming from another time.

Jeff felt his chest tighten. "Sure, Jess, of course I can. I just finished a meeting that will launch me into a huge project." He stopped himself— probably not a good time to tell her that he was in charge of upgrading the Green Springs dam. "Should I come by in the morning?"

"Yeah, that would be great. I think I have my usual physical therapy at nine thirty, so could you come by around ten thirty?"

"That would be fine. I have a meeting in town at twelve thirty, so I'll be coming that way anyway. It'll be good to see you, Jess."

Jeff stood for a while, looking out at the drying forest. There was so much life here this time of year, something regular, rhythmic, and predictable. Yet in the center of the predictability were changes that could have irreversible and permanent effects.

A pair of robins chased each other through the alders. He turned toward his truck and got into the front seat. He waited before leaving, watching the pair dart through the shadows like the many transitions happening in his life. Jess, on the one hand, ripped open and trying to heal, was moving back toward the strength and certainty of her life and risking everything, while the men in the meeting just now were constructing something based on laws and rules that served only a specific interest.

The currents tugged at him as he started his truck. There were some measurements he needed to make up on the Nesika; this year's run of winter steelhead was starting to visit some of the restored spawning areas. Mostly, he wanted to hide from what was happening—the pull of Jess, the surrender to Power-Corp—and rest in the wild cry of the full Nesika.

JESS

⟲⟳

Jess closed her cell phone and placed it on the dark blue plastic tray near her bed. Staring at it, she tried to organize her thoughts and untangle them from the swirl of her feelings about Jeff. His voice had the same warmth, but there was a space between them that felt strange and hurt her. Talking with him brought to the surface memories that she could use to orient her mind, her heart, and heal more than the physical wounds from the mountain lion. In the past few days, she had been able to move on her own into and out of bed, knowing this was what the doctors and therapists were looking for in order to begin to think about a time when she could be discharged. Knowing Leslie was nearby, knowing Jeff had called the wrong place but *had* called, and the daily visits from her mom and various other friends had all served to push her toward the time when she would be able to go home. Her injuries were healing, her leg practically fully usable, but her brain, her mind, her ability to connect her thoughts and her speech, remained damaged. The doctors and specialists assured her that she would progress steadily and could hope for a complete recovery. Jess knew differently; she knew that even though the goal around her was for her to make it back to where she'd been, there was no going back. What had happened to her had changed her; at times, she could follow the impulse of her body to heal itself down into the dark folds of the cat's bite in her flesh. She felt as if she needed a new name, a new identity, but the pieces of her that had existed before the attack didn't fit with those that hadn't.

At the window, she looked down into the grassy courtyard. Rhododendrons and dogwood were beginning to bloom and fill the burgeoning green branches with color and life. She knew she would get out soon and thought of the small square of ground behind her house, the green shoots pushing up between the brown, folded stems of last year's garden. More images stirred: Miko's soft ears, early-morning sun on her bedcovers, the scent of her bedroom, her photos, her work . . .

She turned toward the table where Leslie had left her laptop. *God, the email,* she thought. How could she even begin to sort through what must be there? Her head began to hurt, and she focused on the tangle of branches through the trees outside her window. Closing her eyes, she tried to imagine what could be trying to reach her and why. She tried to locate in herself the person the emails had been sent to, who she had been before the attack. For a moment, she sensed a woman striding through her life, assured that what she was doing was the right thing. She saw that woman making sacrifices—her job, her relationship—for those very right reasons. Then the woman turned and looked at her, and Jess saw that she was leaving, handing Jess a deep uncertainty about who she was, what she was doing, and why.

She opened her eyes, slowly lifted the screen on her laptop, and turned it on. The processor hummed, and the operating system powered on. A very cute picture of Miko illuminated the screen. Her heart ached as she imagined his brown, watery eyes and the spiral tail that could whip in circles so fast, she sometimes thought he might lift off.

Myriad files and programs launched on-screen. She felt as if she wanted to draw lines to connect them with each other; their meaning slipped inside her mind, and she tried to hold on to it. She connected to the hospital Wi-Fi system and checked her email: 214 messages. She watched them scroll past quickly, leaned back in her chair, and closed her eyes.

Too much, she thought, as her stomach tightened. She didn't know this person, needed to let her go. She selected all the messages in her inbox and hit the DELETE key.

"Are you sure?" the computer asked her.

She clicked yes.

The door opened behind her, and she jumped.

"Hey, sweetheart, sorry I didn't call first. Did I startle you?" Jess's mom walked over to her and ruffled the stiff ends of hair that were just growing back in. Jess liked the way it felt, like an animal's fur. She looked up at her mom's dark brown eyes, so much like Monica's, and now laden with sadness. First the loss of her younger daughter, then her husband, and now this. Jess felt a pang of what her therapist called survivor guilt jar her; over the past eighteen years, it had only grown stronger, more present, through causing her mother yet more suffering and activating the unimaginable grief that pulled constantly at Barbara's features. *What she must be feeling when she looks at my lopsided face, my torn skin; what nightmares this must have caused her . . .*

"I brought you some new lotion. I know you like this one, so I went all the way down to the co-op to get it for you. Lavender and rosemary? One year you gave me a bottle for Mother's Day and said it was your favorite. I spoke with Dr. Sheldon, and she says they may be able to let you go in the next week or so."

Jess rested in the familiar cadence of her mom's voice. For a moment, it carried her back to her childhood home. Her dad was in the next room, reading the paper, drinking his evening glass of wine. Her sister was upstairs, on the phone, and their dog, Lappy, lay comfortably on her bed, resting her old body and sighing along with the sounds of the house. One, two, three . . . Jess shook herself, realizing that she should pay attention to what her mother was saying.

"That's great, Mom." She measured her words carefully, trying to remember how to sound as normal as possible, show her mother the progress she was looking for. "I'd love to get out of here. Leslie brought my computer over today. I just deleted all my emails, hope there wasn't anything important."

"You deleted all your emails? Really? Not a bad idea, I guess. Just remember, Jess, sweetheart, you have to have patience. I know it's a good sign that you want to get going, but this is a long process. You've done so well, surprised all your doctors and therapists, but your healing is taking its own time—a time we all need to respect. Once you're out of the hospital, I'm sure you'll feel the pull of your life again."

Jess stopped while her thoughts swirled. She was learning how to control them, how to contain them. It was like riding on the rope swing when she was little. At first she swung around the old maple tree, twisting randomly and out of control, out over the green pool in the river and back, sometimes hitting the rough bark, sometimes letting go into the cool water, sometimes just swinging. Then, finally, she learned to use her body in a way to control her swing. She grabbed the rope, swinging her thoughts from one side to the other . . .

"Leslie called the house this morning after she brought your computer and said it would be a good idea if I brought Miko by to see you. He's been a really good boy, but I know he's missed you. He's waiting for you out in the car, I've cleared it with the nurses and asked them to bring a wheelchair."

An unexpected feeling lurched through Jess's body. It was as if she couldn't control it, or the feeling came on so strong that her damaged mind couldn't even name it. Miko. She could smell him more than she could imagine him; he was just outside. Soon she would be petting his ears, burying her face in his thick fur. The strange feeling coursed through her body: expectation, her old life, memories of his last, shrill, desperate barking from inside her truck.

The nurse came in with the wheelchair, and Jess stepped in carefully. Her body felt suddenly stronger. It had a place to go, a reason to move through the world and toward what she loved. This was the best she had felt since the accident, her mind sliding to one side and allowing a sense of who she was to come into focus. She was quiet while her mother pushed her out into the hall and down to the elevators. She tried to get up when the elevator doors opened and stumbled into the elevator car.

"I can walk, Mom. I don't need that chair."

"Sweetheart, are you sure? I'll bring it with us just in case."

Her mom looked worried and a little surprised. Jess held on to the cold silver railing, which suddenly felt new to her, as if it were her link to somewhere important, the next step. The drop made her dizzy, but she held on and walked slowly out into the lobby, clinging to her mother, who was still pushing the wheelchair. She didn't want to stop and felt the momentum of the swing carry her out over the river, laughing into the sunshine, free of the tubes and the constant exams. Her legs felt strong and determined, like she was making her way up the final switch-back on a difficult trail. Her mom's old red Volvo was out in the parking lot. She could see Miko's black-masked face framed in the backseat window. Tears ran down her face; Miko was waiting for her, as he had been that night; at the end of this tunnel, he would be there for her.

The open space around her startled her, and she felt dizzy. Her mom grabbed her arm, letting the wheelchair roll aimlessly into the parking lot. *There it goes, just like my email,* Jess thought.

"Are you okay? Let's walk more slowly. I know you're excited, but we have a lot of time. Miko has been waiting a long time to see you—he can wait a few moments more."

Jess drew in a breath, and her tears grew stronger. She was coming back, back into her life, yet there was something, a shadow in her mind, that hadn't been there before. She swung farther out over the river and smiled.

When the car door opened, Miko locked her gaze with his and looked for a moment right into her. Then he bolted out and wagged his entire large body, and Jess sat down on the parking lot pavement and let him move all over her, licking her ears and snuffling her neck. She felt a wave of sadness come from him and wash over her. He suddenly lay down on the pavement next to her—his place, she thought. He could protect her now. His big heart, her boy. She bent her head down and buried her face in his neck. They needed each other in ways that no one could understand. And now they were bound into a small pack living in a world that was open to attacks. Right now, on the hard pavement of the hospital parking lot, she believed she could begin again.

Miko swung over onto his side, and she rubbed his belly.

"I know I should have brought him over sooner. But I wanted you to be strong enough, strong enough . . . well, for this." Her mom watched over them protectively. Cars passed slowly by them, looking for parking, noticing the crying woman and her beautiful dog. Jess felt as if she were in a movie and suddenly wanted to run for cover, hide with Miko, and watch from the protection of the forest.

Her mom came over and helped Jess to her feet. Miko jumped up expectantly. "Let's go over there, on the grass in the shade. I can leave you two for a while. I'll get the wheelchair and take it back inside. You have plenty of time."

Jess knew what that meant, having felt time stretch through her days like long yards of thick taffy, though she was never sure if it was from the medication or the damage to her brain, or simply the nature of hospital time. She longed for the quickness of busy days, focused on her work, on the river, loping along with Miko through the underbrush, looking for signs of spawning salmon.

She lay back in the grass, feeling the firm, cool ground under her. She let the weight of her body hold her down, and she could feel how different it had become. Lighter, she thought, and vulnerable and weak on one side. Miko lay down next to her and sighed. She closed her eyes and took in his scent, his softness, his certainty. Rolling toward him, she put her arm around him and let her body relax into the ground. She was home, and she knew that in a few days, this would be the way it was.

She looked up through the branches of the maple above her—a native tree, casting flashing shadows. She thought for a moment of the person who had planted this tree, probably seventy years earlier. That person had decided that a native tree, a tree so many would look out on from the windows of their constricting rooms, would be best. Each year, this tree shed its leaves and pulsed with new life in the spring. Jess could almost feel the coming out-breath of spring in it. She shifted her foot so that it was just touching the tree—another connection, another relationship. Her mom wandered the parking lot, looking for the errant wheelchair, and Jess laughed to herself and brushed Miko's coat.

This moment, she thought. *This moment.*

PIAH

❦

Piah reached out in her sleep to one-year-old Libah lying next to her. The early light was just coming in through the smoke hole above her. The morning sounds of the forest and the waking camp stirred with the others in the small home. Libah rolled in response to her mother's touch and began to nurse. Piah startled as she felt the hot skin of her baby against her own. Her own body pulled away in protective response, and Libah began to cry. *Not my baby*, Piah thought. She touched Maika's shoulder and woke him, placing his large hand on their daughter's back. He looked into her eyes with a kind of shock and desperation. Piah felt a tightness in her throat, and she clutched the edge of Libah's fur blanket in her hands. *Not my baby*. As she continued to nurse Libah, she cried openly. No one in their camp who had come down with the fever and the many ugly sores that covered their bodies had lived. Piah knew that Libah, being so young, would have no chance.

One of the symptoms that had entered her people had been a hot fever and a strange, dark red rash. Ever since the shaman had brought back the visions, the fevers seemed to be getting worse. There was word from the downstream Nesika people that the rash was spreading from tribe to tribe like a wildfire. She focused on sending a cool current of love for her child through her family, trying to soothe her daughter's body, her husband's, and her own.

She wrapped Libah tenderly in a small cedar blanket and carried her out into the rising light. Maika stayed in their home, and she could hear him weeping. She walked the path down to the river. Everything seemed suddenly vivid and loud. The singing birds blended with the rush of the water, and she felt Libah stir and begin to cry. She remembered her vision, almost a year before, when her sister, Tenas, had come to her with a promise that Libah would be the one who would help her people, show them the way through the difficulties that lay ahead. Piah pulled the necklace from Libah's medicine pouch. What did this mean? How could her spirit sister have been wrong?

When Piah reached the water's edge, she sat on a large boulder. She tried to find her power song, tried to listen to the river, to the songs that would come to her to tell her what to do. For the first time, Piah felt lost, betrayed somehow by the wisdom she had come to depend on throughout her life. Libah's hot skin against hers invoked a desperate anger, and the image of the white man's face rose up from the white water at her feet.

Piah called out in her spirit song to her sister, Tenas. She had seen Libah—in the spirit world—as a grown child. Now her child lay dying in her arms, the space between her breaths growing longer. Piah's hand reached down to her vacant belly, where she had carried Libah for nine months.

Where are you going? the spirit of Tenas whispered above the soaring sound of the river. Piah could feel her more than hear her.

Piah, you must let her go.
She is the one—she will open a path between the worlds.
This one who is and the one to come.
This is the only way.

Piah began screaming, holding her child tightly. Libah stirred awake and tangled her small hands into Piah's thick, dark braids. Piah clutched the beaded necklace and wept into the body of her dying daughter. She decided to take her child deep into the forest, where she would care for her, beg the spirits to heal her, fight with them, with the inevitability of the unimaginable.

Piah spent several days in the forest, caring for her child, beckoning to the helping spirits of the plants and animals around her. They wove her into a blanket of healing, lending their bodies to the tender body of her daughter. But then one morning Piah went off to gather a dying salmon from the river, and when she came back, Libah was still, too still. Piah began wailing, howling into the damp gray morning light. Her baby had been taken.

Piah carried Libah's body on her back down to her camp. Maika walked up to her and embraced her as she stood, sobbing, in the open center where the main fire was held. Her father came over to her and took off the back sling that held her baby.

Piah's father looked up at her, holding the small body. Piah felt fury and grief pour through her like a storm. Her father turned and took Libah's body into his tent. Piah heard him drumming and collapsed into the muddy gravity of the earth. She let the visions swirl around her, colorful and comforting. The rhythm of the drum gathered her family around her, and she felt their bond carrying her back from the solitude of her grief. They had lost Libah, but also many others.

Piah stood. Pushing back the heavy, wet skins of her father's door, she walked into the dim light of his home. Smoke swirled in spirals from the small morning fire, and her father did his drumming with tenderness, bidding his granddaughter a safe journey. Piah held the small necklace in her hand.

"I want to give her to the river."

Piah's father looked into her. Strands of black hair clung to his wet skin; gray streaks of ash brushed across his strong, deeply hewn face. He picked up the small, still bundle and handed her to Piah without speaking. So much had been taken from him; the world that had held them both was falling away.

Piah carried the body of Libah to the bank of the Nesika. Though Piah wasn't sure she had been given his blessing, she knew her father would comfort Maika and let the others in the family know what her wishes were. Piah felt the force of the rapids pushing through the granite canyon tearing and cold in her belly. She closed her eyes and began a low chant—beckoning the spirits of the river, the land, her ancestors, and her sister. This was to be an offering, a sacrifice, the opening of a door into another time. Libah, her daughter; Tenas, her sister.

She released her baby's body into the water just below Tenas's grave. Piah closed her eyes and felt the tendrils of the river pull Libah's body from her arms. Piah let go and continued her deep, crying chant, holding the beaded necklace high in the air. Rain poured around and through her, washing her, the small streams feeding the river like the warm blood flowing riverlike through her own body. She prayed and sang until she could barely stand, but some strength in her urged her onto her feet, her belly damp with river mud, and she made her way blindly back to her camp.

She stumbled toward her family and collapsed at her mother's feet.

"Go into the woods for five days." Her mother handed her a small bag of food and fur to keep her warm. Piah couldn't respond; she merely curled her body around the bag and wept into it. She could hear chanting: the women of her home were encouraging her, blessing her, trying to comfort her. Their chants were of healing, how her blood would come back and she could someday bear another child.

Piah felt small and vulnerable as she walked into the forest. The morning light on the river seemed dull and fading. Her body was heavy to her, in a new way, and she wondered if she was coming down with the sickness as well. The possibility tore at her, hands from both worlds: being again with her sister and daughter, being again with Lamoro, gathering willows to heal the sick. She climbed up to the ridge, up to where she'd had her earliest vision, and sat facing the sun. She opened her aching breasts to its warmth, felt it moving across her skin, and had a desire to tear at it with her fingernails. She wanted whatever was happening to stop.

The force carrying this disease into her people was stronger than the spirits, stronger than the river, and had the power to destroy all of her family. She stood up and took off her clothes, lying down on the rock edge of the cliff. A cool breeze blew over her from the river canyon below. Her stomach was taut from not eating, yet she felt an ancient power course through her, moving her to dance. She pulled her hair back from her face and stood up naked above the canyon, then began a slow, unwinding ceremonial dance. A low hum rose in her chest, and she began to chant a new power song while she danced. The chant rang with the grief and sadness she carried from the death of so many, from the death of her own daughter, from the death of her own flesh. As she danced, the wind that blew up from the canyon grew stronger and seemed to hold her in its arms. She rested in its currents and let them lift the pain from her thin, writhing body. She vowed through her song to give everything she had to hold this intruder back by the throat until her people found safety.

Her bare feet slid over the rocks down to the riverbank, and Piah fell forward into the mud and felt the pulse of the current in hers. The long, cool body of the Nesika rushed past her, carrying her baby and her people into an uncertain future.

JESS

~

Everything was so bright. The damp red clay of the road urged her toward something waiting in the dry creek bed. Pungent desert sage blended with a blood scent, and her eyes fixed on a slight movement through the brush. She looked down at her wide gold paws, her long body stretching as she moved. She padded along a dirt path that seemed to lead up into the sky. Just when she was about to go over the edge, she saw a cave-like room off to the side of the path. She entered it, and her senses ignited with the shift from the open air into the confinement of the damp walls.

A sound called her forward. She was perched high on a large rock outcropping, and below her was a vast room like a cathedral, echoing the long, low chants of the people gathered there. They were dancing, and there were hundreds of them.

She leaped from the rock and turned into her human form. She joined the rows of dancers, moving in time with the slow step, the room snaking with bodies forming the shape of a spiral. The room felt like the center of something very important. Jess recognized some people—her dad was there; Miko was there—and a Native American woman took her by the hand and showed her the steps of the dance.

As they danced, the rhythms drew Jess into the center of the spiral, where a stone bowl filled with water sat. The water reflected the night sky, visible through a large opening in the roof of the cave. Three women stood around the bowl, waiting. Jess met the eyes of the Native American woman holding her hand; for a moment they felt like the same person.

"Miko?" she called out. "Hey, boy, c'mere."

She was lying in her room, sweat streaming down her chest. She rolled over and pushed the sheets away, using them to dry her arms and legs.

What was that?

Miko shuffled into her room and laid his big head on the edge of the bed next to her. He was so good. "Miko, my boy."

Her hand was shaking, and she used him to steady her. Her face trembled, and her leg throbbed. She sighed and rolled over to hold on to her dog.

Where had she just been? It seemed like the desert. New Mexico. She could still smell the sage, feel the damp clay road, her long body gaunt with hunger. Where was the cave? The echoes of the ancient dance resonated within her; the Native American woman, her father, her sister, and even Miko had been there. Her brain swung her thoughts around with confusing and contradicting meanings. Images in her mind crashed like two waves coming together, crosscurrents splashing.

She stood up naked and walked into her dark bathroom. The floor was cold, and her damp body shivered. Miko slunk in behind her and plopped down at the bathroom door. It was four o'clock in the morning. Feeling sick, Jess grabbed a dry towel to keep her warm and took it back to bed. Miko lay down next to her, and Jess rested her hand on his back.

Her body felt stiff and foreign to her, and she shifted to try to get comfortable. She thought about taking some sleeping medication the doctor had given her but decided not to.

It had happened a year ago today. Her mind swung in a wide circle around the memory. The stones, the river, Miko barking, the mountain lion. Jess felt her scars tighten, and she curled against the strain of them. She wanted it to stop, all of it.

She needed to go back. The idea tugged at her. There was something waiting in the streambed. She needed to go back today, to the river, to the dam, to the stones. She stretched her legs out under her sheets and fell back into a deep, restful sleep.

BARBARA

⟨◈⟩

Barbara looked down at her hands. How had they aged so much? They looked old, like her mother's hands late in life, folded by arthritis permanently into a clawlike shape. She had often wondered what her mother had tried to hold on to. She remembered that as her mother had slipped through the layers of Alzheimer's disease, she had imagined that she was clinging to her own mother's calico-print skirt or her father's freshly starched and pressed collar. Barbara looked over at her mantel and the scattered photos there, remnants of family members living and dead. For a moment, she was lost among them, different ages at different times, feeling the fleeting independence of her teenage years and the woven dependence of her marriage.

She got up and picked up a picture of her young girls. One was just six, and the other a sassy ten. Their blondish hair whipped around their faces as they held up two prized shells they had found while scouring a beach in Hawaii. That vacation had been so much fun. Barbara had been in the fullness of her life—two amazing daughters and a husband who had helped her become the mother she longed to be. As she looked into the picture, the ginger-flower smells and shapes of Hawaii wafted around her. For a moment, she was there again, away from what her life had become. Her hands grew sore as she realized she was gripping the picture, embedding the feeling of the sand under her feet, the salt wind of that place and that day, and the beauty of her young daughters.

Pain poured through her like molten lava as she put the picture back into its place on the mantel. She stepped back and imagined that beautiful blond hair tangled in a snag at the bottom of the river, an image that would never leave her. In her dreams, she braided Monica's hair, tangled with leaves and sticks from the river bottom. Over and over, Barbara told her how beautiful she was and how strong she needed to be.

All at once, she felt the floor fall out from under her. She stumbled back to her chair and sat. Tears ran down her face, the sobbing racked her, and she felt as if there was no stopping what was happening to her. A cold sweat covered her, and her panic became a sudden drive that her body could hardly contain. She thought she might need to call 911, but then, remembering what the counselor had taught her, she closed her eyes and focused to steady her breathing. Waves, the sound of waves on the beach, always helped to bring her back. And she knew she had to come back, for Jess.

When the doorbell rang, she started. Then she brushed her hair back and wiped her hands on the rough-knit afghan she was holding. The person started knocking, and Barbara shouted out to wait a minute. Who would be visiting this time of day? Usually her days lay down in front of her, lazily uneventful but not very inviting.

She opened the door and was startled to see Suzie. Barbara had heard from Jess about her involvement with the attempt at bombing the dam and her disappearance right after Jess lost her job. Her once-dark hair was dyed white-blond and cut very short. She wore all black and had several piercings along her left ear and a small gold ring in her nose. Barbara stepped back, hardly recognizing her and a little afraid of her.

"Suzie, oh my gosh . . . I'm surprised to see you. It's been a while . . ." Barbara stepped back into her house and tried to take in what this young woman might want.

"Hi, Barbara. Yeah, I've been away, but I heard from my dad about what happened to Jess. I'm so sorry." Suzie paused and looked past Barbara into the house.

"Jess isn't here—but she *is* home from the hospital. Does she know you're back?"

"No. I've . . . well, kept my distance, so to speak. But it's weird, because I was working on a book, and in the book my character is attacked by a mountain lion. It actually came to me in a dream, only I was the one who was attacked. I came back to see Jess and to try to find out more about what happened to her, and maybe why."

"Her injuries were very, very serious. She's getting better, but her therapy takes a lot of her energy. Where have you been? Jess said you just left one day, and then she didn't say much more after that."

"Yeah, Dad mentioned that and sent me the link to the story in the paper. I've been lying low after what happened with Mink and the others. I was glad they weren't able to find out anything about Jess that could have gotten her in even more trouble. Losing her job and Jeff must have been hard . . ."

There was a strong, awkward silence, and then Barbara, realizing she liked that for a moment she wasn't alone, stepped back from the doorway and asked, "Would you like to come in?"

Suzie made a popping sound with her tongue in her cheek and sat down on the worn arm of the floral couch in the living room. Barbara remembered the sleepovers Suzie and Jess had had in middle school; each girl would have her end of the couch and they would scare themselves silly watching old *Twilight Zone* episodes. Barbara had always felt a little uneasy about Suzie; she knew that Suzie had not been close with her family, and then her suicide attempt in high school had left everyone on edge about her.

"Yeah, there was a lot going on, and I had to . . . I had to go for a while. I heard what happened to Jess but didn't think I would be any good to her here or wherever I was. What happened to the cat?"

Barbara sensed Suzie being evasive and kept any more

questions to herself. She was still shaky from her panic attack and didn't have the energy to navigate an entire conversation with anyone, especially this woman. "They hunted her down and killed her. She was a big cat, almost eighty pounds. You know Jess—she must have fought as hard as she could have." Barbara reached back to her neck where Jess's wounds were. She was haunted by her own ache, imagining the roughness of scars, of the misshapen parts of her daughter's still-healing skull fractures.

"Does anyone know why the cat ran away and left her?"

"No, could have been Miko barking, but no one has really talked about that. It must have been a horrible night for her, so cold. Miko was a total wreck when they found him. Thank God the power-company workers start so early. It's lucky Jeff wasn't the one to find her."

"They broke up, right?"

Barbara was finished with the inquiry but didn't have the energy to try to stop it. She stood, thinking of asking Suzie to go, but it was as if one of her old photographs had come to life—there was a person, a friend of Jess's who had at one time meant a lot to her, right in front of her.

"Yes, they did. Would you like some tea or something?"

"Sure, that would be great." Suzie reached out and petted Barbara's black cocker spaniel, Nifty.

"How's the garden going this year?" Suzie half shouted to Barbara, who had left to go into the kitchen and get some tea.

"It's okay. With everything that's happened to Jess, I haven't had the time or energy to do too much, but I do have a small vegetable garden and my usual blueberries, which don't need much attention."

Opening her kitchen cupboard, Barbara felt her heart dip as her hand brushed Jess's favorite lemon-ginger tea. She reached instead for English breakfast and put two cups of water in the microwave.

"I remember this picture of Jess," Suzie called from the living room. "Wasn't this the picture they used in the papers when they printed the story about her being attacked?"

Barbara's heart clenched in her chest again as she recalled that day, the news reporters invading her heart, her home, the calls from the neighbors, the concern . . .

Barbara walked back into the living room with the tea. "Yes, that's the one. It was taken when she was working with her friend Leslie in the Wind River Range, doing some kind of activist work. It's a good picture of her—even though it was years ago. I guess the paper didn't care about that." She paused for a moment, then said, "So, why did you come back, Suzie, and why to see me? Why didn't you just go to Jess?"

"I wanted to find out how she was doing first. And to . . . well, see if you were okay. I heard from my dad how rough it's been for you."

Suzie's eyes seemed too bright, too interested, in a way that was uncomfortable for Barbara. The loud ticking of the old grandfather clock in the hallway filled the silence between them.

Finally, avoiding Suzie's comment, she said, "Jess is doing better. Her leg is mostly healed, but there were some other injuries that are taking longer."

"Does she have brain damage?" Suzie's question seemed too invasive and flat.

"You know, Suzie, I would be much more comfortable with your asking these questions of Jess herself. I'm trying to be careful about what's happening with her condition and the details of her injuries. She's around these days, working from home, mostly."

Suzie looked into her teacup. "I'll go see her. This must be so hard for her. Jess was always, you know, the strong, brave one. Hiking with her was always more of a charge up the side of the mountain, or she would dive into the fastest part of the river . . ." Suzie stopped, and Barbara seized the opportunity to redirect the conversation in a way that would encourage her to leave.

"Do you still have Jess's cell phone number?"

"Yeah, I do, if it hasn't changed." Suzie walked over to the mantel and put back the picture of Leslie and Jess. "Well, maybe I should go. Thanks again for the tea. I'll give Jess a call. See ya!"

Suzie swaggered out the front door—like a pirate, Barbara

thought. She closed the door and locked it. Sitting back down in her chair, she pulled her afghan around her and called Jess's cell phone. She wanted to warn her, for some reason. It was as if Suzie were the cat, looking for Jess, the way her body moved. Yikes, had she been stalking Jess even back then?

She got Jess's voice mail: "Hey, it's me! Leave me a message!" She sounded so . . . well, so *Jess*, and Barbara took comfort in her confident voice.

"Hey, Jess, it's Mom. Look, sweetheart, I just had a very strange visit from your old friend Suzie. She said she was going to call you, so I just wanted to let you know. By the way, what are you doing for dinner on Thursday? Robert's in town, and I thought you'd like to see him while he's here. I think he said you were having lunch with him on tomorrow. Anyway, sweetheart, let me know. I love you." She hung up and stared at the phone for a minute. She felt tired and decided to lie down, rechecking the locked door on the way to her bedroom.

She fell asleep quickly, her body tired from being so scared all the time.

She woke up an hour later, shaking from a disturbing dream. Jess had been playing with a baby mountain lion. The mother was nearby and didn't seem worried. The scene had been Disney-like, cartoonish. Suddenly, Suzie jumped out from behind a large boulder, laughing. She grabbed the baby cat and slit its throat. Jess cried out, but her cry wasn't human; it was the cry of a mountain lion.

Barbara got up and washed her face with cold water in the bathroom. She looked at herself in the mirror and saw the fear in her eyes. They were lined deeply at the edges, and her mouth turned down at both ends. What had been taken from her had been too much. She could see in her face a diving downward, as if gravity were holding her so she couldn't fly off and leave, so she couldn't ascend into the arms that were taking her out of this life, her young daughter's, her husband's, and now that of her eldest daughter, who seemed suspended between the worlds. It was time, she thought—time to find a means of holding on in a way that wasn't so painful, so wrecked all the time. Those first days after the attack, the same sheriff's car pulling into her driveway, the same news reports, had felt like a mantra repeating itself, over and over, in her life.

She opened the mirrored door to the medicine cabinet and pulled out the bottle of Valium her doctor had prescribed after Jess had been attacked. *Just one*, she thought. *Just one.* Barbara closed her eyes and saw her mother's clawlike hands holding hers as she passed away; the clenched hands of her husband, lying in the backyard; the continuous, movie-like image of Monica grabbing for the grasses along the riverbank; and Jess's hand, so weak, so small, holding on to her. They were pulling her down with them into the dark pool. She needed them, just for a moment, to let go.

PART III

JEFF

⁂

The house was quiet in the dark early morning. Stirring his coffee, Jeff looked through the morning paper, letting the ominous weight of the day settle around him like a cloak. He sat there, staring at the paper, until he looked up at the red glow of the digital clock on his microwave. *Shit—I'm going to be late again.* He knew what would be waiting for him: the latest report on the decline of the salmon.

He felt unable to breathe normally, and he stayed too long in the hot steam of the shower. As he waited for the water to work on the stiffness in his back, he knew he had been wrong to believe them and he felt grief binding him like a metal band. The water wouldn't help. Not this morning.

He dried himself and dressed slowly. He was alone, vividly alone. The dark in his room seemed to stretch out for miles, to where Jess was, he imagined, curled with Miko, arranging her thoughts in careful rows, and he wondered if he was woven into them.

Jess had been attacked a year ago today. Just after they had met for coffee at the Nesika Lodge. She had been so ardent, so clear, in asking him for help, but he had sensed that maybe there was more to their encounter. He felt bad that he hadn't been able to figure out how to be with her in the hospital, how to be a friend. Now he knew what to do, how to give Jess what she had asked him for that day.

Pulling into the gravel parking lot, Jeff felt apprehension rise in his chest, and he waited in his quiet truck before going in. He poured himself a cup of coffee in the kitchen, then made his way to his small cubicle, where he had built a name for himself with a now-international company. His walls were covered with posters, pictures of the river, and an old bumper sticker from the Nesika Fly Fishers, saying KEEP THE NESIKA WILD. *Ironic*, he thought. A picture of the Green Springs dam hung right under it, the river reduced to a funnel of spray below the concrete wall. *Keep her wild*, he thought, shaking his head as the constant contradiction rose in his chest.

"Hey, Jeff, how's it going?" Mack Dempsey sidestepped into Jeff's space and half sat on the edge of his desk, pushing the report aside and looking down into Jeff's eyes. Jeff felt as if he had suddenly been called in to the principal's office.

"Fine, Mack, I'm okay, but these new reports are kinda startling. I'm really not sure what to think—other than that what we've come up with isn't working."

"Yeah, it's not as good as we hoped, is it? But what I want to talk to you about is how the company is going to respond to these new reports and the media flare around it. One thing we don't need right now is to give any fuel to those environmental groups. Word has it they've been in contact with this environmental law group, Planet Justice. We can deal with this with . . . well, facts of our own, if you know what I mean."

Jeff felt his stomach drop. Just the week before, he had talked with Jess over lunch about the case with Planet Justice and had wondered how his company would respond. He looked up at the small framed picture on his desk of Jess with Miko, the Nesika, like a poised relative, flashing in the background.

Jeff pushed the report on his desk closer to Mack. "Look, Mack, the population counts are what they are."

Mack leaned back against the wall of Jeff's office. "Well, Jeff, sometimes you gotta do what you gotta do. It's real sad that it isn't different, but you and I both know that this can all turn around in a season."

"That's not true—the facts are the facts here, and to misrepresent them would undermine our credibility and destroy my reputation as a scientist. No, Mack—that's not something we can do here." Jeff felt his face grow hot, and he shifted back in his chair.

"What I'm saying, Jeff, is . . . you know, there are lots of reasons the fish populations are declining. We just need to emphasize some over the others. I need you to work with Beth in PR on a press release. She's expecting your call. The sooner the better on this, Jeff."

Pushing off Jeff's desk, Mack raised himself up to his full height and looked down at him with a kind of dominant male posture that Jeff resented. When Mack had left him alone again, Jeff closed his eyes, leaned forward, and put his head down on his folded hands. He felt a crushing weight bear down on his abdomen, and the fluorescent lights in his office suddenly seemed oppressive and too bright. He needed air.

He got up and walked out to his company truck, POWER-CORP INTERNATIONAL painted on its door in large, excited blue letters, a piece of a power company ultimately controlled by a corporation in Scotland that had bought PowerCorp in the past year. What a contrast—the people who had the most power over the river, and the decisions made about the continued use of the river, were in a foreign country, away from the community of people who worked, lived, and played near the Nesika.

He thought of Jess's small nonprofit, Water Walkers; he imagined her working late into the night, gathering information for the lawsuit. Getting that suit going was what had really brought her back, he thought, given her mind a renewed focus. He sighed, thinking about her long road back, her constant fighting with her body, and the continued unpredictability of her mind. It seemed to him as if some part of her had stepped to the side and was now always watching, like a hunter waiting for something to jump out at her from the brush; she had a new look in her eyes, sharp and fearful. If she knew about his conversation just now with Mack, if she knew what was being asked of him . . . He imagined her claws growing sharp and the twitch of her tail; she would show him no mercy. Her instincts to protect the river, the salmon, and something much deeper had become too strong.

The steering wheel felt cold in his hands, and he realized he was gripping it and just staring out the windshield. He shook himself and started his engine. It was early in the day, and he needed to check the monitoring system up on Lynx Creek Station 9. There had been some unusual fluctuations there, and he wanted to make sure that nothing was out of line. The new system they had installed in the Green Spring power station was working well, but the population counts of the returning salmon and steelhead were still declining at an alarming rate. The automated system determined the flow of the Nesika, the computer, a synthetic brain, overrunning the river's natural fluctuations.

Jeff drove fast up the Nesika highway and turned up a dirt logging road that led to an overlook once used by the Molalla people who had lived in the high river valley for thousands of years. He sat near the ancient rock piles and looked down the fir forest, laced with red vine maples, into the basalt-walled river canyon. His work over the last year had been hard, but he believed that because of it, the relicensing agreement between the Forest Service and PowerCorp had been well crafted. There were mitigating measures in place that he would be in charge of carrying out to help protect the salmon. What he had come to realize was that even though there was sound science backing the design of the fish ladder and the resulting restoration of habitat upstream from the dam, the actual implementation had more to do with PR for PowerCorp than it did with the actual improvement of habitat. His hope had been that it could be both: PowerCorp could keep the dam, and the salmon habitat could be restored in ways that would help increase their numbers and improve the overall health of the river. But the more he realized that the intention had more to do with PowerCorp's bottom line than with saving salmon, the closer he got to seeing things the way Jess did.

Jeff leaned back against the river stones and looked down into the valley below. He imagined the hands that had stacked these stones, what message they were meant to send, and why someone would have carried such heavy stones up this steep hillside. The brown fall grass around him was damp, and a blue jay called out from a low branch in the oak tree above him. He breathed in the cool air and stood up, walking to the edge of the overlook. The blue jay squawked and followed him. Looking out, he shuddered. He knew now that too much was being asked of him. This time, he couldn't justify the decision to leave in the Green Springs dam. His job, his work, had always been important to him. As he looked at the stillness of the water above the dam and the potential for that to become a native habitat again, he knew that he couldn't lie about what was happening to the salmon. Choosing his job over Jess and letting her go had been devastating for him, but he knew why: he had always been the one to hold together his family, be the responsible one who could steady and support his mom. After his dad had died, watching his mother being swept into darkness by her grief had been horrible for Jeff. He wondered if this was why he had chosen his job, instead of supporting Jess, instead of trying to help her as she had been swept away.

He walked back through the tall grass to his truck. He would call Jess and find out if her uncle Robert was around these days. He had moved up to Portland and was living in a beautiful house overlooking the vast Columbia River. His last book had been a cry against the continued use of factory like solutions for a hugely complex problem. Jeff knew Robert was working on the lawsuit with the environmental groups, but he was also a well-respected scientist in his field. Jeff's heart lifted as he thought about having a reason to call her.

He changed his mind about doing the measurements and made his way down to the Nesika Lodge to have lunch.

Anticipating home-baked blackberry pie and coffee felt good to him. He walked in and sat at a table looking out at the old apple tree in the small yard behind the restaurant. The twisted branches had just lost their leaves and still held on to a few small apples. Dark-eyed juncos chased each other through the web of branches and sunlight. Jeff remembered sitting here with Jess a year earlier—her animated smile, her nervousness, the curve of her back as she leaned down next to the river she loved, holding her hand for a moment in the current. Jeff had known in that moment that he still loved her, yet he dreaded the complications of their lives. That night, Jess had been attacked, alone on the bank of the same river she loved.

The morning after the attack, Jeff got the call on his cell phone when he was just waking up, Deb still sleeping by his side. He instinctively jumped out of bed, grabbing his clothes while still talking to Mack. Deb startled awake, and Jeff could see her concern. He stopped suddenly, sitting down and orienting himself to the world he was living in now. The audible click as he closed his phone was like a crack of lightning through the room. Deb put on her robe and sat next to him, trying to comfort him, but he let her words fall between them as the intensity of his shock and his concern for Jess filled him in a way that was surprising. His instinct to go to Jess was too strong; with it came memories and images of their time together, the passion that had flowed constant and sure between them.

Though he stayed away from the hospital and got news of Jess only through some of his coworkers at PowerCorp, Deb had been talking about going back to Alaska, and it had become the beginning of a widening separation in their relationship and future. Jeff wasn't going to leave his job or Penden Valley—or Jess. Less than a month after the phone call, Deb had left for Alaska and Jeff had focused even more on his work and the plans for the mitigation necessary to keep the Green Springs dam in place.

Now, at the lodge, he walked over to the bookcase, picked up a well-read copy of the *Penden Times*, and looked at the front page. Below a picture of a dog leaping in the air to catch a Frisbee was the headline "Salmon Population Continues to Decline; Several Species of Pacific Salmon Designated for ESA Listing." He took the paper to his table and read quickly through the article. There were quotes from the report he had seen that morning. The reporter was careful to stay with the popular line "the reasons for this sudden sharp decline are unclear," and alluded to solutions that were storybook and unrealistic. *The world as we know it is ending, but don't worry—we've got it handled!* Jeff thought.

He put the paper down and sipped his coffee. The juncos raced through the branches of the apple tree. This article was what Mack wanted him to counter with science that didn't exist. He imagined Beth in PR waiting for his call, her makeup replenished and her nails filed and colored to match her jacket. Pictures of her kids and husband decorated her desk; he imagined her smiling in recognition each time she looked at them.

The waitress brought his lunch and he looked down at the plate: open-faced hamburger with lettuce, red onion, and tomato. He waited for a moment, taking it in, asking himself, *How did we get here?* What turns in his life had brought him to this moment, the salmon to this brink? He considered the shifts in the natural forces of life that shaped the contours of this lettuce, gave birth to the farm worker who harvested it, thought about the force that pushed the lion's tooth into Jess's brain.

After his lunch, Jeff drove into town. He wanted to avoid the office and the impending call to Beth in PR. The valley opened up before him as he left the high basalt walls of the upper river canyons. He felt soothed by the widening valley and let the afternoon sun warm his face as he drove. He started heading aimlessly into town and found himself wandering toward Jess's small house—of course. He instinctively wanted to be near her, to calm his fears and reorient his mind. He was afraid of her—of her response to him, of her searing rejection again. Right now it would be difficult for him to lose his job, and he knew that she would ask that of him, instantly.

He sat in his truck just down the road from her driveway and waited. Should he go in? He was on company time and felt a slight nagging to return to his work. He changed his radio to the local rock station, turned his truck around, and headed back upriver.

JESS

Even while she was still in the hospital, Jess had known she needed help. Her recovery efforts in the hospital, coupled with the way her thoughts now swirled in her mind, coming and going like shadows across an open field, had convinced her that finding someone to support her in continuing her work was essential. She had reached out to a lawyer named Kathryn Michaels who worked for Planet Justice, had been involved in other issues surrounding the restoration of salmon, and had a reputation for being unafraid of taking on the savvy, overpaid attorneys from companies like PowerCorp. Even before the mountain lion attack, Jess and the others had known that they would need legal help, since negotiations had gone on without them and had resulted in a settlement agreement between PowerCorp and the state and federal agencies. There had been no consideration given to the opinions and conclusions of organizations like the Nesika Watershed Council and Jess's own Water Walkers. The only move they had left was litigation.

At their first meeting, Kathryn pointed out that they could take the lawsuit in many directions. One was that the Forest Service had made procedural mistakes in adopting the environmental impact assessment the Federal Energy Regulatory Committee had ordered, instead of conducting its own. The other, more dramatic option they could pursue was to attack the process head-on; there were actual signed agreements from the meetings that had created the original document that stated removing the Green Springs dam was the best option for salmon habitat restoration. Those meetings were what had led to the moment when PowerCorp executives had just gotten up and walked out of the room. And Jess still had the notes she had gotten from Rich the day before the mountain lion had attacked her. These notes contained directives by the PowerCorp officials on how and where to change the language of the watershed analysis. *Talk about the fox guarding the henhouse*, thought Jess.

In creating Water Walkers, Jess had had to learn a lot about how the legal process worked. Laws were tools that she and others could use to try to overturn illegal and power-driven documents based on lies and profit. She leaned back in her chair, remembering how much all of this had mattered to her, and now more than ever she needed to find in herself a desire to take a stand, drawing from the certainty of her own mind, trusting what she knew from the science she had studied and her almost ancient passion to save what she could.

Opening her email, she read the most recent one from Martin. Most of his subject lines started with the word "fuck." He had sent her a chart that showed the Pacific lamprey eel was officially considered extinct in the Nesika. These eels were anadromous, like the salmon, migrating to the sea and back to their rivers to spawn, then dying. The Native people who had lived along the Nesika had depended on the eel as a major food source, and the smell of the eels' rotting bodies on the hot summer rocks in the river in Jess's youth filled the room.

Closing her eyes, Jess felt the room fall away and time slip to the side. Since the attack, a door inside her had opened and visions had flooded through her from a place as deep as the source of the river itself. Now, a brightly colored salmon rose up before her and she reached out to touch it. The salmon was dying.

Jess could see its gills working quickly and the death shiver running the course of its body. A beautiful coho, Jess realized, but then the coho became a sockeye, then a fat chum, and finally a shining silver steelhead.

She rested and let the flood of images carry her. This was the death of salmon—not a particular salmon, but the salmon that had been swimming in the fast waters of the Pacific coastal rivers for more than ten thousand years. She reached out and picked up the body of the dying fish. Suddenly, its slick form became the body of her sister, and Jess opened her eyes. She looked back at her desk. Miko stirred and walked over to her.

Petting his head, she said out loud, "Miko, sometimes I don't know if I can keep doing this." She shivered and got down on the floor next to him. He was so certain, next to her need to collapse into him. She breathed him in and let her head rest on his back. She needed to keep moving forward, toward what had been calling her since she was young. There seemed to be a deep fissure in the earth, and, like offended spirits, much of what had been wild was leaving. Jess could sometimes hear the shrill cry of the last Molalla woman leaving the river valley, herded like an animal up through the center of Oregon to a reservation. That woman had had no choice, but Jess did. She knew that even though she had much to do, her heart was steady and sure. Her mind moved through her thoughts differently now, but her convictions, her sense that what she was doing was what was best for now, stayed with her.

The phone rang and brought Jess back into the room. Miko jumped up and went back to his cushion by the window.

"Jess, it's Kathryn. I was wondering if we could get together later this week and go over some of what I have for the opening brief. I think our case here is really good. Did you see the latest report on the overall decline of the salmon population? Scary stuff."

Jess shook herself. "Yeah, it really is. Sure, I can meet up with you later this week. I'm having lunch with my uncle Robert, who's coming down from Portland to give a presentation at the community college. He may have some more stuff for us, based on these latest counts. What about the day after—say, Friday?"

They agreed to meet at Kathryn's office at two o'clock, and Kathryn said she'd be delighted if Jess brought Robert along. Before Jess hung up, she said, "Thanks, Kathryn. We really appreciate your taking on this case. Maybe sometime you can come down to Penden Valley and I'll take you up to the Nesika. This spring should be amazing with the big snowpack in the mountains. The osprey will be nesting and the dogwoods blooming by late May. Just let me know."

"Thanks, Jess. I would love to bring my daughter down. You two would really like each other. You remind me of her in some ways."

Jess knew Kathryn's daughter had just turned twelve and was very interested in her mom's work, but Kathryn's comment caused a stirring in her. Jess closed her eyes and leaned back in her chair, and suddenly there appeared a vision of a girl who she knew to be her own daughter running ahead of her down a trail toward the white water of the Nesika, her short blond hair covered in a blue baseball cap . . .

Jess quietly caught her breath, and Miko got up and came to her side. She shook her head and reached for him to steady herself.

"That would be great," she told Kathryn. "And Miko loves kids. I'll see you on Friday."

When she hung up, the shock of the sudden vision stayed with her. *What was* that *all about?* she wondered. Since the attack, she had been more open to sudden visualizations, but this felt like a visitation, as if an angel had suddenly stepped into the room and given her a message. She stood up, walked over to the back door, and looked out on her garden. As Miko charged out the open door to chase the squirrels running busily up and down a tree, she felt a bolt of loneliness move through her. She was glad she would be seeing her uncle tomorrow.

And Jeff . . . She felt his presence near her, and she knew the girl in her vision was not just her daughter, but *theirs.* In the months after Deb had returned to Alaska, Jeff had moved toward Jess, then away again. She missed his affection, missed his cautious sensitivity, but there had been a chasm between them.

Now, she knew that this vision was the first step toward crossing it, toward their returning to each other.

Jess reached her hand up and brushed across her cropped hair. Since the attack she had left it short, like a nun, she thought—celibate, alone, and devoted. Now, the vision of the young girl had been a sign that life was trying to circle back through her, reach out into the next generation, to someone else who could hold the door open to watch the large bodies of whales and the small, colorful bodies of songbirds slide into extinction. What did that mean? Jess felt so uncertain, yet so compelled, the glaring contradiction of being drawn so strongly toward protecting the same nature that had almost killed her.

She called Miko back into the house. "C'mon, Miko, let's get out of here for a while." She sat on the chair by the door and put on the shoes she used to use for running. Sadness filled her as she wondered whether she would ever run again, feel the adrenaline filling her muscles and sweat breaking out on her strong body. Miko wagged over to her and waited by the door. It was time, she thought, to begin to think of leaving the celibate order.

She opened her door, and Miko bounded ahead of her to her truck. He jumped into the cab, and Jess backed carefully out of the driveway. She turned on the local rock station and turned up the highway toward the river.

She decided to stop on her way to see Rich. It was a strange impulse, she thought, but he had been somewhat forthcoming with the documents from the earlier watershed analysis, and now he was going to be retiring in a few months. She wanted to make sure she had copies of everything she needed before he left.

The Forest Service parking lot was practically empty, and Jess wished she had called first. Oh well. She parked and slowly got out of her truck. Her leg was still weak, and she had to concentrate more on keeping her balance. She opened the large glass door and stepped into the entry area. A new receptionist greeted her in a formal tone. "May I help you?"

"Sure, I'm Jess Jensen, and I was wondering if Rich was in. I don't have an appointment. I was just stopping by."

"I think so. Let me check." The young man turned to his phone and quickly dialed Rich's extension. Jess wanted him to recognize her, know who she was—past worker who had been fired for caring too much, or the young woman who had been in the news for days—attacked by a mountain lion, no sign of the killer cat. But no, he didn't know who she was.

"Yeah, Rich is in. He said to come on back."

Pushing through the swinging doors separating the public from the offices, Jess walked the long, dark-wood-paneled hall to Rich's office in the back.

"Hey, Rich, sorry to drop in like this, but I thought it might be okay."

"It's fine, Jess. Come in and sit down. It's always good to see you. Are you doing okay?"

Jess resented the faux delicacy with which people treated her. "I'm fine. My leg is getting stronger, and I've stopped seeing blue Moonies sailing around my room at night." She always guessed everyone must think she was a little crazy and had decided early on that maybe she was, and, well, she could share some of the fun.

"That's good to hear. I'm actually really glad you came by. I've decided to write an article for the paper about what's happened with the relicensing project, with the dam, and with you and the others who were involved. Now that I'm retiring, I have little to lose, and it seems with the press these days there may be more sympathy to the cause than there was two years ago. I just want to make sure I don't say something about you and your story that you aren't comfortable with."

She looked up at him. She sensed, almost smelled, betrayal—the same feeling she had had that morning. Maybe it was something they were all carrying, a shared participation, a shared knowing, that what they were doing was harmful, and because of that they were motivated to keep working, to care, to try.

"It would be a good idea to let me read whatever you have to say. There are some parts of what happened to me that I would like to keep private. But write what you want, and let me know when you're ready for me to read it. I was also wondering if there are any files or meeting notes that you may have regarding the transaction between PowerCorp and ODFW. I feel like there's still something missing. Maybe it's just a conversation no one knows about, but I wanted to check with you." She felt like an echo in his office, as if she had been in this chair, asking this question, before. She had, and she would keep coming back to this chair until she believed there was nothing left to find.

Rich looked at her with a false smile. Jess felt again as if she wanted to run out of his office, and got up to leave.

"Well, Jess, here are copies of the relevant chapters in the final environmental impact statement, if you think they might be helpful. Let's see . . . here's a folder that has to do with the fish passage recommendations for the Green Springs." He handed the manila folder to Jess. "You know, sometimes these things just happen and you're better off to let them go."

Backing through the door, Jess let his diminishment of her fall flat in front of him. "Let me know when you have that article done." She knew he was waiting for an "atta boy" from her, but it wasn't coming.

Miko was waiting, panting happily, in the cab of her truck. She rolled down the window and turned up her music. They were going upriver. As she drove, she felt the web she was woven into: one that she both was trapped in and had had a hand in weaving. She felt the familiar pull of the Nesika coaxing her upstream, weaving her visions of a child, salmon sliding through a dark slit in the fabric, lamprey eel flowing in dark rivers below this one, rivers of extinction. Jess wanted to stop them from leaving, help them find their way back home. She saw her young, blond daughter standing on the bank of the river, pointing to the splash of spawning salmon. *That's right—you will know what to do, sweetheart.*

PIAH

Piah stood up from the river and brushed off her naked body. Her hair was caked with mud, and her body was tired from crying. A fierceness rose in her, and she stretched her back in the sun. Looking down at herself, she could see the scratches from the rocks. She untangled the mud from her hair, shaking it loose and breathing in the warmth of the living, quietly steadying her breath with her heartbeat and the rhythm of the rushing river. Then, closing her eyes, she began to sing her power song and opened to the spirits and forces around her. The cadence of her singing carried her into the place of visions, beckoning her into a widening vortex. But she no longer felt afraid here; she felt only determination emanating from the scar in her heart. She sat down on the soft riverbank and saw the river spirit walking away from her, summoning her to the edges of her vision. She wanted to show Piah something. Piah followed.

Below them was an opening into a clearing. Through the clearing ran a smooth river that seemed to be made of blue light. Piah extended her hand, and a beautiful tendril of the river of light reached toward her. Recognition and a calling-out passed through her, connecting her to the river and to something else.

She sat down carefully next to the water. The spirit of the Nesika hovered close behind her, seeming to urge her toward the river of light. Piah waited by the river and felt a question rise in her: *What is killing my people, my family, Libah? We always knew how to care for one another until now.*

She suddenly felt very cold and reached back toward the spirit of the Nesika. She was afraid, sensing that something or someone was watching her and knowing something was going to be asked of her—something dangerous and threatening.

From the depths of the river of light, a vision rose up, a brightly colored, woven circle filled with images of salmon, plants, people, and the river itself. Some of the people looked like the bearded man from her other vision, some were women, and some were light-haired children. Piah stared for a long time, as the woven circle grew larger and larger. The light from the river threaded through the images, holding them together, the salmon with the people, the trees with the children and the animals. Piah lay back and watched the circle rise above her, growing larger, almost filling the sky.

As the circle began spinning faster and faster, the light from the river began to dim. Slowly, the salmon and the trees fell away, as if a thread that had held them to the circle had been pulled or broken. The faces of the people began to change, and the children started crying. She saw her own people, the rash covering their faces, turning and walking away. Salmon thrashed along the bank of the river as it receded and left them stranded. A sharp, high howl began to ring all around Piah. The river of light was dying. Piah saw large gray walls holding it back, choking the flow of the river. The howl grew louder. All the changes were happening so quickly. Piah wanted to reach out and catch the falling bodies, but she was held fast to the ground near the river.

When there seemed to be no end to the disintegration of the beautiful image, a woman's face appeared before Piah's. The woman seemed to be Piah's age, light skinned and small; she was terribly wounded on her neck and head. Piah could see the blood running down her neck from what looked like a bite from some large animal. The woman was crying, and her tears were blue light, like the river. Piah wanted to reach out to her, help her in some way, but knew that she couldn't, wasn't supposed to. She saw that the woman was bending over a bundle, a small child or infant, and Piah felt her heart break open. Her breasts started aching, and she felt a kinship with the child. Then another young woman was standing behind her. It was Tenas, her sister, but she didn't look like Tenas. She looked like the woman, in some ways; she was the woman's sister.

The older woman turned and looked right into Piah with her vast blue eyes. The blood from her wound meandered over her right shoulder, and she was shaking. The woven circle kept falling to pieces, and behind the wailing, Piah could hear the strange, rough sound of men laughing. Piah let the woman gaze into her and felt as if they were trying to say something to each other. Piah wanted to tend her wound, stop the bleeding, hold her infant, but she couldn't move; the weight of the descending light held her in place. She felt the momentum of the vision and recognized the presence that had taken her own daughter away.

Piah saw the woman reaching out to the strange gray walls, trying to free the river. She saw her trying to grab on to the salmon with her one good arm as they slid into the darkness. She could tell that this woman was holding on to her life and her child, and trying to hold on to the river. In the blood running over the woman's shoulder, Piah could see a strand of the blue light weaving in and out. The river had hurt this woman, too; her kinship with the river, what tied her to it, was the same wound.

Piah could see that what was happening to her people, to the song of the river, had to do with this woman and her wound. She sensed that the relationship with the child and with this wounded woman was important to what was going to happen to her people, to this land, and to the Nesika.

Piah came back to the present and slowly opened her eyes. It had grown almost dark, and the air was colder. Piah turned to climb up the cliff to where her clothes were. She stopped and listened to a strange sound coming from a clearing near the river.

It sounded like the muffled bark of a wolf and the low growl of a hunting mountain lion. Piah looked back as she was climbing the cliff and saw what looked like a mountain lion dragging a small woman's body off into the brush. Piah stopped and leaped off the cliff, shouting at the cat. Then the image vanished and the barking stopped. Piah watched the quieting pulse of the river in the dying light and finished her climb to the top.

She dressed and sat near one of the many stone piles. Remnants of her vision haunted her, and she tried to make sense of what it had meant. She had cut one of her hands as she was climbing the cliff; the blood running from the wound blended with the blue-light meandering of the river. She remembered the time she had seen Mian on his quest. The initiation into the relationship with spirit was a powerful and important time for Piah and everyone in her tribe. Where were the helping spirits now? How could she find her own power again?

An osprey dipped below her into the river and rose with something large and silver in her talons. Piah watched as the bird found her nest. Giving her babies life, diving into the river, and coming back with more life . . . Piah leaned against a rock pile and heard in the distance the cry of a mountain lion hunting for food for her young.

JESS

꧁ ❦ ꧂

As Jess continued up the road along the Nesika, she turned
down her radio and checked her cell phone for messages.
There was one from her mom, about Suzie. "Shit," Jess said out
loud. *What's she doing back in town?* Her leg ached, and she
shifted in her seat.

She thought about calling her mom back, but images of
Suzie, of the empty room, the bed ruffled and her stuff just gone,
tugged at her. Even though Jess knew why Suzie had split, she
still had a feeling of being torn in her lower abdomen, the sudden
drop of another trapdoor opening under her.

A year ago today. And now she was driving back, in the
daylight, with Miko, to the place where she had been attacked.
She had been through there when she'd needed photos of the
Green Springs dam, but she hadn't taken the time to visit in a way
that she intended to remember. And now Suzie was back, too.

Miko rode alongside her, swaying along with her turns
on the highway. He looked up at her, and she felt an ever-present sadness from him, something that had been there since the
attack. It felt like his big heart was sorry. Jess wondered what he
remembered from that day, locked in the front seat of the pickup,

imprisoned and helpless. But what if he hadn't been there, if he had been out? Jess shuddered at the thought. He could have been killed, or wounded as deeply as she had been. She noticed a slight shade of gray showing around his black muzzle and knew that someday he would go and she would be here without him. Miko let out a sigh and appeared to get more nervous as they neared the dam. Jess reached over to him and felt tears rise in her eyes. They were going back, and they were going back together.

As she drove down the rough gravel, the long afternoon shadows from the Douglas firs danced on the road in front of her. She suddenly felt heavy, as if she were taking on a weight not her own. The rocky parking area opened up from the shadows, and the gold of autumn hung on the banks of the river like curtains. She felt the electrical charge of fear memory pulse through her.

The long light lit up the face of the dam, and Jess sat in her truck for a long time next to Miko, wondering if she should let him out or leave him in the cab. But maybe this was a chance for him to go with her, be next to her, try to find the pieces that had been left behind that day. He sniffed around and appeared more attentive than usual. The high whine of the turbines seemed to harmonize with her nerves, and the decaying smell of the late-afternoon fall river seemed stronger, more present.

She could be where the mountain lion had been that afternoon, pacing hungrily in the shadows, then following the scent of deer down to the water's edge and finding her instead. The turbines' sound blended with the rush of the Nesika, and Jess wanted to call out. Miko started barking at the splash of a spawning pair of winter chinooks in the shallows across the water.

Jess suddenly felt dizzy. The notes that Rich had given her were back in her truck, sitting on the front seat. It was possible there would be something in there that she could use for the lawsuit, something that would help persuade the judge.

She backed away from the river and turned toward her pickup. When she got to her truck, she pulled out the manila folder. She walked down to the edge of the darkening water and reached her hand into the sharp, cold current of the Nesika.

She waited for a moment, then eased the folder of papers into the water. The current took the folder, and the paper swirled like white leaves floating downstream, the river like a woman's hand separating the fibers carefully before beginning to weave. With that, Jess laid down her weapons. Her battle was ending, in some way; she was giving back to the body of the river the words preserving the dam that continued to hold the Nesika's current prisoner. She stood to watch the last pages slip around a small rock, and she hoped that the river would know what to do.

When the papers were gone, Jess called to Miko and walked back up to her truck. How she had decided to put the notes in the river, she didn't know, but she carried a new, lighter, clearer feeling and wanted to make sure she got back home safely.

Once she began to drive, on impulse she reached for her cell phone, called Jeff's number, and left him a voice mail: "Hey, Jeff. I was wondering if you'd like to come to dinner tonight. Call me." She hung up and smiled at Miko. She felt the bridge under her holding her as she reached out to him. Imagining Jeff getting the message, she knew he would say yes. And later, when she checked her messages, he had.

When Jess got home, it was dark. She wished she had left some lights on in the house. She grabbed the groceries out of the back of her truck and unlocked the front door. Just as the key turned in the lock, she heard someone walking up behind her.

"Jess?" said a rough female voice.

Jess whipped around. "Holy fuck, Suzie! Jesus, you scared me. Wow, where have you been? Mom said you were in town."

"Yeah, Jess, sorry. God, are you okay? I've been away—went to Florida, actually. It was all so fucking complicated with those guys getting busted and hurt."

Jess threw on the porch light, which glinted off the many piercings along Suzie's right ear. Her now white-blond short hair and heavily made-up dark eyes seemed like an exotic mask to Jess.

Memories of the attack rose around her, and the right side of her face began to twitch. Since the attack, most of the physical symptoms of her brain damage had disappeared. She noticed it only when she was startled or scared; her face began to twitch, and her thinking became disconnected.

Jess stepped into the shadows, hoping Suzie wouldn't notice. "I know why you went; I just don't get the disappearing act, Suzie. Fuck . . ."

Suzie looked away, and Jess spotted the tip of a tattoo on her neck, a snake or a dragon or something. "I know, but I'm back now. Can I come in?"

"Now is not a good time—Jeff is on his way over, and I have stuff to do. I don't know, Suzie—maybe in a few days, but I'm pretty busy and my uncle is coming to town."

"Jeff?" Suzie prompted, but when Jess just looked at her, she said, "Okay, well, let me give you my new number, and you can call me when you're ready."

Jess handed her a piece of paper and a pen. Suzie handed Jess her number, and Jess looked down at it and then backed away, saying, "Okay. I'll call you in a few days."

Once Suzie was gone, Jess sat down on the couch, thinking about her old friend, once so close to her, now crazy and fearsome. A sudden, striking smell filled the room, the salty-bloody scent of predator and prey. She held her hand to her face as if she were trying to quiet a restless child. She didn't want Jeff to come in and see her like this.

Getting up to put the rest of the groceries away, she reached for a vase in which to put some flowers she had bought at the market, but her hand was shaking and it fell to the floor. She put the vase back up on the shelf and steadied it; she noticed a small crack on one side and reached her hand back up to her face. She closed her eyes and could feel a crack widening inside her, opening to the awareness of something dark and full. She stopped trying to hold on, and let herself slip down the dark slide. She sat slowly down on the cold floor of the kitchen, sensing something waiting in the dark outside her door, stalking her, seeking her familiar scent.

When Jeff knocked on the door, Jess called out to him from the couch. "Come in!"

Miko jumped up and did his dog twirl-dance in greeting, then ran to get his toy. Jess stood up slowly and moved toward Jeff. The air between them was still and full of energy, like the darkness of an early spring storm. Jeff looked at her with kindness in his eyes, and she reached for his hand.

"I'm glad you're here, Jeff. We have a lot to talk about . . ."

"Yeah, we do. I was glad to get your call, really glad. I have so much to tell you."

Her hand in his began to shake. "Jess, are you okay?"

"Yeah. It's so weird—Suzie just stopped by, and she freaked me out. I don't know why she's back." Jess felt Jeff stiffen as he heard about Suzie. "Let's sit down for a minute. I'll be okay." They sat next to each other on the couch, and Jess closed her eyes.

Her mind tilted, and she breathed carefully to try to slow the spinning feeling. She closed her eyes and saw Suzie's face elongate into the face of a mountain lion. Then she felt Monica's presence and saw the flash of her sunny hair as she swung out over the river on the rope swing. Jess smiled and felt the heavy rope travel into her own hands. She took another breath and opened her eyes. Jeff was sitting close to her, and she could feel him breathing with her. She rested and let her body sink into his, and he didn't move away.

After a while, Jeff pushed back and asked, "Would you like some tea or a glass of wine? Maybe I should start dinner and you can rest here."

She lifted her head off his shoulder and smiled at him. "Tea would be nice. There's lemon-ginger in the pantry." Jeff walked into the kitchen, and Miko followed him. Jess felt like she was seeing something that would happen again and again: Jeff feeding Miko, helping with the dishes, taking out the trash. They had found each other in the roar of the fast current and were now riding in the slow pools together. Off in the distance, Jess could hear the sound of a baby girl crying.

"Here's your tea." Jeff set a cup down on the coffee table.

"Thanks," she said, looking up at him, letting the moment rest between them before she continued, "Jeff, my uncle is coming to town tomorrow, and we're going to Eugene on Thursday to meet with Kathryn from Planet Justice about the lawsuit against PowerCorp. I want to ask for your help." She paused, remembering the time a year earlier when she had gone to him. He had been through a lot since then, and she sensed that there was an opening for him.

"I know this could put you in a conflicted position with your job, but, Jeff, you're on the inside and you have access to reports and information that could really help us. Part of what I want you to understand is that we're trying to remove only one dam out of eight. Taking out this dam will restore just a small part of the Nesika. If you look at it like a typical corporate scientist, in the long run the amount of restored habitat isn't that much. Or, from my perspective, you can view it as a turning point, like the beginning of an out-breath, a small turn of the tide."

"I know that's true. This has become a real David-and-Goliath kind of issue. I need to tell you that I did think we could work around the dam and restore some of the habitat, but now . . . the numbers aren't there. What we tried to do isn't working."

Jeff stared at his hands; he looked defeated and hurt. She brushed his back with her hand, and he moved closer to her. She could smell his musky scent from working outside in the rain all day. She remembered the same scent from the hot springs that day.

"This issue for me really has to do with how we look at the world around us, at what's going on," Jess continued. "If we can for one moment begin to imagine the Green Springs dam breached, then maybe we'll be able to hand our children a potential way out. They can continue the breath, and the momentum of this change can carry them and the salmon through the next generations."

She closed her eyes and saw a river of color flowing fast and full of life. Children were dancing with brightly colored flags along the bank, celebrating the return of the salmon. Jeff was quiet.

"It's kind of like the butterfly effect: a small change in one river valley, a small victory over corporate control, can have an impact that we may never see but that we can at least set in motion. I remember a teacher of mine saying once, 'Do your work as if it matters one hundred and fifty years from now.' Jeff, this is a really important time we live in. I know that job security means a lot to you, but there are other ways we can make money, other ways we can live. Please help us."

Jeff reached out and pulled her to him. He buried his face in her hair, and she felt the warmth of his breath on the back of her neck for a moment. Then he sat back up and said, "You know, Jess, I know so much more about who you're dealing with and how futile this all seems from where they stand. PowerCorp is strong and has a lot of industry supporters. It was voted one of the top ten companies of its kind in the country!" He kissed the top of her head carefully. "But I hear you. This has been tearing me up, too. Just today, Mack asked me to write a response to the reports that have just come out about the decline in the salmon populations in the Pacific Northwest. He directed me to contact PR and draft an announcement that reframes the research. He wants me to lie, Jess. He wants me to create the kinds of reports that were used to keep the Green Springs dam in place. We live in a world of contradictions and minefields. I don't know if taking out the dam is the answer, but I do know that to misreport the decimation of a species is more than unethical." He moved in even closer, and Jess sensed the same turning in him that she had begun to feel down by the river. They were both quiet for a while; then Jeff stood to go start dinner.

Jess could sense that he was thinking hard while he was in the kitchen. He finally came back into the living room with some apples and cheese and said, "Okay, I'll help you. But we won't have much time. Once I tell Mack that I refuse to falsify or misrepresent the reports, I'll be fired or suspended. While I have the keys to the office and access to the reports, I'll do whatever I can."

"Wow, Jeff, that's great, but I'm sorry, too. You know I know how that feels. I can't believe those bastards would do that.

Fuck them. And thank you. We can meet with my uncle Robert tomorrow if you can make it. He is so going to believe what is happening to you. And you'll like our lawyer, Kathryn—she's great and has been really helpful with all the legal stuff."

Jess heard rain begin to fall on the roof. The house was warm, and what Jeff was making smelled good. They looked into each other's eyes, and Jess knew that Jeff would be staying over, that the next day he would go to his place and pick up some clothes and bathroom supplies. He would meet Uncle Robert, and they would be able to design a strategy that could breach the Green Springs dam.

Jess got up to check on what was happening in the kitchen. The large poster of the dam seemed to gleam before her. For one moment, she felt as if the dam wanted to come out—something about how unnecessary it was, how outdated, from another kind of time, when the impact of progress had been ignored.

"So, why did you put the notes you got today into the river?"

His voice sounded taunting, and she smiled. "I don't know. It was like I wanted to let go of something, of this fight, of trying to find out what to do, this proving to everyone how right we are. I guess on some level I decided that the direction I wanted to go in was just to say that yes, this is the right thing to do, not because someone changed the reports and they're bad and wrong, but because for the salmon and the health of the Nesika and the ecosystem, there is no other choice. I can't keep trying to find the bad guy to put in jail. That's too much like an old, boring Western. What I—we—are asking is to begin to live differently, to live as if it's obvious that the dam should come down. If we can do that, then maybe some judge in San Francisco will see it, too. Maybe the order will come down through the tragic maze of this administration and we can be there, at the edge of the river, when the turbines are turned off and for the first time in fifty years there is only the sound of the Nesika."

Jeff looked up at her, and she could see the new softening in his warm eyes. He had let go of something today, too: an ardent belief in a system that had betrayed him, a system in which he'd had a sincere belief and had made sacrifices for. Now he was moving toward her, toward a new way of being that was about more than taking down the Green Springs dam. Somehow she knew that they would see the dam come down, would see the salmon spawning in the gravel that came only from the natural banks and contours of the Nesika.

Jess reached up and brushed the hair from his face, then playfully reached down and unfastened the top button of her jeans. Jeff's eyes brightened, and he smiled as he pulled her toward him. She nuzzled his neck like a young animal asking to play. This was new for her, a feeling that this was the way it was going to be for a long time, that this was the way they would be together. She pushed back from him and ran into the bedroom. She knew he would follow. Her body folded readily around him, and they rolled and laughed, tearing the covers off her small bed.

Their lovemaking was slow and tender. Jess shifted for a moment when Jeff moved her hair to expose her neck, but when he kissed her scars and she felt his tears on her skin, she pulled him closer to her and assured him that she was okay. She was alive in his arms and felt the seasons she had missed with him rush through her. For the first time, the light between them ran clear, like the river, wide and open, free of the constrictions that had held it in place. They lay together, tangled in each other, listening to the hard rainfall in the darkening night. They slept for a moment, and then Jeff tucked her in and went into the kitchen to finish making dinner.

JESS

Her cell phone vibrated with an incoming message, and Jess grabbed it and went into the kitchen. She feared it was her mother who had called; she was alone, and Jess worried that something could have happened. Her phone was always on her nightstand when she slept.

The kitchen clock glowed just after midnight. She could see it was Suzie and let it go to message.

"Jess, it's Suzie. Um, sorry to call, but there's something I need to talk to you about. And, it's just that . . . okay, can you call me when you get this? Yeah, sorry again it's so late . . ."

Shutting her phone, Jess sat in the darkness at their small kitchen table. What would Suzie want? After all they had been through, the deception with the plans and her guilty disappearance, it was hard for Jess to trust or believe her. But they had once been close, and Jess missed that, missed Suzie's unpredictability and her straightforward, unapologetic edge. But it was that same edge that worried Jess. She knew that Suzie carried large, unhealed wounds from her childhood and that the pain drove Suzie into corners that Jess was never welcomed into. It made sense that Suzie would have come back fascinated by Jess's bite wounds from the attack.

Jess shivered in her cold kitchen and made her way quietly back to the warmth of her bed with Jeff.

In the morning, she told him about the call from Suzie. "It's like she's stalking me or something. I don't really know what she wants. . ."

"I know. Suzie's always felt a little sketchy to me, coming and going, like a cat playing with prey. But she could also be funny, in a quirky, Suzie kind of way, and she was one of your best friends."

Jess wondered if Jeff was making excuses for Suzie. She took a long breath and waited for her thoughts to reorder themselves. She could smell fear, but this time it wasn't her own.

Then she said, "I have to see her. I don't know how I'll be able to be with her without trying to find out how she got into my computer, if she was the one to give those kids the plans or if they got them another way." She felt a little dizzy and put her hand on her neck where the thick, smooth bite scars were.

"I'm going to lie down for a bit." She walked back into the bedroom and stretched out on the tousled bed. She drifted into a kind of sleep and could hear distant drumming and chanting around a campfire. She rolled onto her side, still half-awake, and let herself go into the dream.

In the vision she was looking at the back of her uncle Robert—he was holding a clipboard and seemed to be counting something. The Green Springs dam was just upriver from him, and the water coming out was a deep blue. Across the river was a small camp that the drumming and chanting were coming from. A young woman walked into camp and was met with a keening recognition. Uncle Robert turned around and beckoned to Jess to come to his side. He put his arm carefully around her, and they watched as the people welcomed this woman back into the camp. They washed her and put skin robes around her. Jess couldn't move, watching the blue-light river and feeling a kinship with the woman being cared for. They sang into her wounds, and the words sounded like gentle falling water to Jess. Her uncle turned to her and said, "See, honey, this is how it was done—how you can heal and take what you know back to the river." There was a rustling behind them, and Jess turned to see Suzie standing there, blood dripping from cuts on her arms.

These dreamlike visions had been happening to Jess since she had gotten home from the hospital. She had mentioned them to Jeff but no one else. Sometimes she wrote about them in her journal, and sometimes she kept them to herself. They were so real, like she was visiting another time. But this was the first time Suzie had been there, too, or Uncle Robert.

Jess got up and took a shower. She ran her hands over the scars on her neck, face, and leg. She had healed and become stronger and found her way back from serious damage to her brain. She thought of Suzie in her vision, and of her wounded arms—wounds that she had given to herself. When Jess had asked her about them, Suzie had said that the pain she felt from the cuts was something that was real for her and that she could control. Jess could only imagine what it was that Suzie *couldn't* control in her life.

Stepping out of the shower, she dried herself with a rough blue towel. She looked into the mirror and saw her short hair and wounded face—her eyes seemed to be a darker blue, and the scar below them looked like a brand or tattoo. She thought about how the Molalla women had tattooed their faces after going through the passage into adulthood. Jess ran her hand through her wet hair and down her face, tracing the edges of the scar with her finger. It had taken a long time to heal. She could hear the echoes of the chanting from her dream vision and closed her eyes. *We all have scars*, she thought. *Their resilient skin shapes us and makes us strong.*

BARBARA

C liff was an old friend of her husband's who now spent most of his days fishing up on the Nesika. They had daughters the same age and had been close because of the two girls. Now they were both growing old in a quiet back eddy of loneliness. She had reached out to him many times, but he had kept his distance. Now, knowing what was happening with Suzie, Barbara had reached out in a more deliberate but gentle way.

Sitting in his living room with him, she wanted to start their conversation by staying close to what they had in common. "How's the fishing going? Given all that's going on, I'm surprised there are still even fish in that river."

"Oh, you know, Barbara, there will always be some kind of fish, but it's changed a lot since Jack and I used to fish up there. Seems there are times we're catching more small-mouth bass than trout or steelhead."

Barbara let the memory of her husband, Jack, settle in a sweet and tender place in her chest. She put her hand over her heart as if she were making a pledge.

"I can't imagine. It seems like just yesterday I couldn't cook and clean the trout and salmon that Jack and the kids caught fast enough . . . I just don't understand how it got to be so messed up. Anyway, it's good to see you, Cliff. Sorry it's taken me so long. With Jess and all her appointments, we've been pretty busy. But there's something I need to talk to you about. It's about Suzie."

Sighing, Cliff straightened in his chair and put his large hands in his lap. He looked like a man at prayer.

"She's back in town, working on a book project, a novel, actually, and in her book there's a young woman who gets attacked by a mountain lion. I know she and Jess have been friends for a long time, but this is just a little creepy, especially after what happened for Jess at her job and whatever role Suzie might have had in that . . . I know you and Suzie aren't close, and how hard it's been for you since your wife died." Barbara didn't want to say "suicide" or "killed herself," let alone bring up the fact that Suzie had found her mother's body lying in a pool of blood when she was only four years old.

Cliff nodded and said, "Do you know Jess's friend Martin? The guy who runs the Nesika Watershed Council? I see him from time to time, and I know that he talks with Suzie now and then. I think she was even working with him for a bit, just before all that stuff went down with those Earth in Mind kids. I can talk to him, find out more about Suzie's plans. I'm really sorry about all this . . . How is Jess doing these days, anyway? I know she's had a rough time. I just keep remembering when the kids were little— so innocent, so full of life—and now . . ."

"Jess is doing okay. You know her—she's so persistent and cares so much about the river—but I worry about her. She's still strong, but since the mountain lion attack . . . That was awful." Barbara sank into the memory of the lonely, sleepless nights blending into exhausting days, each one like going into a dark cave, her grief walking by her side and never letting go.

"I'm so sorry."

"I'm sorry, too, Cliff. It seems like we're always just ahead of our last disaster. Thank you so much for having me over today—I didn't really want to push you into this, but I didn't know who else to talk to."

As she sat in the chair across from Cliff, his gray eyes looked sad and Barbara suddenly felt even more sorry for him, because she knew him, recognized his pain, understood his wounds, and felt the horrible echoes of loss ringing through every living room.

PIAH

⟨◎⟩

As she dressed, she felt the call of the river, strong in her veins. Piah knew that this was her initiation into her role as the medicine woman for her people. The power of her visions showed her she was to pass on to the woman in the vision the wisdom and knowledge that her grief had given her. Libah's death had torn Piah apart in unimaginable ways, and now she had to tend both to her own wound and to the wounds and losses of her people. She looked down at the blood dripping from her hand and felt the pain radiating through her skin. The pain in her body was her kinship with all of the life around her, before her, and after her. Her ancestors were standing behind her, and they were holding the gifts of their wisdom.

Piah sat near one of the stone piles and looked back down at the Nesika. The river looked different to her now—it was the grave of her young daughter. She stood and walked to the circle of stones in the clearing. Facing each of the directions, she asked the north for guidance, the east for ease and clarity of vision, and the south for the passion to move forward to keep living. And before the west she laid down her grief and asked for healing and the power to let go. In the center of the stone circle, she sat and accepted the gifts of her ancestors and felt the lure of the future, of the generations to come. She asked for courage to face the danger, the widening gulch of darkness, death, and loss.

All around her, the birds were calling to their mates to come and roost in their homes for the night. She could hear the padding of footsteps, the night animals coming out to hunt. She pulled out strands of her hair and left them in the circle as an offering to the spirits. Barefoot, hungry, and sad, but also empowered, she walked barefoot down the path toward the small lights of the night fires in her village.

JEFF

⟨◎⟩

A s he was leaving the house for work, Jeff felt as if something larger than he was moving him. For most of his adult life, he had tried to find a way to veer toward what he thought was right, the agenda he had set for himself. Now he felt a blending of purpose—not just that he was doing what he thought Jess wanted him to do, but that he was doing what had been waiting for him all along.

When he got to his office, he hesitantly checked his phone messages.

"Hi, this is Beth in PR. Mack said you'd be contacting me today about a press release he wants to get out? He has quite a deadline on this one. I'll be in my office until about four thirty. I've got to pick up my kids from soccer practice by five. Give me a jingle!"

"Hi, Jeff, it's Mack. Look, I was thinking maybe we should get the newspaper out here to do some photos of the gravel augmentation program. Those big piles of gravel make it look like we've been doing our hard work." Mack's rough voice trailed off into mocking sarcasm, and Jeff grimaced.

No other messages. Jeff sighed and switched on his computer. The door behind him swung open, and he felt the heavy presence of Mack Dempsey himself move into his office. Mack was with Ken Gamaika, the guy from ODFW who was in charge of tracking the mountain lion that had attacked Jess. Jeff smiled in recognition.

"Hey, Jeff. Ken came up this morning to meet with us about the press release you're working on with Beth. He has some ideas and some information he wants to share with us about the impact of the hydropower system on the runs of salmon and steelhead in the Nesika. How's that going?"

Jeff felt a sinking in his stomach and looked up at Mack from under his cap. Ken was someone Jeff had worked with before. He was a sloppy scientist, more interested in making his quota by giving tickets to unlicensed fishermen than in working on protecting the habitat of the Nesika.

"Well, I wanted to talk with you more about it first. I've been looking over the report, and where it references actual return counts in the Nesika, I don't see how anything can be done. It really is as bad as it looks."

Jeff felt the air leave the room, and Mack turned to look at Ken.

"Maybe we should go into the conference room, and I'll call Beth in from PR so we can begin to draft a statement." Mack turned and walked out of Jeff's office. Ken stayed and locked Jeff with a look that was both demeaning and threatening.

"Jeff, you know there are always problems with return counts. We can't claim for sure that the Green Springs dam is responsible for these low numbers. That's all we have to say. PowerCorp is really vulnerable right now, having just undergone the relicensing of the project. We can't back up now. There's too much in the media that contradicts itself. We have world-class scientists breaking their necks trying to establish genetic differences between stocks of fish, while the Federal government sends out reports that hatchery salmon are the same as native fish. You know, Jeff, it really is all a story, and our interest is in preserving the power system in order to keep the lights on in town!"

Jeff swung around in his chair and looked up at Ken. "Ken,

you know not one electron of power generated by this project lights one lightbulb in Penden Valley. This power goes into the grid and is bartered by power brokers whose names we don't even know. Don't try to feed me this bullshit about the community depending on the power this river generates. And I'm not going to lie anymore about what's happening to the salmon. You and I both know the salmon is the canary in the coal mine and that, for all intents and purposes, with the populations diving the way they are, this fucking canary is dead. We have two choices: get out of the coal mine and let the ecosystem die a slow death, or stop what we're doing, clear the air, and find a way to restore the oxygen."

Jeff heard the sliding of chairs across the floor in the next room and knew that Mack and Beth were waiting for them. He stood up and brushed past Ken, who was looking down at his boots, smiling.

Walking into the conference room, Jeff felt as if he were entering a foreign country. He had worked so hard for this company and his career, and now he felt everything falling away from him. In a few hours, he would be meeting Jess and her uncle for lunch at the lodge. He sat at the hard plastic table under the bright, offensive lights. Beth looked almost exactly as he imagined her: wearing thick makeup that looked even thicker in the fluorescence; colored, stiff hair; and a stern look of self-importance that he immediately disliked. These were not his people; he was in the wrong place. He listened to Mack going over some of his ideas with Ken and Beth, and they sounded hollow. Jeff knew this was the old story—a story of deception, destruction, and greed. But finally, rather than playing his part in the drama, Jeff understood it as only one story of many. He was choosing to live according to another story—a story in which there was value in life, honesty, and interdependence.

"Mack, Ken, Beth, look—what you're doing is unethical and possibly illegal. There are laws that have to do with how we make decisions and what we choose to do about the information we receive. What's happening today is much bigger than trying to cover up a report about the salmon populations. If you hide this, something else will come up, and then you'll have to hide that. While you're dancing around, trying to put out these fires, the river continues to die. This decision you've made is extremely dangerous. It's a violent blow to the salmon and the rivers they depend on for their survival. I can't do this. I can't continue to play this game with you or anyone else." He stopped and let his words bounce around the sterile room.

Mack shifted his chair back and looked at Jeff with a small smile. "You know, I've always wondered about you. It doesn't fucking matter if fish come from the river or the hatchery. Hell, it most likely doesn't matter if there is a single goddamn fish in this river. We have to keep the turbines spinning, and we will. Don't even think for a moment that some stupid report will have any effect on the decision to relicense the Nesika Project. I think it's time you packed up, Jeff. I hoped you would work out. You're a talented scientist. But we both know that if you're climbing that girl's tree, she's going to have more than your ear on this one."

Jeff felt his face grow hot, and he felt sick to his stomach. Being in this room, in the presence of people like this, drove home his conviction that he was making the right move. It was like waking up from a dream. The masks had come off.

"I agree with you, Mack. This is not the time for me to be working for PowerCorp. And you'd better fucking leave Jess out of this." He stood up, knocking his chair back.

Jeff slammed the door to his office and sat down. He knew he could get some boxes from the copy room, and he looked around again, sorting out what was his and what belonged to the company. Looking through his files, he felt a sudden rush of anxiety. What was he going to do? He had a small savings account, and he still had the money that he had gotten when his father had died. He thought of his dad, of his warmth and concern for what was right. At times like this, Jeff felt the empty, lonely hole from his father's death even more acutely. But now he was moving toward work that had to do with more than being right—he was certain his dad would understand, encourage him, and love Jess. So Jeff would begin to work with Jess and the others, trying to push the heavy door open, trying to find the opening in the dam, to begin to let the flow back into the waiting lives there.

As Jeff pulled out of the parking lot, he felt released from something that had been holding him down. He had packed his boxes and cleared the files from his computer, but not before emailing to Jess anything he had that he thought might be helpful for her case. He had time before he met her and her uncle for lunch, so he drove out to the trail to Lemolo Falls. He loved this place and had imagined getting married here one day. *Lemolo*: Chinook for "wild" or "untamed" . . . As he walked up the trail, he felt the heaviness leave his body, as if the rush of Lemolo Creek were washing away the debris of the past year, and laughed to himself. He could envision the wedding—at the base of the falls; simple, a few people—and could hear, blending with the rush of the water, a young girl laughing.

JESS

ꙮ

J ess smiled, glancing over at Uncle Robert as she drove her truck. She had seen him a few times since her attack, but this was her first chance to hear in-depth about how his work was going and how he might be able to help with the case. All along, she had known he was with her, encouraging her and sending her articles and updates to support her grant applications and research.

The day was cool and rainy, and the river was high and fast from the recent fall rains. When they reached the Nesika, Jess pointed out the now-abandoned osprey nest and a glimpse of the clear-cut that she had worked on with Martin the day of her attack.

Jeff had left for work earlier than usual that morning. She was concerned that something might happen to him there, a reprimand for not contacting Beth in PR, for not siding with the company, for not playing the game according to its rules. She would find out soon enough what had happened, when Jeff met them for lunch at the Nesika Lodge.

The lodge was warm and filled with the murmur of customers—fishermen, tourists, and local workers. Jess and her uncle sat a corner table and waited for Jeff. When he walked in,

Jess felt a wave of relief and expectation carry her across the room to his arms. He hugged her close, and she felt the tension in his body relax. He didn't look angry or upset anymore; he seemed relieved and determined. She breathed in the musky smell of his worn jean jacket and held him for a moment longer.

"Hey, you look all right. How'd it go?"

Jeff turned and greeted Robert, before sitting down. "Well, as I thought, when push came to shove, they shoved and I pushed. There was really no room to work with them—there never was. I've been deceiving myself for too long, trying to figure out how to cooperate with them and change them at the same time. Guess it's not as simple as that." He stopped and ordered a cup of coffee. "Anyway, Mack came in with Ken from ODFW to help me with the press release, and I said that I wasn't going to do it. I even attempted to tell them why. Guess it wasn't the time for them to hear it. I have my stuff in my truck and emailed some documents that might be useful to you—well, *us*—for the case." He let out a long sigh, and Jess reached for his hand.

"Well, I know I'm not surprised," Jess said. "I'm almost surprised they gave you time to pack your office."

Robert turned to him and said, "Jeff, I had what was possibly the same conversation you had with the people at the agency when I quit. The story is the same everywhere, and it's not because they're trying to be mean. They really believe that what they're doing is right and that they deserve to have it their way. Hell, just this morning I read that forty-one percent of the people in this country believe that the Iraq War was the right thing to do. People will and can believe in anything. And their arguments are not necessarily incorrect. We need power, we need dams, and it's less clear to most of them that we need salmon or what role the fish play in our lives. Our job is to find a way to tell them that it really isn't about being right or making decisions based on exclusively human need."

Jeff shifted in his chair, and Jess checked him for his reaction. She had spent many years having conversations like this with her uncle, and she squeezed Jeff's hand to connect with him and comfort herself. They sat in silence for a moment, until the waitress came to take their order.

Jeff looked up from his coffee cup at Jess and said, "Well, I know there are decisions we make, and sometimes we make the wrong ones. But today, after I left my office, I went for a walk up to Lemolo Falls. As I was walking up the trail, I realized that the water that flows through the creek reaches the Nesika just below the Green Springs dam. The creek is completely free from being restricted by dams or other obstructions. The rush of the water sounds different in some ways from the creeks upstream from the power project. And I wondered how it was that I could tell the difference."

Jess looked up at her uncle and smiled. "Jeff, I guess there are some things we just know, and most likely have known for a very long time. Let's figure out what we're going to say to Kathryn tomorrow. We know what's right for the Nesika, but we still need to make some sort of plan. There has to be a way to turn this decision around."

JESS / JEFF

⟨☙⟩

They walked up the trail together. It was late afternoon, and
the fall sunlight played through the forest canopy and lit up
the golden alders and twisting branches of the vine maples. A
winter wren called out his song. Jess reached for Jeff's hand as
they turned into the clearing just before the hot springs. It was
the middle of the week, and no one was there. Jeff looked down
into her eyes and smiled, pulling her into him.

"Can I kiss you?" Jess cradled his face gently, and they
kissed, long and hard. She loved the way his hand felt holding
the back of her head, keeping her safe, supporting her in the
ways she now needed him to. He stepped back and undid the
top button of his jeans. An osprey cried out; her mate downriver
answered her. Steam from the hot spring swirled in the slight
breeze as Jess stepped out of her clothes. She felt something like
shame twist through her and reached for Jeff's hand.

"What is it, Jess? Are you okay?"

"Sometimes I feel a little dizzy, and you haven't seen me
like this in so much light." She looked down at the scars on her
leg, jagged from the cat's teeth.

Jeff reached to her. "Jess, hey, what happened is part of you
now. I know it must be hard for you not to feel like yourself, but

you are so strong and so beautiful. Out here in this light, this is where you belong."

They slid into the hot spring together. Jess loved the sulfur smell, the almost slick feeling of the water that came from deep in the earth. Below them in the canyon, the ever-present rush and cadence of the Nesika rose up and folded over them.

They sat in the spring in careful silence, allowing the life of the forest to embrace them. Jess let go into the center of the moment, remembering the passion and excitement they had felt here seemingly so long ago. Time had pushed and pulled them together and apart, but the vivid memory of what had been born then had stayed with them and held them in this place.

A young deer walked into the clearing next to the spring and grazed on the grasses at the edge of the forest. Jess thought about how she must always be vigilant now, aware of what might harm her.

Jeff moved toward her. She loved him so much, was so grateful for this moment.

"Jess, will you marry me?"

"Of course I will."

The deer lifted her head for a moment and then went back to grazing.

PIAH

⟨◦⟩

When she reached her village, she could smell salmon cooking and heard the low singing of her people's night songs. She went to her small home and sat quietly near her mother. No one came to her, and no one comforted her. They knew that she was new to them, that she came with vision and power to guide them through this time of loss and healing. The willow bark had helped with the fevers, and fewer of her people seemed ill. As her village filled with a comforting calm, Piah sensed that she was holding her people, protecting them, and imagined a wide bowl of light surrounding them in the growing darkness.

Her father walked across the camp toward her, and Piah stood to greet him.

"You are back" was all he said. As he embraced her, she inhaled the scent of his cedar clothing and of the smoke from the evening fires in his long, heavy hair.

"I am and I am not," Piah responded, and he looked into her eyes.

"Medicine is coming from you, and you chose to come back. You have returned from a great distance, and we will create a ceremony to welcome you. A great part of you was lost with your daughter, your sister, and the many who have died from the fire disease. But for now the disease has released us, because you were able to put Libah's body in the river and gave yourself to the mourning, the necessary pain that you must go through to heal."

The next morning, they all gathered in the ceremonial shelter in the center of camp. Piah's father was wearing Raven's mask and began his drumming, calling their people to the ceremony that would bring Piah back and welcome her as their medicine woman.

Piah felt tendrils of power, like tree roots, flowing beneath her feet. The circle of the cedars around her seemed to sway along with her father's drumming. As she stepped into the circle, she felt her body blending with the tree roots, like the rivers and streams flowing down the canyons and mountains all around her. They were the rivers and mountains of her time and of the future.

Her father began to dance, and Piah sat down and let the medicine flow through her and into the bodies of the people around her. The vision of the woven circle unfolding came back to her, and she knew that what she was being given was for what was coming, though for what and whom, she didn't know. She felt the presence of Libah flying high above her, and the tear in her heart ached, but she let her go. She knew that Libah was the one to carry the knowledge and wisdom into a time that Piah could not be part of.

As the drumming slowed, Piah's father, as the spirit of Raven, spoke to her: "You were born as a child into this time, and children will keep being born into their time like the melting snow of the high mountains flows down the mountain streams into the Nesika. Along the banks and in the body of this river, many people will be given lessons, visions, and the power to bring clarity through the wounds of their bones and hearts. Your sacrifice has given our people hope and healing. The wisdom of this sacrifice will ring down through the many twisted ladders of generations to come. I can see you, Piah, and I can see that others will, too."

The drums grew louder, and Piah's father/Raven danced again, and the howling that rang from his heart stirred in her a strength from the pain of her scars, and off in the distance the cadence of the Nesika moved in time with their drums. Piah closed her eyes and saw a kind of opening, like the mouth of a cave, where the young, bleeding woman from her vision was standing. Piah felt a stirring in her womb and let the spirit of Libah fly toward that light.

JESS

⟨❦⟩

J ess bent down slowly to open her mailbox, her eight-months-
pregnant belly preventing her from getting around easily.
Carrying the weight of her growing girl on her small frame was
making this last trimester of her pregnancy difficult. She went to
the mailbox each day looking for the copy of the decision made
by the Ninth Circuit Court of Appeals that Kathryn had sent
to her. Judge Martha Baston had ruled that there was enough
evidence to create a judicial order to remove the Green Springs
dam on the Nesika River. The actions taken by PowerCorp and
the Forest Service had been "arbitrary and capricious."

Today it was there, a large manila envelope with an offi-
cial-looking return address. Jeff had gone up with Miko to help
Martin ground-truth another renegade timber sale. She wished
he were here to look at this document with her, and thought for
a moment about waiting for him. No way. She took the mail back
into the house, poured a glass of water, and sat in the warm sun
next to the window overlooking her fall garden.

That spring, after the wedding at Lemolo Falls, Jeff and Jess
had had a large reception at their house. They had completely

redesigned the back garden, clearing old brush and layering the yard in raised beds. They had decided to get married on May 30, which was Monica's birthday. They wanted to include her memory and presence in their life together.

The wedding had been colorful and dreamlike. Jess's mom had designed a bright blue, green, and gold banner with symbols of the river: salmon and bright spirals. It had flown like a flag in the mist and breeze of the falls, and Jess now imagined it flying over the dam at the ceremony when the deconstruction would begin and the Nesika would be freed.

Now the banner played in the wind just above the spent raspberries. She had gotten pregnant quickly, before the wedding, and they had been able to keep it a secret until they had come home from their brief honeymoon on the Oregon coast.

Jess lowered herself carefully into a soft backyard chair. She loved that the sun was out, and for late January the day was bright and warm. She opened the envelope and took out the document. Kathryn had said it was long for a decision of this type, which was a good sign that the judge had taken the details of the case into careful consideration. Because she had done such a thorough job of writing the decision, there would be less of a chance for a successful appeal.

Closing her eyes, Jess held the paper in her hands and felt her pulse in her head and a slight shiver in the right side of her face. It had been two years and three months since the mountain lion had attacked her. She felt a chill and moved her chair into the sun again, looking down at the document in her lap, noticing how near her baby it was.

The phone rang loudly from the living room, and she stood up and went into the house to answer it. It was Suzie's number, and she let her answering machine pick up. Jess had never reconnected with her; there was too much history there, and Jess had the reserves to tend only the relationships in her life that supported her and kept her grounded and moving forward in her work. Jess was glad, though, that Martin had assured her Suzie was okay, living in Eugene with those kids.

Lying down on the couch, Jess read the cover letter from Kathryn:

Dear Jess,

Yay! This is such good news, and we couldn't have done it without you and Water Walkers. I know this must be a dream come true for you. And we all know that the likelihood that the dam would ever come out, according to PowerCorp, was so small it couldn't even be comprehended. With their stable of high-priced corporate lawyers, they claimed there wouldn't be a judge on Earth who would rule in our favor. I'm so glad we were able to take the position we did. You were right—by giving the judge the whole picture of how important the Nesika is, how important all of life is, from a kind and compassionate perspective, we were able to show the judge how simple her decision could be. Thank you so much, Jess. I have learned a lot from you and this case. It has been an honor to work with you.

Sincerely,
Kathryn

Jess looked up from the letter at the wedding pictures on her desk: Jeff and she, standing in front of Lemolo Falls; her mom, Uncle Robert, and Martin, smiling and happy while the mist from the falls dampened their hair and blew like a cloud around them; and Miko, of course, looking handsome and regal, his round black bear face smiling into the camera. She smiled. Then, holding the letter and the decision on her pregnant belly, she closed her eyes.

Her baby stirred, and Jess put her hand protectively on the moving foot or elbow. She rode the slide-like feeling into sleep. Just as she was beginning to let go, she felt a jolt and found herself standing on the bank of the Nesika, in the same place she had been attacked. It was earlier in the day, and the river was moving quickly, and Jess noticed that the Green Springs dam was gone. Salmon splashed and pushed through the shallows, spawning fiercely, the water a blur of silver bodies moving up- and downstream. Jess wondered for a moment what kind of time she was in. She felt a tingling as she recognized that she wasn't dreaming, at least not the kind of dreaming that was familiar to her. She reached down and felt that her belly was flat—but she knew Libah was fine.

She heard a sound and looked across the water. She spotted a woman lying naked in the mud. She didn't seem to need help; she just needed to be seen. The woman stood and looked across at Jess. Jess could see a dark blue line running from the woman's chin down to her chest, and three other dark, wide line marks on her chin. She was grieving; Jess could feel the woman's searing pain run through her own body. She was grieving the loss of her child.

Jess realized that she was seeing a Molalla woman who had lived in the high mountain canyons of the Nesika River Valley more than two hundred years earlier. She saw the spirit of a baby girl hovering over the woman, and then the blue light of the river took her downstream. The woman cried loudly, and the spawning salmon seemed to shift in response. Jess watched her, wanted to help her, but she couldn't move from her place. The woman started walking away from the river and turned suddenly. The sound of the Nesika grew louder and louder, drawing the women's attention to the current, and for a moment the salmon disappeared and the water changed as the dam rose up and then came down. Then, in a breath, the salmon returned and continued spawning in the shallows.

The two women looked at each other for a moment more, a shared recognition of kinship with the river binding them to each other. Another young woman appeared; this one looked like Monica, but older. Jess's heart leaped, and she wanted to call out to her. The young woman looked up and smiled. Jess recognized a kind playfulness that she had known in her younger sister, but she was tending the Molalla woman, too. Jess knew that this was Monica and someone else, a sister to the Molalla woman. The sister and the river were bound to each other; Jess could see the river's blue spirit light winding around the sister like a fast-growing vine, then meandering around both Jess and the Molalla woman. The sister lay down in the current, as if she were resting, and disappeared, and Jess knew that this loss, this sacrifice, was the opening. The Molalla woman tossed something high into the air, and Jess caught it. It was a small beaded necklace. *For Libah*, Jess heard a singing voice from across time saying to her.

This was the same river, the same current, that both women loved. Jess stayed for a moment after the woman climbed up the cliff to the place where the stone piles were. She heard a sudden sound in the bushes behind her. A large mountain lion walked up to her. A female, Jess knew. She brushed near Jess's leg and stayed for a moment, before stalking down to the river's edge to take from the abundant run of salmon.

ACKNOWLEDGMENTS

In order to tell this story, I had many mentors, supporters, critics, and powerful guides along my way. I will never forget the first day that I started to write this book when I was having a hard time beginning and my husband, Robert Atkins, encouraged me to "just play." His constant confidence in me and my work, and his support and love, imbue each page of this book. I also want to express my deep gratitude to my doctoral committee Joe Meeker, Sarah Conn, Betsy Geist, Susan Morgan, and the late Patricia Monaghan. They cheered each draft and kept me going to the finish line of my PhD.

I am grateful to my first editor Ellen Parker, who after reading my first draft declared that I had indeed "written a book." Since then I have had many supporters and guides cheering and aiding me along this path, including my next marvelous, talented, and awesome editor Gail Hudson from Girl Friday Productions and the tenacious, brilliant editor from She Writes Press, Annie Tucker, who helped me write a book worthy of this story.

And, my lovely, talented daughter, Emma—this book is for you and your generation. My hope is that it can serve as a guide on how to embrace your wildness, and the strength to find the way through and share that with others.

I found inspiration from my lifelong awe for the deep-green meandering North Umpqua River that winds through my heart, soul, and mind in so many ways. And for my family that lived on the banks of that river, my mom, dad, and our beloved Robin who lost her life in that river when she was eleven. This book is for you, dear, for your flash of brightness in our lives and for gracing us all with the power of this story.

I also want to acknowledge the Molalla people who lived up on the upper reaches of the North Umpqua and serve to inspire the character of Piah and her people. This fictional account is a rendering of a much more complex and deeply rich hidden story of the people who lived there before any contact with the white Euro-American settlers. The stories of Piah are based on my research for my PhD. Even though there isn't much directly known about them, the Molalla live on in the hearts of their descendants, in the flash and whorl of the currents of this river—and in the folds of the canyons of the Cascade Mountains where the wildness that we crave lives in the darkest fissures of what we have lost and strive to remember.

Also, I thank the stalwart group of intrepid explorers who helped forge the creation of ecopsychology—Mary Gomes, Allen Kanner, the late Theodore Roszak and Dolores LaChappelle whose echoing "Go Deeper" rings through my mind like a mantra.

Finally, I recognize the constant companionship of my dear dogs that have been by my side throughout this process—Bentley, and Brook; your love shines through my life every day and inspires the many moments in this book in the character of Miko. He is all of you. And, to my dog training friends and family—so many times I would glean strength from our time together, from the experiences of connection, reflection, and accomplishments of training and staying committed to playing the game and taking what I love seriously.

ABOUT THE AUTHOR

Lisa M. Reddick has lived in loved and written about the Pacific Northwest most of her life. Her personal essay "The River" was published in the anthology *Landscapes of the Heart: Narratives of Nature and Self*. She is working on her next novel *Burning Wisdom*, which is a continuation of *The Same River* focusing on the issues of climate change. She currently lives in Edmonds Washington with her husband and two fabulous Australian Shepherds.

Author photo © Lara Grauer Photography

SELECTED TITLES FROM SHE WRITES PRESS

She Writes Press is an independent publishing company founded to serve women writers everywhere. Visit us at www.shewritespress.com.

The Black Velvet Coat by Jill G. Hall. $16.95, 978-1-63152-009-9. When the current owner of a black velvet coat—a San Francisco artist in search of inspiration—and the original owner, a 1960s heiress who fled her affluent life fifty years earlier, cross paths, their lives are forever changed . . . for the better.

Arboria Park by Kate Tyler Wall. $16.95, 978-1631521676. Stacy Halloran's life has always been centered around her beloved neighborhood, a 1950s-era housing development called Arboria Park—so when a massive highway project threaten the Park in the 2000s, she steps up to the task of trying to save it.

A Drop In The Ocean: A Novel by Jenni Ogden. $16.95, 978-1-63152-026-6. When middle-aged Anna Fergusson's research lab is abruptly closed, she flees Boston to an island on Australia's Great Barrier Reef—where, amongst the seabirds, nesting turtles, and eccentric islanders, she finds a family and learns some bittersweet lessons about love.

Anchor Out by Barbara Sapienza. $16.95, 978-1631521652. Quirky Frances Pia was a feminist Catholic nun, artist, and beloved sister and mother until she fell from grace—but now, done nursing her aching mood swings offshore in a thirty-foot sailboat, she is ready to paint her way toward forgiveness.

The Lucidity Project by Abbey Campbell Cook. $16.95, 978-1-63152-032-7. After suffering from depression all her life, twenty-five-year-old Max Dorigan joins a mysterious research project on a Caribbean island, where she's introduced to the magical and healing world of lucid dreaming.

To the Stars Through Difficulties by Romalyn Tilghman. $16.95, 978-1631522338. A contemporary story of three women very different women who join forces in a small Kansas town to create a library and arts center—changing their world, and finding their own voices, powers, and self-esteem, in the process.